Kingfisher Blues

A Chupplejeep Mystery

MARISSA DE LUNA

Murder, mayhem and Goan village life

Copyright © 2023 Marissa de Luna

All rights reserved.

Lost Button Publishing
No part of this book may be reproduced or transmitted by any means, without the prior written permission in writing of the author.
The author's moral rights have been asserted.
This is a work of fiction. All persons appearing in this written work are fictitious. Any resemblance to real people, living or dead, is entirely coincidental.

Cover design by JD&J

For James

CHAPTER ONE

Five men wearing white dhotis stood at the back of the stage. Drums hung around their waists, tied with maroon fabric. The little girl was mesmerised by the dancer in the ornate gold and red skirt and green painted face. Jagdish Sharma stood centre stage, his legs apart, making slow and deliberate movements. The performer's eyes were enhanced by thick black makeup against the green. He moved his eyes like she had never seen before. Right, left, right, left, up and down with such speed, keeping in rhythm with the beat of the *dholki*, drum. The performance was coming to the end of the first act. The crowd were clapping along with the little girl, who was standing to get a better view.

'The costumes, the colours,' she gushed to anyone who would listen. A toothless granny sitting to her left smiled at her innocence and reached out from under the folds of her white sari to pinch her cheek, but Sangeeta deftly moved to avoid the wiry hand.

'Why you brought her here?' a woman asked. Two musicians entered the stage and sat next to the tablas and sitar, which had been hidden under a black cloth until now. 'This is not the show for such a young girl.'

'It's okay,' her mother replied. 'Sangeeta likes the dancing.'

The girl turned to her mother's friend. 'I love kathakali,' she said. 'I'm going to be a dancer like him one day.'

The woman, whose face Sangeeta noticed was round like the dumpling she was about to eat, laughed and turned back to her plate of food. 'Maybe some women are doing kathakali these days.' She nodded sagely to herself. 'These interval musicians are good too; better, in fact,' she said through a mouthful of food. She swallowed. 'I'm not sure why I came. This eye dancing is too much for me. I wanted to see what all the fuss was about, but I think it's making me quite nauseous.' The woman bit into her second dumpling. Sangeeta made a face as soon as the woman's back was turned, meriting a small slap on her knee from her mother.

The girl stood up. 'Mama,' she said, 'I'm going to get an ice cream.' She pointed to a hawker standing at the end of the row. Her mother nodded and gave her a fifty-rupee note. Sangeeta made her way to the ice cream walla, but when she reached him, she had a better idea. She looked over at her mother, who was busy laughing with her friend, and skipped down the steps of the open-air theatre to the stage. When she reached her destination, she decided to explore a little further. She opened the door to the rear of the stage and made her way down a dimly lit corridor.

'Jagdish is in his dressing room,' she heard a woman call. It didn't take Sangeeta long to find the door with his name. The little girl knocked, quietly at first, then a little louder. When there was no response, she tried the handle. It opened without any resistance. Two steps and she was inside. The room was painted the colour of rust, and it smelled of jasmine and sandalwood. Sangeeta saw the great Jagdish Sharma slumped on the chaise longue in the corner of his room, taking a nap. She was surprised, but she understood. Making those *navarasams*, facial expressions, and dancing was hard work. Hard work warranted a little sleep. Her father always took naps. Her mother said he was just lazy, but Sangeeta knew it was her mother who was the idle one. Her father worked while her mother sat around all day eating cashew nuts and gossiping with their neighbour.

The great Jagdish could take a nap mid-performance if he wanted; after all, what were breaks for?

'You're on in five,' boomed a voice. Sangeeta looked up and saw a speaker fixed in the top right corner of the room. Jagdish didn't stir. The little girl looked around his dressing room. There were several vases full of fresh flowers, and his heavy gold headdress lay on his dressing table amongst some other gold jewellery. She walked towards the table and peered at the jewels laid out. Then she turned towards the dancer.

'Uncle,' she said.

Jagdish didn't move.

'Uncle,' she tried again, louder this time. Nothing.

'What is this?'

Sangeeta heard a voice behind her. She turned. A woman in blue jeans, stripy shirt and a sparkly nose ring with a clipboard in her hand was staring at her.

'What are you doing in here?' the woman scolded. 'Get out of here at once.'

Sangeeta didn't move. 'What's that?' she asked instead, walking towards the great dancer. The girl pointed to Jagdish's chest, noticing that underneath his chains and garlands was a dark stain on the red fabric of his costume. She took a closer look and saw an ornate handle sticking out of his chest. The girl let out a scream.

'What?' the woman asked, taking a step closer to the performer. 'Oh,' she said. 'This one likes to play a joke. Jagdish, you're on,' she said, but there was a tremble in her voice. When the dancer didn't move, the woman with the clipboard poked him with a pen. 'Come on,' she tried, her voice wavering. Sangeeta didn't take her eyes off the dancer.

Clipboard woman took a step back. Sangeeta could see her shaking.

'Go,' the woman turned to her and commanded in a barely audible whisper.

Sangeeta didn't need to be told twice. She covered her mouth with her hands and ran, gasping for breath as she pushed through the throng of people. She ran back along the dimly lit corridor and through the stage door. She stopped to take a breath when she was outside again, then she resumed running; up the stairs and past the hawker selling the ice cream. She shoved her way past the other theatregoers and took her place next to her mother, out of breath, a lump in her throat.

'How was your ice cream?' her mother asked.

'This Jagdish is not so great if he can't make it to the stage on time,' her mother's friend said.

'I don't think he's going to make it at all,' Sangeeta said softly, tears beginning to stream down her cheeks. She closed her eyes and pictured the filigree gold handle sticking out of the dancer's chest, the dark blood staining his garments.

'Why's that?' her mother asked.

'He's dead,' Sangeeta sobbed. 'He's dead.'

Chapter Two

Chupplejeep heard a scream. He dropped his paper and ran to the bedroom. Christabel lay on the floor, her arms by her sides, her feet apart. The scream came again. Chupplejeep looked towards the cot.

'Bonita, what's the matter?' he asked as he stepped over Christabel. He picked up the baby, and she instantly calmed. 'And what's the matter with your mother, *beta*?' He nuzzled Bonita's neck as she made sounds similar to papa, but not quite. She hit him on the nose playfully, and he held her hand.

'Her mother has had enough,' Christabel said from her corpse pose on the floor. 'I thought some yoga would help, but I think I need a miracle instead.'

Chupplejeep looked at the infant in his arms. 'She's not so bad,' he said.

'Oh here comes father of the year,' said Christabel. 'And how many times were you up in the night?' she asked. 'Your snoring was almost as bad as her crying. I feel like I'm living in a mad house.'

Father and daughter shared a conspiratorial smile. Chupplejeep put Bonita in her cot and held his arms out to his wife. His wife made a face but eventually took his hands and allowed him to pull her to her feet. She sat on the bed next to her husband. 'Why do I find parenting so tough?'

Chupplejeep pulled her towards him and kissed her head as she leaned into him. 'Everyone finds it tough,' he said. 'They just don't like talking about it.'

'Like Ethel, who baked two cakes, one *bebinca* and made an *apa de camerao* yesterday in between feeding her nine-month-old twins. These kids want food continually, and the mess this one makes…*oof*,' Christabel said, looking up at her daughter.

'Knowing Ethel, her mother made all those goodies and put them in the freezer so she could impress her friends.'

Christabel laughed. 'I was so desperate for children. I thought being a mother would come naturally to me, but I'm a mess. Look at my hair, my nails. And the kids…'

'The kids, what? They adore you. They're well fed and dressed, and most importantly, they have fun with you. What else do you need to do to prove you're a good mother?'

'Bake some cakes,' Christabel said. 'Good ones.'

'You made good cakes before we had Bonita and Nicholas?' Chupplejeep asked.

Christabel pulled away and hit him playfully on the shoulder. 'I want to be angry at you,' she said. 'I do all the parenting around here and you swoop in for the fun bits. Have you even read those parenting books I left by your side of the bed?'

'Listen,' Chupplejeep said. 'Take some time out. Go to the spa, the hairdresser, shopping and I'll look after this one.' Chupplejeep twisted one end of his moustache. 'I'll even make dinner for when Nicholas is back from school.'

Christabel laughed. 'Who are you?' she said, looking at him. 'I don't recognise this person. Where is my useless husband?'

'Hey, I can take back my offer,' he said, trying to make light of a situation he had caused. Chupplejeep knew his faults. He was a terrible father. He loved his children, he would throw himself under a bus for them, all the usual clichés, but they were hard work.

No one ever said how difficult it was to raise children. He suspected it was to keep the human race going. Of course the kids were worth it, but at five in the morning when Bonita was screaming, he wasn't quite sure, and once in those early days of never-ending feeding and crying, he could almost see why his parents had left him at an orphanage. *Almost.*

Bonita started fussing. Chupplejeep picked her up and bounced her a little.

'I'm going for a nice hot shower and then I'll be off,' Christabel said. She gave him a wide smile as Bonita's whimpering turned into full-blown sobs. Christabel closed the door to the bathroom behind her.

Chupplejeep made his way to the kitchen with Bonita in his arms. He took a biscuit from a tin and gave it to the crying child, popping her into her highchair. Instantly the child stopped crying. It wasn't so hard after all. Subconsciously, he could hear his mother-in-law chiding him though. 'This is how you create a comfort eater,' her voice echoed. 'You want your daughter to take after you?' Chupplejeep looked at his blissfully happy daughter. He considered taking the sweet treat away then reconsidered. There was no way he could risk that now. Whoever coined the phrase 'taking candy from a baby' clearly never had any children of their own.

Chupplejeep heard the shower stop just as Bonita had finished her biscuit. Most of it was in a paste around her mouth. Sighing, he reached for a cloth and wiped her face, which was met with fresh tears. He was only five minutes into a very long day. Chupplejeep scooped his daughter out of her high chair and considered putting Baby TV on.

'It's amazing what a shower can do,' Christabel said as she sashayed out of their bedroom looking like a new woman.

Chupplejeep smiled. He could do this. His wife had been doing this for the last eighteen months after a terrible pregnancy and even worse labour that he didn't dare think about again. He looked back at Bonita, whose bottom lip was quivering as she saw her mother heading towards the door.

'Come on, Bonnie,' he said, picking up a children's book from the sofa. 'We're going to have some fun.'

Christabel turned back to her husband and child and kissed Bonita on her head. 'Bye, baby,' she said, cooing over the infant.

'Oh,' Chupplejeep said. 'Could you just take her a moment? My phone's ringing.' Christabel made a face but took her daughter and gave her a cuddle. 'One minute,' he mouthed to Christabel as he answered the call. 'Private Investigator Arthur Chupplejeep speaking,' he said, walking over to the window.

'I see,' he said. 'Dead? How terrible... Now?' He turned to look at Christabel, who was scowling at him.

'Right now?' he said again, making a face at the telephone. He looked at Christabel again and held his left hand up as if to say he was helpless. Chupplejeep found a pen and piece of paper, made a note and assured the person on the other end of the line that he would help. Disconnecting the call, he turned to Christabel again.

'No,' she said before he had a chance to say anything.

'But – ' he started, but she cut him off by raising her hand. She handed their daughter back to him.

'I'm off,' she said. Bonita giggled this time and pulled Chupplejeep's hair.

Christabel stopped at the door. 'If you're that desperate, you know who you can call,' she said, and with that she turned on her heel and left.

Chapter Three

Chupplejeep parked outside the beige building where a skinny man was waiting for him in a checked shirt, black trousers and sandals.

'Hurry, sir,' the man said to Chupplejeep as he got out of his new Maruti Baleno. It had been a sad day when his four-by-four had packed up. Chupplejeep had deliberated for days on which car he should get to replace it. In the end, he needn't have worried, because Christabel had already decided: a nice family saloon, a five-seater, to accommodate the children. She had even picked the colour. He supposed this was what happened to the freedom of choice when you got married. He couldn't complain too much though. The Nexa blue was very much to his liking, and it had air conditioning, something his old vehicle lacked. He even got a good price; whether or not that was because the car had been discontinued in many other countries he wasn't sure, but with a solid guarantee, he couldn't argue.

Chupplejeep grabbed his brown leather briefcase from the passenger seat and followed the wiry man in the sandals into the building. He was about to ask what the rush was when the man stopped, turned to him and in a serious tone told him that Mr Kapoor didn't like waiting. This instantly irritated Chupplejeep. Clearly this fellow didn't have children, because with children you had no choice but to be patient. Chupplejeep thought back to last night when Nick was telling him a story about another boy in his class. The story was worth five minutes of his time; instead it took at least half an hour. Chupplejeep had even forgotten what he was supposed to be doing when the story was over. Truth be told, though, no one in India liked waiting. It was a national problem, even though more than half of Indians were never on time, especially in Goa. Everyone knew this. So why was Mr Kapoor so special that his assistant had to explain this to him?

After walking through a long corridor and then up a flight of stairs, they arrived at a green door. The assistant knocked and opened it. He let Chupplejeep in and without another word scurried away to another room.

'Ah, you're here,' the man behind a large teak table said. The walls of this office had been freshly painted a pale yellow, and there was a faint smell of aniseed in the air. The man behind the desk made no attempt to get up to shake Chupplejeep's hand but instead motioned to the seat in front of him. It was for this reason that Chupplejeep decided not to apologise for his tardiness nor explain that he had to wait for his mother-in-law to arrive to look after the baby before he could leave the house. He shuddered thinking of the lecture Christabel's mother had given him as he handed Bonita to her. Sylvia Saldanha was a necessary evil.

Kapoor studied him from behind his desk. When Chupplejeep had decided to become a private investigator, he believed he could pick and choose his clients, but it turned out he couldn't. He wasn't yet demanding a high enough fee, and so he had no choice but to accept each one. Plus, he now had an employee that he had to consider.

'You're late,' Kapoor said, glancing at his watch. 'But I suppose you're here now. Kapoor.' Chupplejeep stretched out his hand and Kapoor took it. 'I understand you're the best and very reasonable.'

'My rates have gone up,' Chupplejeep said. It had been Christabel's idea. He hadn't wanted to hike his prices so soon after starting out, but his services were in demand, and Christabel had become his unofficial manager of sorts. She had decided that he could command a higher price and still get the work. 'You're worth it,' she had said, imitating the woman on a shampoo commercial. 'Don't sell yourself short.'

From his briefcase, Chupplejeep took out a pre-printed appointment letter with his newly increased fees on it. He handed it to Kapoor, who barely glanced at it, signed it and handed it back. 'Still, very reasonable. In Mumbai you'd pay double. So now that's out of the way, let's get to the point. A superstar has been killed on my premises. You must know of Jagdish Sharma?' Kapoor asked.

'I've heard of him,' Chupplejeep said. He had only just read about him this morning when the call from Kapoor came through. The famous kathakali dancer had lived between Goa and Delhi for years, but he hadn't performed in the state in over a decade. It was only recently that Jagdish had agreed to perform a series of shows in Goa. Chupplejeep had never been into the arts so couldn't claim to have known about this apparent superstar.

'I can't afford to get a bad reputation because of this one unfortunate event. The police are doing an okay job, I suppose. But I can't trust them to find the killer fast. And one of the sub-inspectors who attended the crime scene was so star-struck, his jaw was hanging open every time one of the other dancers walked past. Like this.' Kapoor imitated the sub-inspector he was referring to before closing his mouth and regaining his composure. 'It doesn't fill me with confidence. So you think you can handle it?' Kapoor asked.

'Where was the body found?' Chupplejeep asked.

'In his dressing room. His assistant alerted us last night halfway through the show.'

'Witnesses?' Chupplejeep asked.

'None that we know of.'

Chupplejeep stood up, his bag in hand. 'Shall we go to the scene of the crime?' he asked. Kapoor stood too. Standing, Kapoor looked much shorter and stockier than when he was seated. He wore a brown shirt with white polka dots, brown trousers and a brown belt with a gold buckle. Chupplejeep couldn't help but compare Kapoor to a chocolate snowball he had seen in the bakery yesterday. His stomach rumbled.

Kapoor led the way back down the stairs to a room behind the stage. Kapoor lifted the ticker tape and gave the guard outside a look. The guard looked away as Chupplejeep followed Kapoor into the crime scene. The room with its rust-coloured walls and huge bunches of flowers looked like it hadn't been touched.

'Is this how the room was when Jagdish Sharma was found?' Chupplejeep asked.

Kapoor nodded. He pointed towards the chaise longue. 'He was there. Knife sticking out of his chest. It was Jagdish's knife, I might add.'

'Was it a kirpan?'

'He wasn't a religious fellow and not Sikh either. He was Hindu. But he liked this ornate knife. He took it everywhere with him, said it was good luck or something. He got that wrong, obviously.'

'And a young girl found him?' Chupplejeep asked. 'Do you have her details?'

Kapoor nodded. 'She won't be able to tell you much. She's barely ten. The production assistant found her loitering in here. She was probably after an autograph or something.'

'Your production assistant followed her in?'

'No, she found her when Jagdish failed to appear at the stage door.'

'Ah,' said Chupplejeep, this telling him all he needed to know about the security on the night.

Chupplejeep motioned to the half-drunk drink that looked and smelled to be some kind of lassi. 'The crime scene officer didn't take any of this away?'

'Now you know what I'm dealing with,' Kapoor said, turning towards Chupplejeep. 'Look, whoever did this needs to be caught, and not only that.' Kapoor lowered his voice. 'The murderer cannot be tied to this theatre. I run five theatres in Mumbai and Delhi, and next month I plan to open another here in Goa. I can see you're an intelligent man. I don't need to tell you how it works.'

'The perpetrator is the perpetrator,' Chupplejeep said as he made his way around the room. He took photos of the sofa where Jagdish's body was found. When he had enough photos, he turned to Kapoor. 'When I find the killer, I can't change who it is,' he said. 'Are you going to be okay with that?'

Kapoor made a face. 'No. I suppose you can't. But you'll come to me first,' he said. 'That way I can make some arrangements before it hits the press.'

'So long as it doesn't compromise my investigation.'

Kapoor laughed. 'It won't.'

'Can I ask where you were last night?' Chupplejeep asked.

Kapoor frowned at the investigator. 'The cheek,' he said. 'I've hired you to find out who did this, not interrogate me.' Kapoor took a breath. He studied the investigator again. 'I was in my office the whole time. Ask my girlfriend if you don't believe me.'

Chupplejeep nodded, noting Kapoor's wedding ring. At least Kapoor was honest enough to admit he had a girlfriend.

Kapoor laughed. 'Jagdish was making me money. I had no reason to get rid of him.'

'So, tell me,' Chupplejeep said. 'Do you know who did?'

Chapter Four

An hour later, Kapoor excused himself, taking a call on his mobile phone, leaving Chupplejeep alone in Jagdish's dressing room. Chupplejeep opened the door and peered out along the corridor. There was no CCTV at the venue; Kapoor had confirmed that. Chupplejeep turned right out of the room, passing several other dressing rooms and a canteen. All manner of personnel had authority to be backstage. Kapoor had said it had been buzzing yesterday, to use the owner's turn of phrase. 'Opening night,' Kapoor had said. 'It's always buzzing. The staff, the performers, the audience, everyone is on a high.' At the end of the corridor there was a staircase that led upstairs to the offices.

Chupplejeep had found the production assistant in the canteen and had asked her about how she found Jagdish. It was obvious the woman had been shaken up and was unclear why she had turned up to work today. Chupplejeep had said as much.

Kingfisher Blues

'I'm very reliable,' the woman said, straightening in her chair.

'You're human, also,' Chupplejeep said kindly. 'And you were the one to find Jagdish. The little girl...'

'She was having a good look round Mr Sharma's dressing room, and she was shouting at him, trying to wake him up,' the production assistant said, tears springing to her eyes. 'I too thought he was playing a joke,' she added, dabbing her eyes with a handkerchief. 'During rehearsals he could be a bit of a joker.'

'Was Mr Sharma nice to work with?'

'You know these celebrities,' she said. 'They are of a type. Nothing I would complain about.'

Reliable *and* loyal, thought Chupplejeep. A credit to Kapoor, no doubt. Chupplejeep asked if Jagdish had been himself the day of the murder. The production assistant hesitated with her response but said that he was his usual self. Had she noticed anything out of place in his dressing room when she found him? The woman closed her eyes, trying to recall the room.

'I only remember the knife and the body,' she said. 'That's all I remember.'

'It must have been a shock,' Chupplejeep said. 'If you do remember anything else, call me.' He doubted she would. 'One last question, if I may? Did you move anything in Mr Sharma's room. You or the girl?'

'I told the girl to leave as soon as I realised what had happened. I didn't touch anything, nothing at all. But I don't know how long that girl was in the room for,' she said, looking at Chupplejeep. 'You know what children are like, poking their noses in everything.' She said it as if she was speaking from experience.

'They're curious,' Chupplejeep responded. 'Rest assured, I'll find the girl and ask her.'

The production assistant gave him a weak smile.

Chupplejeep made his way back towards the dressing room. At the other end of the corridor there was a path that led towards the stage. Chupplejeep twisted one end of his moustache. Not only did the staff have free access to Jagdish's dressing room, but theatregoers could have accessed the rear of the stage, like the little girl had.

Kapoor had hired a bouncer to stand guard at the entrance that led from the audience to the dressing rooms, but the security guard had eaten at a cart earlier in the day and so he had spent much of the evening in the toilet. Coincidence? Chupplejeep didn't think so. It wouldn't have been difficult to spike the food or drink of a security guard who liked to eat. The bouncer had briefly entered the room while Chupplejeep had been talking to Kapoor to express his sincere apologies for failing in his duties. Kapoor had fired him on the spot.

Chupplejeep returned to Jagdish's dressing room. The police guard took his details before he entered the room this time. Chupplejeep didn't argue. He manoeuvred himself under the tape. Fingerprints would have been lifted from the scene, and he could see some of the powder residue from lifting latent prints. There was no harm in taking his own if he could get a decent set. He would have to call on Kulkarni for another favour. Opening his briefcase, Chupplejeep removed a vial and a pipette. He used the pipette to extract some of the now curdled yoghurt drink and put it in a clear plastic bag, which he tucked into his case. Once again he slowly walked around the room. When he got to the chaise longue, he walked behind it and squatted so he was eye level with the pale red velvet upholstery. His eyes scanned the seat, looking for anything out of place, anything the forensic team may have missed. The chair had been soaked through with blood, but much of this had been cleaned up, or at least someone had attempted to clean it. The smell of bleach lingered. The floor was no better. It was obvious where the blood had pooled by the staining. The clean-up team's shoddy work was to his benefit, he supposed, taking another photo.

The forensics team had been pretty useless too, Chupplejeep concluded, considering they had left the half-drunk lassi untouched. Chupplejeep was about to stand up when something caught his eye. Behind one of the legs of the seat was something small and shiny. The investigator examined it. It looked to be a small green stone, an emerald perhaps. A precious or semi-precious stone dropped by the killer, or one of the jewels on the embellished handle of Jagdish's knife, the one that was used to stab him? Chupplejeep put the stone in a little plastic bag and slipped it into his pocket.

As Chupplejeep considered the importance of this clue, he heard the door handle rattle. He stayed in his crouched position behind the chaise longue and waited. A moment passed and then the door slowly opened. He craned his neck to see a tall man in a pink shirt and *lunghi* hurry into the room.

'Damn it.' The man swore as he made his way to Jagdish's dressing table and started rummaging through the drawers.

Chupplejeep was struggling to remain as he was. His knees were about to give way. He steadied himself by holding on to the seat, but the chaise longue moved in the process, the wooden foot of the seat scraping against the stone floor. The man in the pink shirt startled, and Chupplejeep stood up.

'Who are you?' the man demanded.

'I could ask the same of you,' Chupplejeep said, stretching out each leg in turn. He really had to do something about his knees. He was too young to have weak knees.

'I work here,' the man said. He looked around him. 'At this theatre.'

'Ah, not in Jagdish's dressing room then?'

The man stood with his legs apart, arms folded across his chest. He stared at Chupplejeep. 'I was looking for something. Not that it's any of your business. You?'

'Kapoor hired me. I'm a private investigator.' Chupplejeep took a step closer to the man in the pink shirt and stretched out his hand. 'Chupplejeep,' he said.

The man eyed him suspiciously. 'I think you need to leave,' he said.

'I just told you why I'm here –' Chupplejeep started, but the tall man cut him off.

'Security,' he shouted.

There was an audible silence. The man walked towards the door and shouted louder this time.

Chupplejeep could hear footsteps in the distance. 'Kapoor has hired me to find Jagdish Sharma's killer, and I'm not sure why you don't want to talk to me.'

A broad man in a black polo and black jeans looked into the room. 'Problem, Darsh?' he asked the tall man.

The man stared at Chupplejeep. He held up his hand to stop the security guard. '*Nai*.'

'Why does Kapoor want you here?' Darsh asked. 'He should leave it to the police.'

Chupplejeep didn't respond, and there was an awkward silence until Darsh spoke. 'I'm taking over from Jagdish,' he said gruffly. 'You know what they say, the show must go on.' Darsh shoed the security guard away.

'You were Jagdish's understudy?' Chupplejeep asked.

'His stand-in. I've been doing my own shows for some time. I was signed up to this a long time back, and I had to fulfil my contract, but I'm more than just an understudy, as you put it. People pay good money to see me. Sure, they'll be saddened that they can't see the great Jagdish Sharma, but they'll leave this theatre in awe.'

'You've played such big theatres before?' Chupplejeep asked.

'Are you implying that I killed Jagdish to take this show from him?' Darsh clenched his fists by his sides.

'This show is big money from what I hear, and it's getting a lot of press coverage.'

Darsh straightened. He stared at the investigator.

Chupplejeep held his hands up. 'I'm here today to understand what kind of fellow Jagdish was and to find out who wanted to harm him. It's my job.'

'I had no reason to kill the man. I was going to overtake him as the number one kathakali dancer in India regardless.'

'Can you tell me a little about this great man?'

'You'll hear it soon enough,' Darsh said, his shoulders dropping a little. 'Jagdish threw his weight around like most celebrities do. Expected everyone to be at his beck and call, including his family. You know, the usual "fetch my cigarettes, bring my whiskey, send a car for my mistress." Belching and farting when it suited him. No consideration for others.'

'Kapoor tells me he has a wife and three daughters.'

Darsh nodded. Chupplejeep noticed the dancer's eyes focus on the framed photograph on Jagdish's dresser. It was a picture of the deceased's wife and kids. They were no longer children but young women. All three children had inherited their mother's good bone structure. Being good looking was not a requirement of a kathakali dancer, which was fortunate for Jagdish and explained how the man had become so successful despite his average looks. With all that heavy makeup and ornate headdress, the audience were only concerned with the dancer's eyes, and even though Chupplejeep had only seen Jagdish Sharma in pictures, the man's eyes had been mesmerising.

'He was loved,' Darsh said, his eyes lingering on the photograph. 'They didn't see that side to him. The public adored him.'

'And let me guess, his family forgave him all his sins.'

Darsh smiled, but Chupplejeep noticed him tense again.

'Did his wife know about his indiscretions?'

Darsh shrugged. 'The wife's always the last to know, right?'

Chupplejeep asked the dancer if he knew who Jagdish was having an affair with, but Darsh claimed not to know. He asked Darsh if he knew Jagdish Sharma's wife.

'Rupali Sharma comes to the shows and the afterparties. She's there when directors, theatre patrons and owners throw parties.'

Chupplejeep nodded. 'Being Jagdish's stand-in, you would have spent quite a bit of time with him, no?'

'Nothing doing,' Darsh said. 'I practiced on my own away from his critical eye.'

'I see,' Chupplejeep said. 'So you don't know if anything in his behaviour changed in the run-up to his death.'

'No idea,' Darsh said, turning away again. Chupplejeep noticed Darsh's eyes wandering towards the dresser again. 'You were looking for something?' he asked.

'Makeup,' Darsh said, without hesitation.

'Makeup? Don't you have an artist to do all that for you? I've heard it takes hours to paint a kathakali dancer's face.'

'It does,' Darsh said. 'It's an intense process. For the makeup artist and for the performer.'

'And you were missing some key makeup?' Chupplejeep asked.

'Yes,' Darsh said. He glanced at the dressing table one last time and then turned back to Chupplejeep. 'It's not here. I'd better get back to my room,' he said, his tone hostile again.

Chupplejeep watched as the man in the pink shirt retreated to the door.

Chapter Five

Chupplejeep headed towards the stage. Standing at its centre, he looked out onto the empty concrete seats. He moved his eyes to the right and then the left, up and down. Then he closed them. Just doing that once was giving him eyestrain. How kathakali dancers moved their eyes like that was beyond him. To perform at such a theatre was a big deal. Chupplejeep himself wasn't a performer. He recalled a school play he was once involved in. He had refused to play a part in the stage performance and instead opted to help with the lighting and sound. It had been a wise decision; being in the spotlight was not his thing. Even now, despite the theatre being empty, he felt anxious.

He opened his eyes and thought about going home. He could only ask his mother-in-law to babysit for so long. Sylvia didn't think much of him, though, so there was no reason to head back quickly. There was no chance that woman was going to change her opinion of him even if he were to become a saint, so what was the point in trying. Nicholas would be home from school though, and he wanted to be there for him. The boy wasn't settling well in his class, and Chupplejeep empathised. The last thing he wanted was for his mother-in-law to give his son the third degree as to what was troubling him.

As Chupplejeep rushed through the exit, he bumped into a tall woman. He apologised and stood back as the woman made a face and rubbed her arm. The woman wasn't just tall but beautiful as well. Her skin had a dewy complexion so clear he was tempted to reach out and touch her face. The impulse alarmed him. He had never before wanted to touch the face of a stranger. It took Chupplejeep a moment to realise who this woman was. Her red-rimmed eyes gave her away. This was Jagdish's wife, Rupali Sharma.

'Sorry,' he said again. He meant to add *for your loss*, but didn't.

'You're that detective,' Rupali said, turning to face him. 'I've read about you. Investigating my husband's death?'

'I'm no longer a detective with the force,' Chupplejeep said.

She nodded before turning back towards her destination.

~

Rupali returned home and used the staff entrance to access the house. She put her finger on her lips as she

Kingfisher Blues

passed one of the maids along the cool marble corridor. Sitting at her dressing table, she examined the bags under her eyes. At least she didn't have to fake those, but a little exaggeration wouldn't hurt. She retrieved her makeup palette from one of the drawers and dabbed a dark shade under her eyes. She pouted, retouched her lipstick and turned away from the mirror.

What a chore it was hosting so many well-wishers when she was supposed to be grieving. She thought this part would be easy. Accepting people's condolences, sitting and pretending to pray with them, but she found she couldn't even bear to wear the traditional mourning colour of white. Dressed in aquamarine, her mother had scolded her this morning. It was why she had left the house under the pretence of visiting Kapoor, the other side of the Mandovi River, when in reality she was desperate to get inside Jagdish's dressing room.

Outside, she could hear fireworks and music in the distance; locals were celebrating the start of Diwali. The fragrant smell of simmering spices was drifting up from the village. What she would have given to be able to go out with them and dance the night away instead of carrying on with this charade. Did the stream of people that had started to arrive since the news of her husband's death know what her husband was really like to live with? Did they know about his tantrums and narcissistic personality? The way he emotionally bullied his wife into giving up her successful acting career, her friends? Did they know Jagdish had several lovers? Would they care?

The last lover she had discovered had been the final straw. There was no way she was going to stand around and let him make a fool of her yet again. His choice this final time was repugnant. The woman was nothing, a nobody, a dirty... Rupali stood up and walked to the window.

How many people in the village tonight would be looking up at her house and pointing the finger? She had motive – she hated her husband. She had wanted a divorce, but there was no way in hell that her husband was going to give her one. The villagers didn't know that though.

'What will people think?' Jagdish had said.

'You've been divorced before,' she had responded.

'That was a long time ago. Nobody remembers that.'

'Nobody will care,' Rupali argued. 'Divorce is commonplace now. Every second person is divorced.'

'No,' Jagdish said, staring at her with those menacing eyes. Once he set his mind to something, it was final. She had been stubborn like that back in the days when she had the upper hand. She had certainly set her sights on this up-and-coming kathakali dancer, and she had been determined to make him hers. She had to laugh at the irony of it.

And so for a while after that conversation she had accepted that Jagdish was her fate. That there was no way out. But then she met someone who changed all that.

She sighed. It seemed like a distant memory now, a different life. She was free now, free to do whatever she

Kingfisher Blues

wanted. Within reason, she supposed. Jagdish should have died sooner. A small smile rose to her lips.

Those well-wishers, who no doubt were still sitting in her lounge on her new white carpet, would be waiting for her to return, assuring her mother that they didn't want to leave her alone. In reality, they were waiting for the gossip so that they could *WhatsApp* their friends the minute they left the house. 'Can you believe,' they would type as fast as their fingers would allow, 'that his wife wasn't even wearing white and she left to do some errands instead of crying with us. It wouldn't surprise me if she was the one...' Rupali stopped her mind from racing. Perhaps her mother was right. She walked to her bed and looked at the three white outfits her mother had selected earlier in the day.

She heard a knock on the door. 'Come,' she said.

'Madam,' her maid said as she opened the door. 'Your room?'

Rupali looked around at the windows. The grills hadn't been pulled across, her bed hadn't been turned down. 'Are they still here?' she asked.

'Madam, they are waiting.'

Rupali nodded. 'I better go and see them then. And the girls' rooms?'

'They are ready for their return.'

Two of her daughters were on their way from London after being told that their beloved father was dead. Her youngest was already here, having taken a flight to Goa from London in order to surprise her father after his show. So far, her youngest hadn't left her bedroom. Her daughters didn't deserve to be fatherless so young. They would suffer for a time, but Rupali was hopeful that with their new lives in England, they would be able to move on. She had to think that way in order to hold it together. Rupali turned back to the white outfits and then padded over to her cupboard. She selected a black *shalwaar* with gold embroidery and a thick orange shawl. She dressed and wrapped the scarf around her head, then she headed towards the staff entrance and made her way out into the night.

Chapter Six

The girl of ten who had found the body of Jagdish Sharma looked up at Chupplejeep with her big dark eyes. Sangeeta's mother sat behind her, staring directly at the private investigator.

'So,' she said menacingly.

'Like I said, I just want to ask your daughter a few questions about last night,' Chupplejeep said.

'So ask,' her mother said.

'Can you tell me your exact movements when you entered Mr Sharma's dressing room?'

'I opened the door,' Sangeeta said.

'It wasn't locked?'

Sangeeta shook her head. 'I knocked first, but there was no answer. When I entered, I saw Jagdish lying on his chair, having a nap. I thought he must be exhausted with all the dancing. He deserved a nap.'

'*Tche*,' he mother said from behind her.

'I called his name,' the girl said, ignoring her mother. 'Then that woman with the clipboard came in. She went straight over to him and poked him with a pen, said he was a joker. Then she realised what had happened and asked me to leave.'

'So what did you do?' Chupplejeep asked.

'I ran,' Sangeeta said.

'And before that, did you notice anything strange in the dressing room? Did you touch or move anything?'

Sangeeta folded her arms across her chest. 'I'm not one of those children. I didn't touch anything. I didn't move anything.' The girl's eyes shifted, suggesting to Chupplejeep that she *was* one of those children, but he could see that she was unwilling to say anything more on the matter.

'Will she get paid for answering these questions?' Sangeeta's mother enquired as she let him out.

'No,' Chupplejeep said incredulously, unable to come up with any other words. 'No.'

~

'Jagdish Sharma was legendary,' Pankaj said to Chupplejeep later that evening as they raced towards Miramar beach. As they approached, the string lights, in various colours, told of the festivities ahead. In the distance they could hear the thud of music. The smell of fried foods filled the air. 'Legendary people have enemies.'

'Because they are treated like gods, they think nothing can touch them. Commanding everyone around them,' Chupplejeep said.

'Like his disgruntled understudy Darsh,' Pankaj said. 'Sounds like he was looking for something other than kohl in Jagdish's dressing room. I told Manju you were on the case.'

Chupplejeep took his eyes off the road and glanced at his colleague.

'I know, I know,' Pankaj said. 'But he can help us if we need it. He was a big fan of the man's work.'

'I can imagine,' Chupplejeep said, thinking fondly of the administrative assistant who worked for him when he was part of the police force. Manju, if anything, was in the know about all things fashion and celebrity. They had found this out when Chupplejeep had been investigating the death of a woman who had been murdered in the changing room of a fashion store.

'It will be a terrible blow to the hotel he was due to perform at,' Pankaj said. Chupplejeep frowned. He had believed that Jagdish was exclusively contracted to perform at Kapoor's theatres. He said as much to Pankaj, but his colleague soon put him straight. Chupplejeep knew he had hired Pankaj for a reason. In the short space of time, Pankaj had done his research. It turned out that Jagdish had agreed to a ten-week residency at a hotel about forty minutes from the theatre.

'Which hotel?' Chupplejeep asked.

'Baytown. Popatrao –' Pankaj started but Chupplejeep cut him off.

'Popatrao's broke, and the hotel hasn't got its five stars, or so the rumour goes. Why would Jagdish Sharma want to perform at a place like that? Something to look into,' he said to Pankaj.

'I'll get onto it first thing tomorrow,' Pankaj said. 'Now we have more pressing things to attend to.'

Chupplejeep noticed a bead of sweat on Pankaj's forehead despite the air conditioning. 'It's going to be okay,' he said.

Pankaj didn't respond. He just looked straight ahead.

'Park over there,' Pankaj said to Chupplejeep, pointing towards a huge effigy of Narkasur.

'Are you crazy?' Chupplejeep asked, turning the car around and pulling up next to a row of hawkers selling *pani puri* and limcas from their *gados*, carts. 'They're going to burn that thing in about half an hour, and they'll pay no attention to what's next to it.'

Pankaj stepped out of the car. He surveyed the area as Chupplejeep paid twenty rupees to a toothless man wearing an orange cap in return for a parking permit, which he placed on his dashboard.

'Come on,' Pankaj said, turning to his boss. 'I don't want to be late.'

'Relax,' Chupplejeep said. 'Your wife's in safe hands. Christabel won't let her get swept up in this crowd.'

'It's not the crowd I'm worried about,' Pankaj said. 'Shwetty has been acting different lately, and I'm worried.'

Here we go again, thought Chupplejeep. 'You're concerned she's going to leave you?'

'Not that,' Pankaj said.

'Then what?'

Kingfisher Blues

'The other thing.'

'Oh,' said Chupplejeep. There was only one other thing that Pankaj worried about consistently, and that was when and whether his wife would agree to have a child. Pankaj had assumed that he and Shwetika were on the same page when it came to the matter of starting a family, but six months into their marriage, Pankaj realised he was wrong.

'Never assume,' their old administrative assistant Manju had told him. 'It makes an ass of you and me.' Chupplejeep had to agree with this. He wished the young apprentice was with them now. Manju had started working at the police station as an administrator just before Chupplejeep had retired. The boy was bright and well connected, as they later found out, and when Pankaj handed in his notice, Inspector General Gosht fast-tracked Manju through the academy. The boy was starting out as a sub-officer. Having someone on the inside at his old police station had proved to be useful, especially on the last case he was hired to investigate, where thousands of rupees had gone missing along with a wealthy miner's daughter.

'Baby?' Chupplejeep said in a low voice. That word still didn't sit comfortably with him.

Pankaj, who was highly sensitive to the word, would have heard Chupplejeep whisper it a mile away. 'Shwetty is going to tell me something tonight. She said it was important.' Pankaj stopped and turned to Chupplejeep. 'Sir, she touched her belly when she said this.'

'You think she's changed her mind?'

'I can only hope,' said Pankaj, turning towards the crowd again. 'I can't afford to do anything to upset her.' Pankaj stopped again and stepped up onto a short wall by the beach. He looked out over the crowd.

'We're on time,' Chupplejeep said. 'Give or take half an hour, and we know where we're meeting them.' If Shwetika was going to be irritated by Pankaj's tardiness, he could only imagine how Christabel felt with two children to manage as well. From what he had seen of Shwetika, there was no chance that she would be helping with Nicholas and Bonita. No, she would be discussing her nail colour, more likely.

'There they are,' Pankaj said, his face breaking into a wide smile. 'Look, Shwetty is holding Bonita.'

Chupplejeep felt panicked. 'Come on then,' he said. 'Let's not stand around.'

Shwetika and Christabel were standing exactly where Chupplejeep had instructed. It was a quiet spot in the entrance to an exclusive apartment building called Sapphire Towers in Miramar. Its residents were in air-conditioned comfort watching the parade and fireworks, avoiding the crowds and the smells. The owner of the building had appointed Chupplejeep a year ago to investigate a sensitive matter involving an accusation of theft against him, and Chupplejeep had swiftly cleared the old man's name. The doorman at the building knew Chupplejeep, and he also knew of his employer's feelings of indebtedness to the private investigator.

Chupplejeep nodded a hello to the familiar watchman who opened the gate for them. As they

Kingfisher Blues

walked over to their wives, Christabel's friend Violeta was telling Nicholas all about the legend of Narkasur, a demon king who spread terror and torture and kidnapped young girls.

'Violeta,' Chupplejeep said sharply.

'What?' she said. 'Not even a hello?'

Christabel frowned at him.

'Careful of what you're telling my boy,' he said, ruffling Nicholas's hair. 'He's only young.'

'You interrupted me,' Violeta said. As usual, Violeta was dressed in violet satin. It was her trademark to dress in the same colour as her name suggested. She wore the colour with pride. 'Anyway,' she said, turning to the little boy. 'Lord Krishna cut off Narkasur's head and slit his tongue and then smeared the blood of the demon on his head as a symbol of victory. The girls he had taken were released.' Violeta gave Chupplejeep a wide smile. 'See, it's a story of good triumphing over evil. So don't be afraid, Nicholas.' Chupplejeep lifted up his boy, who looked a little pale.

'After the demon was killed, people lit lamps in their houses to mark the end of darkness and the beginning of light in Goa,' Chupplejeep said. 'The festival of light.'

'Diwali,' Violeta said.

'Can we go home?' Nicholas asked. Paper flames surrounded a papier-mâché float of this demon with his large black and white eyes painted against his bright pink skin. They watched as it passed them on the back of a lorry. Chupplejeep noted the effigy's razor sharp teeth, clawed hands, horns and black hair and pushed his son's head into the crook of his neck. Other children were running about and laughing, paying no attention to the nine-foot demon. Bonita was pointing at it and laughing, but Nicholas was a sensitive child. Chupplejeep spotted a hawker past the wrought-iron gates selling hot buttered corn and motioned for the watchman to open the gates for him. Once outside, he made his way towards the cart. His mother-in-law's words about comfort eating came back to him.

He shuddered at the thought of Christabel's mother. Following his visit to Kapoor's, his mother-in-law had lectured him for a good half-hour on how unsupportive he was as a husband and father. He had to spend another thirty minutes whilst she told him in detail of how good Christabel's father was. Of course he had heard these stories before. Chupplejeep had even fallen asleep during one rendition, not long after Bonita was born, when he had been sleep deprived. Christabel's mother had woken him up with a sharp poke to the ribs. He rubbed his chest; just the memory was enough to provoke some discomfort in him. Depending on his mother-in-law's mood, stories about her late husband varied. Earlier today the man was a saint, but according to Christabel, her mother often referred to her father as useless. 'There was a reason my father lost his hearing so young,' Christabel would often say with a smile.

Chupplejeep and his son, now distracted with his snack, returned to their gathering.

'So you're late,' Christabel said.

'Sorry,' Chupplejeep started, but his wife waved away his words. 'I expected you to be late. It's why I let Violeta tag along, to help with the kids. Shwetty, on the other hand…'

'She has something she wants to tell Pankaj before her trip to the south tomorrow,' Chupplejeep said.

'Oh yes, she does,' Christabel said. Her eyes shifted to the couple, and Chupplejeep followed her gaze. Shwetika was holding Bonita as far away as possible from her as the baby tried to grab her necklace. Shwetika's face was serious. She was saying something to Pankaj. 'She…' Christabel started. Chupplejeep leaned in closer to hear better over the din of the parade and crowds.

'What?' he said. 'I don't think I heard correctly.'

'Sir, sir,' a voice came from behind them. Chupplejeep turned towards the voice, as did the others. A woman with a thick fringe half covering her eyes was standing at the entrance to the apartment building in a black chiffon dress that skimmed her bare feet. Her lips were painted red, and she had thick kohl around her eyes.

'Can I help you?' Chupplejeep asked. He quickly glanced over at his kids to check they were safe.

The woman stared at Chupplejeep. 'We need you,' she said.

Chupplejeep wondered how the woman could see with that hair in her eyes. 'Sorry –' he started but the woman cut him off by raising her hand.

'You're a private detective, aren't you?'

Chupplejeep nodded.

'Then you better come with me.'

'Why?' Pankaj asked.

'A crime has just been committed.'

Christabel rolled her eyes. 'Here we go,' she said under her breath.

Chapter Seven

Chupplejeep made sure his family were safe in a taxi before heading upstairs with the woman.

'What's happened?' he asked as they rode the elevator to the tenth floor. The woman's perfume filled the lift with the smell of vanilla and caramel. It was a little cloying, and Chupplejeep couldn't help but cough to clear his airways. He watched as the display showed the floor level they were passing. It was amazing what a little *baksheesh* could buy when the maximum number of stories you could build in Goa was seven, or so the planning authority said.

'She'll tell you,' the woman said.

'Who is *she*?' Chupplejeep asked.

The woman with the thick fringe laughed. 'You're the detective, no? I thought you were on good terms with her father.'

'Mr Gopaldas's daughter?' Chupplejeep said. 'She lives in Mumbai.'

'She's here for Diwali.'

'And you are?'

'Her good friend, Nita Das. You can call me Nee.' Nita shook her head, and her fringe moved slightly away from her eyes. She offered her hand to Chupplejeep. He took it, introducing himself and Pankaj.

Chupplejeep glanced over at his colleague, who had turned quite pale. Was it his discussion with Shwetika that had made him so ashen, or was it something about this shoeless woman that had unsettled him? As the elevator doors opened, Nita pushed her way past the men and walked through the open door to the penthouse.

The investigator and his colleague followed, taking in the polished marble floors and ornate chandelier. The lights were bright and the ceilings high. Several earthenware tealights littered the hall for Diwali.

'Thank goodness,' a woman said in high-pitched voice. 'Nee, what would I do without you. You're here.'

Chupplejeep turned towards the voice. A petite woman stood in front of him, her head tilted to one side, her long hair appearing like it was weighing her down. She was dressed in white, unlike all the other guests, who wore black.

'You must be Miss Gopaldas,' Chupplejeep said. 'Your father and I –' he started, but the woman cut him off.

'Please,' she said. 'Call me Reena.' She turned to Pankaj. 'Yes,' she said, 'like Reena Kotecha the actress.' Reena looked back at Chupplejeep. 'I know my father has great respect for you. You saved him once and look,

Kingfisher Blues

again we need saving. But I think it was meant to be. You standing down there like that. It was destiny.'

There was a collective murmuring of agreement. At a party like this, Chupplejeep expected to see some evidence of drug taking and discarded champagne bottles. He wasn't disappointed. All the telltale signs of a rich kid's party were evident. The guests were inconvenienced and ready to get back to their revelry. A tall man with round glasses had just rolled a spliff. He sniffed the air and stepped onto the balcony.

'I only had a couple,' Reena said, as if reading Chupplejeep's mind. 'I had kept a clear head tonight, but still this bad thing happened.' Reena paused, her eyebrows knitted together.

'Nee, what do you think that means?' she asked, turning away from the investigator. 'It was a kombucha day and I drank champagne. You think that had something to do with it?'

'What exactly has happened here?' Chupplejeep asked, his eyes shifting to the clock and back again.

'Darling,' said another voice from the crowd. 'You mustn't do this to yourself. There will be an explanation.' A woman in her fifties with red hair and orange skin wearing what looked to be a black sarong made her way to Reena and clasped her hands in hers. 'We must not delve too deep at this point. The detective is here for a reason.' Reena looked unsure. She turned to Nita.

The partygoers seemed to lose interest at this point and resumed their normal conversation, as if whatever it was that Reena was worrying about was trivial. Perhaps they were used to this kind of drama at this kind of party.

'How will this look?' Reena whispered, as someone dared to turn the music on, albeit at a low volume. There was laughing coming from somewhere in the flat.

'On Insta?' Nita asked, pursing her lips as she considered the question, much to Chupplejeep's amazement. He had just cut short a family outing thanks to Nita, and here she was considering how this situation was going to look on social media. 'You're thinking of Ruby's party,' she said. 'The one where the clarinet went missing.'

Reena nodded. 'It's such a similar situation,' she said.

Nita held her hand up. 'This is not the time to compare. That party was over a year ago in Bandra, and it was a clarinet.'

'An expensive clarinet,' Reena said.

'There's never a good time to compare,' Nita said, her eyes drifting around the room. 'Think about your breathing. We were so close to a breakthrough, so close and now this is a setback.' Nita looked over at Chupplejeep. 'I'm her social media coach,' she said by way of explanation, like it was a common career choice.

Chupplejeep took a breath. 'I have to get on,' he said. 'I was under the impression that a crime had been committed here, but it sounds like you have everything under control, so my colleague and I will take our leave.' Chupplejeep turned before Reena had time to respond. Pankaj followed as he headed towards the door that someone had closed behind him.

'Sir, sir,' he heard a voice call from behind him. Chupplejeep stopped and gritted his teeth. He didn't want to turn around and get involved in some small-scale crime that had been blown out of proportion by someone used to the world working in her favour. Then he pictured Mr Gopaldas, the kind and gentle old soul. This image was quickly followed by one of Chupplejeep's daughter. He hoped that people would look out for Bonita too as she grew up.

'Yes,' he said, turning.

'My ring,' Reena said. 'It's missing. I was wearing it this evening and it disappeared, right here, barely an hour ago.'

Chupplejeep took in Reena's slight hands and arms. They were free from any jewellery.

'What kind of ring was it?' he asked.

Reena was silent.

'A diamond, a ruby?' he encouraged.

'I was wearing the Kingfisher Sapphire,' she said, a sob escaping from deep within her. 'And now it's gone.'

Chapter Eight

'Come, come,' Nita said, ushering Reena away towards a peach velour sofa. 'Let us breathe.' Chupplejeep listened as Nita tried to soothe her employer with her positive mantras, to little effect. Chupplejeep cleared his throat and quietened the room.

There were at least twenty guests in the room, and his eyes flitted from one to the next as he explained what he was about to do. His heart sank a little at the task that lay ahead of him. Reena had confirmed that no one had left the party since the disappearance of the ring, so there was a good chance the ring was still in her apartment. Instantly one guest declared that he had to leave.

'There's another party I need to get to,' the impatient guest with a pointy goatee said, making a show of looking at his diamond-studded watch. 'I don't have time to be searched and interviewed. Have you seen the time?'

'Whose party?' Reena was quick to ask.

'You don't know her,' came the response. Reena picked up her phone, and Chupplejeep noticed that Nita put her hand over the device. 'She's not on any social media,' the man said.

'Then does she even exist?' another person said. The crowd laughed.

'Come with me,' Chupplejeep said to the man with the goatee. 'If you're in a hurry, I can speak to you first. Your name is?'

'Daniel. Daniel Chatterjee,' he said. He glanced at Nita, who was watching Daniel from under her fringe.

Chupplejeep was sure he had heard the name before, but he couldn't place where and in what context he had heard it. He put his arm out to show Daniel into one of the spaces that he was using as an interview room.

'Did you notice the ring Reena was wearing earlier this evening?' Chupplejeep asked once they were seated in the office at the back of the apartment.

'I saw it,' Daniel said. 'It wasn't hard to miss. This big blue stone with two dazzling diamonds either side. It was what the party was about. This massive rock that all the women wanted to try on.'

'And did they?'

Daniel shrugged. 'Who knows? I made the right noises and then made my way to the bar.'

Chupplejeep noted Daniel's bleary eyes and slurred words. It was difficult to tell whether or not he was lying.

'Reena throws a great party. Right here in the centre with all the commotion going on outside, the demon god being burned in the distance. We didn't have to mix with the crowds. We could watch it all from this place. Then about half an hour ago there was a scream. Reena was almost hyperventilating. Her ring was missing.'

'She believes it was taken,' Chupplejeep said, taking his notebook from his pocket.

'Don't you use your phone to make notes?' Daniel asked. 'So much simpler. Yet you cops don't want to make your lives easier.'

'I'm not a cop,' Chupplejeep said.

'*Aacha*,' Daniel said, leaning back in his chair. 'That's right. I don't have to speak to you.'

Here we go, thought Chupplejeep. He took a breath and trotted out his well-used line. 'But why wouldn't you?' Chupplejeep said. 'It's not like you have anything to hide.'

'No one took Reena's Kingfisher Sapphire. She has issues, that's all. Her aim in life is to capture it all on social media to make other people think like her life is amazing.'

'Isn't that what all the youngsters do these days?' Chupplejeep asked.

Daniel laughed. He leaned forward and crossed his legs. He took a cigarette from his shirt pocket. 'Mind?' he asked. He lit up without waiting for an answer. Daniel took a drag, turned and blew the smoke away from Chupplejeep. 'Hang around with Reena long enough and you'll see she isn't your ordinary social media junkie. She's obsessed. She only ever does anything so she can post about it. She thinks everyone is looking at her feed, but you know what?' Daniel asked.

'What?' Chupplejeep asked.

'Reena looks at her own posts more than anyone else.' Daniel grinned. 'Listen,' he said, stubbing his cigarette in a nearby glass bowl. 'We all love Reena because we knew her from before, when she was this fun-loving and carefree woman, but last year she turned forty, realised she had no purpose in life and made social media her "thing." She has a problem and she knows it. That's why she's got Nita in her life. Nita is supposed to get Reena to stop comparing herself to other people's lives on social media. But Nita is becoming another obsession and an unhealthy one.'

'Yes,' Chupplejeep said, turning a page. It was hot and airless in Gopaldas's office. Chupplejeep tried to open the window. 'The social media coach,' he said, jimmying the handle. 'Do you know Nita?' Chupplejeep recalled the look she had given Daniel when he agreed to talk.

'It's crazy what some people can make money from,' Daniel said. 'I once tried my hand at publishing. It never worked. My first and last author was Alani Ali. Great name, although I think she made it up. She was spouting information on positivity and how it can be bad for you, something like that. The book flopped. I can't say if it was the marketing or the content. Maybe India wasn't ready to be told that you can't tell your kids to stop crying. That was ten years ago. The author distanced herself from the whole ordeal and is now making her money in other ways. Still with the mad theories. She liked the high life though. She isn't going to slog it out her whole life.'

'And what do you make money from?' Chupplejeep asked, half listening to Daniel's story. A diversion tactic, possibly. The window eventually gave way and opened.

'Has this got anything to do with the Kingfisher Sapphire?'

Chupplejeep ignored the question as he sat back down.

'I own Mango Book Stores,' Daniel said. 'I'm a bookseller, not a publisher.'

'Oh,' said Chupplejeep. So that was what his story was about. Was Daniel trying to show Chupplejeep his vulnerabilities by saying his first attempt at publishing had failed? The retail chain had started in Mumbai, and they now had stores all over India. The man sitting in front of him was a millionaire. Christabel had been talking about him only recently which was why Chupplejeep had recognised the name. Normally the richer the interviewee was, the more they threw their weight around, insisted they had better things to do with their time and looked down their noses at their interrogator. Daniel was surprisingly cooperative given his wealth.

'Do you read much?' Daniel asked.

Chupplejeep shook his head and Daniel laughed. 'Neither do I,' he said.

'And do you live in Goa now?' Chupplejeep asked.

'I live all over India. For now I'm in Goa, yes.'

'So if I need to contact you again –'

'I stay at the Hyatt when I'm in town.'

Chupplejeep nodded.

Kingfisher Blues

'If you ask me, the ring flew off Reena's finger and is probably hiding in some plant pot. Reena was quite drunk, and have you seen how skinny she is?'

Chupplejeep couldn't deny that. Reena did have slender fingers, but he doubted she would have worn a ring that was too loose for her, especially one so famous as the Kingfisher Sapphire. If he remembered correctly, it was a family heirloom which had some connection to a great Mughal. The apartment complex they were sitting in now, Sapphire Towers, was named after the ring. It was due to be displayed in the Chhatrapati Shivaji Maharaj Vastu Sanghralaya Museum in Mumbai in three weeks' time. The gem had been in the local papers. It wasn't news that Chupplejeep was interested in, but Christabel had been talking about it.

'Who would want such an expensive ring?' Christabel had said. 'You'd be too worried it would get lost, and the wearer would have no fun. It's a joy depriving ring.' Given what had happened here tonight, Christabel had been on to something.

Chupplejeep assured Daniel that the plant pots would be checked before asking if he could check Daniel's pockets.

'Get lost,' Daniel said.

Chupplejeep didn't waver. Eventually Daniel stood up, lit another cigarette and put it between his lips. He shoved his hands in his pockets, pulling out the inner fabric. Then he pulled out a wodge of notes from one back pocket and a phone from the other. 'Nothing here, I'm afraid.'

Daniel pocketed the money and held out his hand. Chupplejeep shook it, surprised by the man's courtesy. Daniel turned to leave. 'My driver's waiting downstairs,' he said, holding up his phone to show Chupplejeep a WhatsApp message of the thumbs-up emoji.

Chupplejeep considered the retailer as he walked away. Daniel was pleasant and rich enough to buy a Kingfisher Sapphire of his own. There was no need to steal one, but the Kingfisher Sapphire wasn't for sale; it was a treasured artefact. It was priceless. It was a well-known fact, if you read the gossip pages of the newspaper, which Christabel often did, that Mr Chatterjee collected art and whatnot. So it was quite possible that this man had wanted the jewel for his private collection. He made a note in his book. But it was too early in the investigation to make any wild guesses.

Chupplejeep glanced at his watch and sighed. It was past one in the morning. It was going to be a long night.

Chapter Nine

The interviews were tiresome. Some guests refused to cooperate. It took much cajoling on his part, and that in itself was exhausting. One guest, Aman Khosla, had let them pat down his pockets but had refused to talk to them and stormed out of the flat as soon as Pankaj had asked him his full name. The other partygoers didn't seem the slightest bit bothered by their presence and continued to eat and drink until it was time to be interviewed. Then they answered Chupplejeep's questions with relish, keen to be involved in something so dramatic.

'What a blast,' one woman said. 'This is quite something. This morning I had a glass of kombucha at a café in Anjuna, and I swear it was spiked with something. I knew then that this was going to be a great day. I'm so delighted to be here with Reena in her time of need.' The woman shook her head. She sounded like she spent most of her time at acid parties. The perfect candidate to steal a ring to sell to feed her drug habit. Chupplejeep questioned her further and found that she owned a successful beauty line, so perhaps she didn't need the money. Apart from a handful of guests, all Reena's acquaintances, because he doubted they were real friends, were well-off – not just well-off but seriously wealthy. The kind you would see on *Bollywood Wives*.

Very few guests had financial motivation to want that ring. He and Pankaj had scoured the apartment. The plant pots had been carefully examined, as well as any hiding place that someone could go back to later. They also had the arduous task of searching in guests' handbags. It hadn't been an easy feat. Most of the guests were reluctant. 'Who are you to ask to look into my bag?' one partygoer had asked, clutching her purple patent bag to her chest. Chupplejeep had to remind himself that he no longer had the law behind him. He was a private investigator with no authority to search people whatsoever.

Eventually the lady with the purple bag had conceded, and the reason for her reluctance soon became apparent. She was carrying a small amount of marijuana hidden in an ornate red and white pillbox. Chupplejeep eyed her as he opened the small container.

'For medicinal purposes,' she said, looking the other way. Chupplejeep replaced the lid of the box and handed back the bag to the guest. Then there was the blister pack of Viagra they had found on another guest, another explanation to their initial reluctance to be searched.

It had been a hard task, but they had got there in the end. Everyone, it seemed, wanted to be cleared of having taken the Kingfisher Sapphire, and if their other indiscretions had been discovered in the process, well, it was a small price to pay, or so they believed. But someone at the party had taken that ring. Chupplejeep just had to find out who it was.

'Do you know of anyone who would want to take the ring?' Chupplejeep eventually asked Reena when the other guests had filtered out. Reena had insisted that Nita accompany her for moral support. The women held hands, or rather Reena was holding on to Nita. The social media coach noticed his gaze and beamed. Reena needed her, and Nita was thriving on it.

'Everyone,' Reena exclaimed. 'They were all so jealous of it.' The woman looked at her bare hand and sniffled. 'Don't let them fool you. They may all be rich, but they still want it because they can't have it. The piece is one of a kind. It is part of history.'

'Why would you wear a ring that everyone wanted?' Chupplejeep asked.

'Good question,' Nita said, flicking her fringe away from her eyes. 'Evil eye is still a worry. You don't want someone to curse you with their envy. Reena and I discussed this.' Nita clasped Reena's hands in both of hers.

Reena pulled her hands away. 'Nee didn't want me to wear the ring. She didn't want any photos of it on social media either. She thought someone would wish bad thoughts on me, but I didn't listen.' Reena reached out and squeezed Nita's hand. 'But the whole point of the party was the ring. I thought about wearing a fake. But the thought came too late, and there was no time for our jeweller to make it.'

'And Nita,' Chupplejeep asked. 'Where were you when the ring disappeared?'

'Are you accusing me?' Nita asked.

'I'm asking everyone the same questions,' Chupplejeep said.

'I was doing a crystal meditation on the balcony at the time,' she said.

'And you, Reena?' Chupplejeep asked. 'Where were you when you first noticed the ring was missing?'

Reena looked away. 'I was pouring myself a glass of champagne,' she said. 'I looked down and it wasn't there. I panicked. I screamed. And all the guests started looking here, there and everywhere.'

'Nita,' Chupplejeep started. 'How well do you know Daniel Chatterjee?'

There was a flicker of hesitation in Nita's eyes which Chupplejeep caught despite her fringe. Reena was looking intently at her friend.

'I hardly know him,' Nita said. 'The first time I met him was at the party.'

'I see,' said Chupplejeep. He noticed a look of relief on Reena's face. Were the three of them in this together? Or did Reena have a crush on Daniel and was worried her social media coach had beaten her to it? Both were possibilities.

'I notice you don't have any staff here tonight,' Chupplejeep said. It was odd for someone of Reena

Gopaldas's standing not to have waiters and waitresses and bar staff.

Reena's eyes found Nita. 'I told them to go and enjoy the celebrations downstairs with their families.'

This wealthy client knew how to treat her staff at least.

'They'll be here soon to clean up this mess though. I'm not lifting a finger after tonight.'

'Ah,' Chupplejeep said.

'You can't expect me to,' Reena said.

'At least this tragedy cannot be blamed on them,' Nita said.

Chupplejeep smiled. 'Do you have regular staff here?' he asked.

'The daughter of the woman who practically raised me, and another. He too has been with us for some time,' Reena said.

'And can I speak to them?' Chupplejeep asked.

'If you must,' came the response. 'They'll be here shortly.'

'Not today. I must get back to my family,' Chupplejeep said. 'Tomorrow, perhaps,' he added, remembering the death of the kathakali dancer he was also investigating.

Chupplejeep stood as Pankaj entered the room. The young man motioned to him that they hadn't found anything in the bedrooms. 'Well, the ring isn't here,' Chupplejeep said. 'We've searched as best we can.'

'So that's it,' Reena said. 'You're just leaving me.'

'Like I advised earlier, you need to report this at the police station. And you need to get some rest. Maybe speak to your insurers,' Chupplejeep said, although he believed two of those suggestions were pointless. The police would have little time to investigate something like this, and it was highly unlikely that the Kingfisher Sapphire was insured. The premiums were too high, and there were very few companies in India that provided that level of insurance. Most wealthy citizens in India had little or no insurance for their jewels. They were often rich enough to replace anything that went missing. The Kingfisher Sapphire was irreplaceable though. Christabel had been right. It should have been locked in a glass cabinet, not on the skinny finger of a socialite with a social media addiction.

Reena had seen through his recommendations. She looked at him with her big brown eyes.

'I know your father,' Chupplejeep said. 'I'll do my best to find your ring for you.'

'We'll pay generously,' she said. 'Daddy is going to kill me when he finds out. He told me not to wear it, but… I couldn't help myself.' She turned to Nita. 'Nee's helping me,' she announced as if she were talking to her support group.

Chupplejeep turned to his protégé. Pankaj had dark circles around his eyes. He would want to get back to Shwetika before she left for her girls' trip tomorrow. He assured Reena that she would hear from them again. The tealights in the hall had been extinguished.

'Does this party have a hashtag?' Pankaj asked.

'Kingfisherblue,' said Reena. She reached for her phone and opened it, beaming at the display as it lit up. 'Four thousand likes and fifty-two comments,' she said, turning the screen towards Chupplejeep. The picture that had garnered the love was one of Reena, her right hand held up for everyone to see the Kingfisher Sapphire.

Chapter Ten

It was nearly ten o'clock when Pankaj entered the office at the rear of Chupplejeep's house. The nameplate that Chupplejeep had nailed to the door had tarnished after the heavy monsoon that had just passed. Pankaj ran his fingers over it before he stepped inside. Closing the door behind him, he sat at his desk, which was positioned to the left of the room.

The office was small, designed for a single desk, but when Pankaj said that he had lost faith in the system and wanted to join Chupplejeep as a private investigator, Chupplejeep insisted that he share his space.

'We could rent somewhere in town,' Pankaj had suggested, but Chupplejeep had shaken his head.

'Not while we're starting out. We can't spend money unnecessarily. It's free here,' Chupplejeep had said, looking at an imaginary stain on his desk.

Pankaj had felt embarrassed then, that he had suggested something that would cost his boss money he didn't have. Chupplejeep was doing his best to pay

Kingfisher Blues

Pankaj despite barely covering the costs for some of the cases they took on. It had been a foolish suggestion. Pankaj had quickly countered it with another idea that turned out to be just as bad as the last.

'We need to stop taking on cases for free. Like when we found out who was stealing coconuts from that old lady's house. And when we caught the culprit who stole the local pao-walla's cycle.'

'We may not have been paid in cash,' Chupplejeep had said. 'But that old woman gave us the best pot of xacuti I have ever tasted, and every month that pao-walla delivers me fresh hot bread.'

Pankaj had busied himself with some paperwork after that, knowing that Chupplejeep wasn't interested in the thick coconut curry or the fresh bread. He just liked helping people. The food gifts were just a bonus. Deep down, Pankaj had felt the same. But he was a husband now, and a husband was a provider. Working for food did not pay the bills. He had to admit though, that the old woman's xacuti was the best he had tasted.

Pankaj stared at his boss, who was talking animatedly with someone on the telephone. If only he were more like Chupplejeep. It was hard though when Shwetika wasn't at all like Christabel. She didn't understand the late nights and constant phone calls, and she definitely didn't understand the poor salary he took home every month. Shwetty was a woman who wanted a full life, a rich life, one filled with luxuries; a husband who doted on her. Pankaj did dote on her; he had put her on a pedestal when they had been dating, and that was where it had started to go wrong.

'In a relationship you need to be equals,' his mother had said to him. 'You are not better than Shwetty and she is not better than you. You are a team.'

The problem was that Pankaj did think that Shwetty was better than him, and she believed the same. Shwetty also believed that Pankaj loved his job more than her, and he had proved her right by returning home in the early hours of this morning. When Pankaj said he wanted to start a family, Shwetty wanted to know if he had time for a baby. Yesterday, at the parade, Shwetty had given him an ultimatum: his job or a family. Early this morning, his wife had left for the south – a girls' trip with her friends – and Pankaj didn't have the chance to ask her if she had meant what she had said. He had also been afraid of her response. Especially as he had been out for most of the night before, leaving her to return home with Christabel. Pankaj put his head in his hands.

~

Chupplejeep disconnected the call and shifted his gaze to Pankaj. He didn't have to ask why his colleague was looking so glum because he already knew. Shwetty was the root of all Pankaj's problems. No doubt she had berated him for leaving her at the parade yesterday.

'Are you ready?' Chupplejeep asked.

'Where are we going, sir?'

Kingfisher Blues

'I'll tell you on the way,' Chupplejeep said, picking up the keys of his Baleno and heading for the door.

As they walked along the veranda around the outside of the house, Christabel called out to them.

'You two want some fresh coconut water?' She was standing next to their occasional handyman who tackled the difficult jobs around the house, including shimmying up the coconut trees and picking the heavy fruit before they fell on the house or worse, one of them.

The two men stopped. They looked at each other then the children. Nicholas held a green fruit in his hands; pink and white straws peeked out from the top of the tender coconut. Bonita greedily grabbed at her straw with a chubby hand.

'It's tempting,' Chupplejeep said, 'but we'll be late if we don't leave now.' Chupplejeep kissed Bonita on her forehead and ruffled Nicholas's hair. 'Be good for your mother,' he said to both of them as a large fruit was thrown to the ground with a heavy thud.

'We're going to see Jagdish's ex-wife,' Chupplejeep said to Pankaj as he started the engine. A quick internet search had told him that the star had previously been married, and the woman lived locally. It was a lead they had to follow, especially as Chupplejeep had been unable to get hold of Rupali, Jagdish's widow. 'Her name is Sonal. Her husband Abhijeet Johar answered when I rang. They're meeting us at the Shake Shack in twenty minutes.'

'Abhijeet Johar?' Pankaj asked. 'He was a big-shot manager for Bollywood actors and actresses back in the day.'

'Was?' Chupplejeep said.

'He has a son who has or had some form of addiction problem. Abhijeet took some time out to deal with him, but by the time he returned to work, most of his clients had left him or no longer wanted to work with him. You know what these celebrities are like. They want attention all the time; they don't want to compete with their manager's wayward offspring.'

'It sounds like there *is* a market out there for a social media coach. I've heard a lot of strange job titles in my time,' Chupplejeep said, 'but a social media coach?'

'Sir, it's a sign of the times.'

'What did you think of our social media coach last night?'

'Nita?' Pankaj stared out of the window. 'There was something about her that wasn't quite right.'

'The way she needed Reena as much as Reena needed her,' Chupplejeep said.

'You noticed it too. And something else. I can't quite put my finger on it,' Pankaj said.

'Disingenuous, perhaps,' Chupplejeep said. Nita had been hired by Reena to help her combat her addiction, and from what Nita was saying, it appeared like she was trying to help the heiress. But there was something under Nita's show of calm and positive mantras, something about the way her eyes darted this way and that from under her heavy fringe that told Chupplejeep that Nita was hiding something.

'Do you think the Kingfisher Sapphire will turn up?' Pankaj asked.

The ring was beautiful and expensive. Any one of the partygoers could have taken it. There was no security and no staff around to keep an eye on things. But at the same time, most of Reena's guests were loaded and appeared to have an affection for their host. Would they really steal from someone they cared for? He explained his thinking to Pankaj.

'Gore Vidal said, "every time a friend succeeds, I die a little." Or something like that. Envy is a strong motivator,' Chupplejeep added.

'I can't have it, so you can't have it either,' Pankaj said. 'It's a childish mentality.'

'Mr Gopaldas called me this morning. He wants the ring found and has made me a generous offer if we can locate it. I put a call out to a local jeweller I know. I told him to contact me if any stone matching the description of the Kingfisher Sapphire is discussed in his circles.'

'If one of the guests took it, it could be thousands of miles away by now,' Pankaj said.

'Mr Gopaldas knows that, but he has promised the ring to the Chhatrapati Shivaji Maharaj Vastu Sanghralaya in Mumbai, and Mr Gopaldas doesn't like to break his promises. He's a man of his word. It's why he's made us such a good offer. If we can find the ring, we could get the office in town you were talking about.'

'Sir,' Pankaj said, colour rising to his cheeks. 'That was a *faltu*, rubbish, suggestion. Your house is just as good as any office. And there is a kitchen close by.'

'It would be good to have space to move in our office though, wouldn't it?'

Pankaj smiled.

Chapter Eleven

The Shake Shack had been recently refurbished, with pink and white walls and framed milkshake prints, but still Sonal Johar looked out of place. She wore gold hoops in her ears and an intricately embroidered shalwaar kameez in deep purple with silver stitching. A red ruby caught the sunlight and dazzled Pankaj. He averted his gaze towards the ground and noticed that Sonal's shoes were modest flat black sandals. A stark contrast to the rest of her outfit.

Chupplejeep introduced himself and Pankaj and thanked Sonal for agreeing to meet. 'Like I said on the phone,' said Chupplejeep, 'Mr Kapoor has asked me to look into this matter. Is your husband here?'

Sonal shook her head, her lips pressed firmly together. 'Something came up,' she said after a long pause.

Before Chupplejeep and Pankaj had a chance to sit down, Sonal stood again. 'It's a little too cool in here with the air con,' she said. 'Let's go outside.' She motioned to a waiter, who took their order for three mango shakes before they made their way to the outside seating area that had a water feature and a rock garden. 'There's a resident tortoise that lives in that garden,' she said, pointing to the green behind the rocks. She stood on her tiptoes and peered into the space, then she scanned the area for a table she liked the look of and sat down. 'I like watching water flow. It's so soothing, don't you find? Here we have a place by the water, and it truly calms my soul. When we're in Mumbai it's a little different. Life there is fast paced. Everybody wants something from you. Goa suits my son better, so we mostly stay here now.' Sonal stared at the water flowing out from an earthenware pot, blackened by mould.

'Your ex-husband,' Chupplejeep started. Despite her sunglasses, he noticed she was wearing thick makeup around her left eye. He didn't want to stare too much, but he was certain she was covering a bruise. He could just make out the yellow and blue skin above her cheekbone.

Chupplejeep wasn't subtle enough. 'Silly accident,' Sonal said, adjusting her sunglasses. 'I slipped getting out of the tub the other day, fell and hit my face. It was weeks ago now. Taking time to heal.'

The investigator nodded politely. 'We want to know about Jagdish,' he said.

'Ah yes. You too want something from me. It's like we are back in Mumbai.' Sonal Johar gave a small laugh. She tilted her head to one side and pushed a strand of her silky black hair behind her ear. 'Of course I want you to help catch my ex's killer. Jagdish was many things, but he didn't deserve his fate. Definitely not.'

'And what was he?' Chupplejeep asked.

'Sorry?' Sonal asked, straightening in her chair.

'You just said that he was many things. What was he?'

'A husband, a father.' Sonal looked into the distance. 'He was protective of his girls. Most of the young men around here have been put off approaching his daughters because of the questioning he gives every young suitor.'

'That surprises me,' Chupplejeep said. 'In my day a young man would see that as a challenge.'

Sonal shrugged. 'Jagdish loved his daughters, from what I saw.'

'He was a good father?' Chupplejeep asked.

Sonal looked away. 'Jagdish was a friend; sometimes a bit of a narcissist. They say you shouldn't speak ill of the dead. But if there were no bad feelings between us, we would have still been married.'

'He liked getting his own way?' Chupplejeep said.

'Lording over people, controlling them.' Sonal stared at Chupplejeep. 'You should be asking Rupali all this. I knew Jagdish over twenty years ago. It's possible that he was a different man then.'

Chupplejeep took out his notebook as the waiter placed the three yellow shakes on the table. 'So you haven't been in touch with Jagdish in the last few years?' Chupplejeep took a sip of his sweet drink. It was excellent.

'We spoke now and again. Sometimes he helped with my son. Bhavan can be a bit of a handful, and in the last year Jagdish has been meeting with him, talking to him, trying to get him to change his ways. It's not easy for a twenty-four-year-old to take advice from their parents. Bhavan seemed to listen to Jagdish though.'

'They were close?'

'Who?' asked Sonal.

'Your son and your ex-husband?'

Sonal swatted Chupplejeep's words away with her hands. 'They talked, that's all.' Sonal turned away, her eyes directed towards the running water.

Chupplejeep let the silence be for a moment. 'You never wanted children with Jagdish?' he asked.

'I don't really think that's any of your business,' Sonal said.

'And even without the shared responsibility of children, you stayed in touch?'

'Not always. After we split, we didn't talk for years, and then a few years ago we bumped into each other. We kept in touch after that. You know how it is as you get older… And Jagdish was good with Bhavan, so…' Sonal gave Chupplejeep an exasperated look. 'You want people in your life that you like.'

'So the split with the occasional narcissist was amicable?'

Sonal turned sharply to Chupplejeep. 'We were married for over ten years. We met when we were young. We both made an impression on each other's lives. He had his faults, but I suppose we were friends.'

Kingfisher Blues

'Jagdish started training as a kathakali dancer from a young age,' Chupplejeep said. He had read his full Wikipedia page this morning alongside his bowl of cornflakes. Bonita had been trying to get his attention, and having failed to do so, she had thrown her porridge on the floor. He had suffered a cold look from Christabel, and so he had made a quick exit to his office, waiting with the door shut, until Pankaj had arrived.

'It was Jagdish's vocation. He had been pushed into it by his mother, but really it was the job for him. He loved it. He was passionate about it. I always came second.'

'*Aacha*,' Chupplejeep said.

Sonal pulled her sunglasses from her eyes and cleaned them with the edge of her shalwaar. She replaced them and took a modest sip of her shake. 'I knew what I was getting into when I married him. His mother made me aware of what I would have to sacrifice if I chose to marry her son. Her son was destined for great things, she said, and she was right. It came at a price though. I was young, and I believed I could put my career aside for love. But at the end of the day, you need more than love to sustain you. I started to resent him and then…'

There was a long pause. Chupplejeep fully expected Sonal to continue with her story, but apparently she was done. 'So you left him?' he asked.

'Is this really relevant, Mr Chupplejeep?' she asked. 'I want to help you find my ex-husband's killer, but I don't see what the past has got to do with it.'

'I'm trying to get a picture of the man Jagdish Sharma was, the man he became, so that I can better understand why anyone would want to hurt him.'

'A lot of people would want to hurt him. He was an arrogant man, a rich and powerful man too. Rich, powerful, arrogant men are not well liked. You're a private investigator; surely you know that.'

'To dislike someone is one thing,' Chupplejeep said, 'but to take their life is something else.'

Sonal rubbed her temples with her hands. 'So what do you want to know?'

'When was the last time you spoke to Jagdish?'

'A few days before his show was due to start.'

'What did you talk about?' Chupplejeep asked.

'This and that,' Sonal said. 'Nothing in particular.'

'Does your husband mind you talking to your ex-husband?' Chupplejeep asked.

'My husband knows there's nothing between us. He trusts me.' Sonal stood up. She made a show of looking at her watch. 'I need to get going,' she said. 'I said I'd give you twenty minutes of my time, and you've had it.'

'You need to be somewhere?' Chupplejeep asked.

'I need to meet my son at the centre.'

'The centre?'

'Yes. It's a good place for him right now. Occasionally my son requires some rehabilitation, not that it is any of your business. The Atul Centre gives him the space he needs to get better.'

'How did your son take the news of your ex-husband passing? If Jagdish had been helping him, I can imagine they had become quite close.'

Sonal studied her fingernails. 'I really must go,' she said.

'Of course,' Chupplejeep said, standing. 'One last question, if I may.'

'Go on then,' Sonal said, impatiently.

'Where were you on the night of the 12th November?'

'12th November?' Sonal asked.

'Jagdish's opening night. The night he was killed.'

'I wasn't at Kapoor's, if that is what you are thinking.' She hesitated. 'I was with Bhavan. His centre was hosting their own Diwali show. We had bought Bhavan a motorbike; a new black and silver one. He had this red snake put on the gas tank, commissioned someone to do it for him. A bit of an extravagance for us, but he had been after one for some time, and he's twenty-four now. We couldn't deny him forever. He had taken it out and, excited with his gift, agreed that we attend the show with him that night. Sometimes he's not so keen on us coming, but those shows are legendary, and I wanted to see it for myself. After Bhavan got the bike, he was so happy he would have agreed to anything. The day of the show came, and he had changed his mind about us attending, but he had previously agreed, and so there we were. We were at the show. There were lots of staff there; just ask them if you don't believe me. Can I go now?' Sonal asked.

'And did the show live up to your expectations?' Chupplejeep asked.

'I – er, yes,' Sonal said. 'It was different, that's for sure. Actors dressed up as birds in the middle of the gardens, no stage as such. The garden was the stage apparently, or something. A little alternative for me.'

'But you stayed till the end?' Chupplejeep asked.

Sonal nodded but didn't meet his eye.

Pankaj, who had remained quiet this whole time, had finished his mango shake. He stood. 'Years ago, your husband used to manage Jagdish. Is that right?'

Sonal stared at Pankaj. She stuttered as she spoke. 'Y-yes, that's right,' she said.

'So did Jagdish know Abhijeet first or you?' Pankaj asked.

Sonal looked at Chupplejeep. Chupplejeep gave her a half-nod. 'We all met around the same time; in Mumbai at a bar many years ago. Jagdish and Abhijeet were never close. It was a business transaction between them, nothing else.'

'But even now, with nothing holding you together, you were all still friends.'

Sonal swallowed and then forced a smile to her lips. 'Is that so strange?' she asked.

'A little,' Chupplejeep said.

Sonal turned on her heel. 'I really must go,' she said. 'Please check my whereabouts at the Atul Centre.'

'I will,' Chupplejeep called after her.

Sonal didn't look back.

Chapter Twelve

Darsh hunkered down in the driving seat of his Honda, careful not to be seen, as Chupplejeep and his colleague left the shack. He caught his reflection in his recently installed mirrored music system and grinned. He looked good, there was no denying it. Stalking this private investigator was not doing anything for his look though. Hunched down like this, there was no way he would get the creases out of his shirt. He cast aside any thoughts of his appearance. There were more pressing things at hand.

Sonal had left the establishment just moments before. Darsh hadn't mentioned Jagdish's ex-wife in the brief conversation he had had with the investigator, so the detective had figured it out another way. Would Sonal assume that he had tipped them off? Darsh wouldn't be in suspense for long. She would call him the minute she felt she could. She usually did.

As the investigator got into his car, Darsh's phone began to ring. He pulled the phone from his pocket and looked at the display, then he put it back. He wasn't in the mood for threats and false promises today. Sonal was the one who had got him into this mess. He straightened and started the car as the dark blue Baleno moved off. Keeping his distance, he followed the car as it made its way over the bridge towards Porvorim.

Darsh had hoped that he had fooled Chupplejeep into thinking he was after some makeup when he had been caught searching Jagdish's dressing room. Darsh had been proud of his quick thinking. Makeup was a big part of a kathakali dancer's costume. Their faces were painted masks. Darsh wasn't fully in control of his body when his face was painted green with exaggerated red lips and black eyes. An alter ego took over when that headdress was placed upon him. It wasn't just his eyes and lips that took on a life of their own, but he too felt like a different person. One he sometimes didn't recognise.

The papers had reported that Darsh's movements were spectacular, that he was the next big thing, but Jagdish Sharma had continually refused to make way for him. Jagdish had even muscled in on the Baytown contract that he had been offered. Popatrao had approached Darsh to offer him a residency at his five-star hotel. Jagdish found out, and a day later the contract was withdrawn. Jagdish must have been desperate for Darsh not to have any kind of limelight in signing up to what turned out to be a bum deal. The hotel didn't have all of its stars, and Popatrao had no money to pay.

Of course Jagdish had his legal team on it. Had he not died when he did, he would have got out of the contract one way or another, and he would have dragged Popatrao's name through the mud while doing so. Darsh didn't have connections like Jagdish did. He would have had to go through with the contract and in doing so would have probably been a laughing stock.

Jagdish had done him a favour. Darsh hadn't seen it like that until his girlfriend had pointed it out. It was little consolation. For two years Jagdish had done his best to get in Darsh's way, and there was only so long that Darsh could put up with it. So when Sonal Johar came to him with a plan, Darsh didn't think twice about accepting, because he had nothing to lose and everything to gain.

Darsh didn't know that things would end up like this though. The police were ineffective. He didn't think for one moment that Kapoor, of all people, would hire a private investigator to look into the matter. Jagdish wasn't that important. It was a line he told himself again and again, but he was beginning to see through this lie. Kapoor didn't want the name of his theatre sullied. If this investigator, if this Chupplejeep fellow, found out who killed Jagdish, Kapoor would get the credit, his theatres would thrive, and the great Jagdish would be glorified forevermore.

As Darsh pulled up a few metres behind the Baleno, now parked outside the pathology office, another thought crossed his mind. Until now, Darsh hadn't been worried about Sonal because he had trusted her implicitly. Until now, Darsh didn't think that with a little pressure Jagdish's ex-wife would crumble and throw him under the bus. But she could. To casual observers, Sonal didn't seem fragile, but she was – fragile and a little unpredictable.

The thought gave Darsh an uneasy feeling in the pit of his stomach. The leftover cold prawn *balchao* he had had for breakfast suddenly didn't seem like a good idea. He opened the door to his car and retched, emptying the contents of his stomach onto the pavement. Wiping his mouth with the back of his hand, he swiftly closed the car door, started the engine and made his way back home.

Chapter Thirteen

'Great work,' Chupplejeep said as they pulled up outside Kulkarni's office. A single hanging star signified the celebration of Diwali, but knowing Kulkarni, he had just used an old Christmas decoration.

Pankaj beamed. 'There had to be another connection between Sonal, Abhijeet and Jagdish. So I thought why not risk it and ask her the question.'

'You didn't know Abhijeet used to manage Jagdish?'

'It was a guess.'

'A good one. I couldn't see anything about it online when I looked previously. And what about that black eye?'

'Abhijeet or Jagdish could have given that to Sonal,' Pankaj said.

'Or her son. He has behavioural issues. If he was spending time with Jagdish recently then perhaps there could be motive there too.'

'It should have been the other way around,' Pankaj said. 'Jagdish should have wanted his ex-wife and manager dead. They betrayed him. But sir, do you really think that there would be bad feelings between the friends two and a half decades later?'

'The word "friends" doesn't sit well with me. I find it difficult to believe that the three of them remained friends.'

Pankaj shrugged. 'My mum has been reconnecting with all her old friends. It could be an age thing.'

'These people are not retired with nothing better to do with their time,' Chupplejeep said, getting out of the Baleno. 'No offence to your mom. Jagdish Sharma was at the peak of his career. He wasn't looking for old friends.'

'They say it's lonely at the top. His ex-wife and his ex-manager would have known that. Maybe he reached out to them in a moment of loneliness.'

'Maybe,' Chupplejeep said, 'or maybe it's something else.' He made his way into Kulkarni's office.

~

'Five months you've ignored me, and the minute you have a dead body on your hands the telephone goes.' Kulkarni stretched out his hand and Chupplejeep took it. 'So, boss,' he continued. 'Every time I want to see you I need to hang around the morgue, eh?'

'Kulkarni,' Chupplejeep said. ' You know it's not like that.'

'Then what is it like?' asked Kulkarni, enjoying the game. 'Tell me.'

'He's a father now,' Pankaj said. 'A busy man.'

'Oh yes. How are my favourite two?'

Chupplejeep couldn't help but smile. 'They're good. Christabel's an excellent mum, but you never told me what hard work it is. Really, it's something else. Those kids, they always want something.'

'It's a thankless task,' Kulkarni said, flashing Chupplejeep a wide smile. 'But you're not here to talk about your babies. You want to know what I know about the death of the famous Jagdish Sharma. I never saw any kathakali dancing. I was considering going to watch his performance at Popatrao's hotel.'

'You were going to pay to watch a kathakali dancer? I wouldn't have put you down for that.'

'I wasn't going to pay, Baba,' Kulkarni said. 'My wife knows Popatrao's wife. She was going to get free tickets.'

'Ah, that's the Kulkarni I know.'

Kulkarni playfully hit Chupplejeep's shoulder. 'Do you want my help or no?' he asked. 'Do you want to know what was in the lassi drink you found in Jagdish's dressing room?'

Chupplejeep and Pankaj settled themselves on two metal chairs in Kulkarni's small office. 'Tell,' Chupplejeep said.

'Yoghurt, water, salt and a pinch of…'

'Poison?' Pankaj enquired.

'Still so keen,' Kulkarni said. 'Not poison, just *bhang*.'

'Quantity?'

'Not enough to knock out someone as big as Jagdish Sharma. Just something to relax him. He probably drank it before every performance.'

'I was certain that drink was laced with something. Something to put Jagdish into a slumber so that the killer could easily stab him to death,' said Chupplejeep.

'Jagdish would need to keep his eyes focused for all those movements, but he would have certainly been relaxed with that amount of bhang in his drink,' Kulkarni said, 'And there wasn't much of a struggle, from what I've seen in the report.'

'You've seen the autopsy report?' Chupplejeep asked.

Kulkarni laughed. 'You say jump and I say how high, no? That's the kind of relationship we have.'

'Kulkarni –' Chupplejeep started to protest, but Kulkarni cut him off by raising his hand. 'You're lucky I like you.' He stood up and walked over to his desk, reaching into the open drawer to retrieve a brown file. 'You were right,' he said.

'Like I said, Mr Sharma probably had a little bhang before every performance. Whoever attacked Jagdish took him by surprise, maybe they added some extra bhang to his drink. He was feeling good on the opening night of his show, the first half of his performance down. He wasn't on guard; the bhang saw to that. The killer approached the dancer, perhaps confronted him about something. The killer reached for Jagdish's knife to stab him. My guess is your perpetrator pulled the weapon out from its sheath quickly, before Jagdish had time to register what was happening. Just three stab wounds

Kingfisher Blues

were found on his body. The one made to the heart was fatal. The killer meant business. He or she was not very happy with our kathakali dancer.'

'Do you think they meant to kill?' Pankaj asked.

'You don't stab someone in the chest to teach them a lesson,' Kulkarni said. 'The stab wound to the heart led to blood filling the pericardium.' Kulkarni looked at his audience. 'That's the sac around the heart. This compressed the heart and compromised its function. Simple.'

Pankaj flinched. Even now, after all these years, he still felt nauseous at the thought of death, especially where large amounts of blood were concerned. The thought of Jagdish being stabbed and blood rushing out of his wounds made Pankaj straighten and take a deep breath. Kulkarni laughed.

Chupplejeep twisted one end of his moustache, the way he did when he was thinking. 'A narcotic sedative in the right quantity injected or ingested could kill someone, no? Why not use a fatal poison instead?'

'A narcotic sedative could suppress the respiratory centre of the brain,' Kulkarni said. 'If the correct amount was administered to Mr Sharma, he could have simply fallen into a deep sleep, slipped into a coma and then stopped breathing. There are many ways to murder someone. I don't need to tell you this. The killer could have suffocated their victim also. But this would have required persistent strength and could have taken some time, and the killer wanted a quick death, it seemed.'

'Or maybe the killer didn't know what he was doing,' Pankaj said. 'After all, he or she didn't come prepared with their own murder weapon. They used Jagdish's knife.'

'It's likely...' Kulkarni started.

'...but with the internet you can find out anything.' Pankaj finished the pathologist's sentence for him.

'Not necessarily,' Chupplejeep said, thinking of the rash Bonita had developed ten months ago. He had put her symptoms into a search engine and had instantly regretted it. It came up with all manner of illnesses, and ultimately the best course of action was to take her to a doctor to get her checked out. It turned out to be heat rash. Chupplejeep had realised then that parenting involved a lot of unnecessary worry.

'How did you get this information?' Pankaj asked the pathologist.

'It's better you don't ask. But your boss here owes me more than one beer.'

'Your contact in Miramar?' Chupplejeep asked.

Kulkarni nodded. Chupplejeep gave him a pat on the back.

'Could a woman have done this?' Pankaj asked.

'I don't see why not. Jagdish was a big man, but with the sedative in his system, it would have been easy to overpower him, and I think he knew his attacker. It was why he was taken by surprise. Whoever killed him, the great Jagdish Sharma wasn't expecting them to harm him.'

'Was there anything else in the file?' Chupplejeep asked. He had tried calling Jagdish's widow several times now hoping to speak with the woman, but each time the phone rang out. Was the woman lost to her grief, or was it something more sinister than that? He wondered if any of Rupali Sharma's jewellery was missing a small green stone like the one he had found in the dancer's dressing room.

'What are you after?'

'The murder weapon was an embellished knife. I assume it was studded with precious stones.'

''Es,' Kulkarni said. 'I thought you'd be interested in it. I took copies of the photos they have on file. I'll send them to you. As far as I can recall, there were stones on the knife.'

'Were any stones missing?' Chupplejeep asked, thinking of the small green stone again. He recalled a conversation he had had with a yoga teacher with a fascination with crystals on a past case. What had she said about green stones? That they were thought to bring about positivity and healing, something like that.

Kulkarni shook his head. 'So who wanted him dead?' he asked, interrupting Chupplejeep's thoughts.

Chupplejeep turned to Kulkarni. 'That's what I'm trying to find out.'

Chapter Fourteen

'What a place,' Pankaj said as he stepped out of the Baleno and walked down the palm tree-lined drive with his boss. A large gulmohur tree stood to the right of the entrance of the building. 'This must be costing the Johars an arm and a leg.'

'It certainly isn't a place I had imagined. This is something quite different. More like a luxury retreat.' Chupplejeep and Pankaj walked up the stone steps towards the lobby of the Atul Centre. Painted cream with filigree balustrades, it didn't look like the institutions Chupplejeep was used to visiting. Inside, the air was cool with a faint smell of jasmine, which tickled Pankaj's nose.

'What exactly is this place?' Pankaj asked in a low voice.

'This is a first-class centre,' came a voice from behind them. The two men turned to see a sizeable lady in a red and white shift dress beam at them. Her lips were painted a cherry red and her cheeks were dabbed with some kind of shimmer. Cynthia, she said, holding out her hand. Her smile was infectious.

Chupplejeep and Pankaj introduced themselves and enquired after Bhavan.

'The Johars' boy,' Cynthia said. 'He stays with us now and again. Though he's not so much a boy anymore.'

A woman with fair hair and a large white plaster on her cheek walked past. She smiled as she went, pulling her sun hat further down as she noticed the intruders. 'On my way to the pool,' she said in a European accent.

'Of course,' Cynthia said. 'Do enjoy the fresh watermelon juice,' she called after her.

'We have a couple of questions,' Chupplejeep started.

'I'm sure you do,' Cynthia said, stepping towards a two-seater sofa in the foyer. She bent down and plumped the cushions. Stepping back, she admired her handiwork. Two women walked past and whispered something. Chupplejeep was sure he heard one of them swear as she gave him a sideways glance. The woman's eyes were red rimmed, her lips quivering. A woman in a blue nurse's uniform followed. 'See to them,' Cynthia commanded, her smile faltering only for a moment.

'Yes, yes,' the nurse said, hurrying along.

Cynthia turned to Chupplejeep. 'Don't mind them,' she said. 'Nurse will remind them of their manners. Donna's good, she's just a little lost. We had better go somewhere private. Come with me.' Cynthia started walking towards the imperial staircase.

Once Cynthia's office door closed, she sat behind her large teak desk and let out a sigh. Behind her was a large open window that looked out over the lush valley where neem and mango trees were growing side by side.

'Ke-ke-ke,' Pankaj said, mimicking a bird who was making a noise somewhere in the distance.

Chupplejeep shot his colleague a look.

'Is that a jungle babbler?' Pankaj asked.

'A what?' Chupplejeep said.

'Your friend here knows his birds. Well done,' Cynthia said. 'And if you listen hard enough, you can also hear the song of the noisy white-browed bulbul.'

Pankaj blushed, and for a moment the three of them were silent as they strained their ears to listen to the birdsong.

'I can't hear any –' Chupplejeep started but was shushed in unison by Cynthia and Pankaj.

'I hear it,' Pankaj said, his lips turning into a smile. 'I hear it.'

Cynthia placed a hand on Pankaj's and looked him in the eye. 'Would you like tea, my boy?' she asked.

Pankaj nodded. Cynthia used the intercom on her desk to ask for three cups of tea. 'I love my job,' she said, 'but it can be tiring.'

'And what exactly is your job?' Chupplejeep asked. 'I had a look at your website, but it didn't tell me much. And it took my colleague and me quite a while to find this place.'

'Nestled in the hills with nature all around. You will find serenity here,' Cynthia said.

'That's what it says on your website.'

Cynthia smiled as her assistant carried in a small tray with three cups of tea and a plate of biscuits which she set down in front of them.

'Help yourselves,' Cynthia said. 'You must be tired after your drive. These orange blossom biscuits are divine.' Cynthia helped herself to a biscuit and sat back in her chair. 'So let me tell you,' she said. 'Our centre here is something special. A place for those who are not coping so well in the real world. It gives them a safe space to retreat and find themselves.'

'That doesn't tell me —' Chupplejeep started but Cynthia raised her hand to stop him.

'Here we allow our residents to heal. We are a wellness and rehabilitation centre.'

'So your residents check in of their own accord?' Chupplejeep asked, thinking of the lakeside yoga retreat at Toem Place that he had once visited.

'Yes and no,' Cynthia said. 'Of course we have some residents who come back time and time again, but mainly it is at the request of their agent or parent.'

'What kind of healing do they require?'

'Spiritual, physical, behavioural,' Cynthia said, looking into her cup of tea. 'In our lives we experience many different traumas right from when we are born to when we die. Do you know birth is a trauma for babies?'

Chupplejeep nodded. He couldn't argue with that. It was quite a traumatic process, from what he had witnessed.

'We all experience big and little traumas in our lives. Some don't affect us. Some have a huge impact, and sometimes it isn't just the big trauma that has the big effect. Sometimes it's the little trauma that we suddenly remember, or a series of little traumas. Sometimes it's the straw that breaks the camel's back. Do you know that saying, Mr Chupplejeep?' Cynthia turned to Pankaj. 'You understand. I can tell you have a knowing heart.'

Pankaj's cheeks coloured. Chupplejeep rolled his eyes. 'And how do you help these people heal with their big and little traumas?' he asked. 'Do you have medical doctors here? Is that the service you are offering? Certificated practitioners?'

'I can assure you that all our therapists here are certified,' Cynthia said, looking a little aggrieved.

Chupplejeep nodded. It wasn't hard to get certified in India; all you needed was a bribe.

'Do you carry out any medical procedures here?' Chupplejeep asked, thinking of the woman with the fair hair and white plaster on her cheek. Medical tourism was real, and it was becoming a problem. With lower costs and better facilities, many tourists from the west were making their way to Goa for a medical holiday; getting their teeth fixed or mole removed while enjoying two weeks in the sun to recover. Chupplejeep could see the business and end-user logic behind this, but not all medical tourists checked out who was performing surgery on them. And how difficult was it to fake a degree or qualification in India? Only recently four doctors were arrested for practicing without a valid licence. Their patients were outraged, saying they were receiving first-class care under these imposters.

'I must say, Mr Chupplejeep, that your questioning seems more like an attack than a quest to find useful information.' Cynthia's smile had well and truly faded now. She looked like Bonita when her favourite soft toy had to be washed.

'Let me explain why we're here,' Chupplejeep said. He told Cynthia about the murder of Jagdish Sharma and how he had been employed to find his killer. He also explained that he had spoken to Sonal Johar and that her alibi was that she and her husband had been here with her son, Bhavan, the night the murder took place. 'Could you verify that for me?' Chupplejeep asked.

Cynthia opened her drawer and took out her diary. She opened the book to where a dark blue ribbon kept her place. 'Which day was it, did you say?'

'The night of the 12th November,' Pankaj said, craning his neck to peer at her diary. Cynthia pulled it towards her protectively.

'We did have a show that night and yes, the Johars were here.'

'The whole time?' Chupplejeep asked.

'I wouldn't know. It wasn't a policed event,' Cynthia snapped.

'Do all your residents take part in a show here?'

'Oh no,' Cynthia said. 'You are mistaken. For every big festival or holiday we have performers come to the centre to put on a show. Set in the grounds, amidst torches of fire, we have an area where performers do some theatrics. On the date in question we had a great little performance company in. They were so good we are running the show again in a few days. Theatre and art is good for the soul, Mr Chupplejeep. It helps one heal from all kinds of trauma.'

'Oh yes, the trauma. And can you expand on what kind of trauma Bhavan is suffering from?'

Cynthia's hand flew to her mouth. 'Most certainly not. He is currently a patient here, and I cannot divulge such information.'

'How often is he a patient here?' Chupplejeep pressed.

Cynthia stood up. 'I'm afraid I'm going to have to ask you to leave. Our clients are like family to us, and we are very private.'

'But his mother –' Chupplejeep started, but again Cynthia cut him off.

'Well then, maybe you should ask his mother,' she said. 'Now, I'm a busy woman, and I must get back to my duties. The Atul Centre won't run itself.'

'Of course,' Chupplejeep said, standing. He shook Cynthia's hand, and her smile returned. 'Can I speak with Bhavan before I leave?' he asked.

Cynthia's smile disappeared again. She glanced over her shoulder. 'He's not here,' she said.

'An outing?' Chupplejeep asked.

'Yes, yes,' Cynthia said.

'Can I arrange to come back to see Bhavan when he is here?'

Cynthia nodded. 'Of course, if Bhavan wants to receive guests.'

'I've explained why we're here,' Chupplejeep said. 'It's imperative that we speak to him.'

'You're not the police,' Cynthia said. 'Now I really must get on.' Cynthia stood up from behind her desk and moved towards the door. Opening it for the two men, she asked her assistant to take Pankaj and Chupplejeep back downstairs.

'See that they leave the premises,' she directed, before closing the door behind them.

~

'Sir, do you understand what they do there?' Pankaj asked as they made their way in the Baleno through the narrow lanes to get to the main road. 'I'm not sure I understood what she was on about with the big and little traumas, but it did make me think of Shwetty.'

'How so?' Chupplejeep asked.

'I've put a lot of pressure on Shwetika because I want a family, and my wife has a point – do I really have time for a baby with this job? I'm causing the person I love a big trauma.'

'Maybe you need to check in at the Atul Centre. I think Cynthia would give you a good rate given your knowing heart.' Chupplejeep laughed, and Pankaj couldn't help but join in. 'I think you have an admirer there.'

'Why don't they want us to see Bhavan?' Pankaj asked, moving the conversation on.

'Because they're afraid of what he might say,' Chupplejeep said.

'The centre?'

'The Johars,' Chupplejeep said. 'There's something the Johars don't want us to know.'

'They'll never let us back in to speak to Bhavan.'

'No, but I wasn't joking when I said you should check in. Cynthia liked you. And she is one of those people who like a challenge. You have a real problem too. You'll appear genuine, and that place may give you some answers you're looking for.'

'You're serious?' Pankaj said.

Chupplejeep looked at the road ahead. 'Give them a call.'

Chapter Fifteen

Sonal watched Bhavan as he parked his beloved motorbike. So he was back from the centre and this time alone. No doubt he had been with that girl again, the one who worked there. Bhavan spent most of his time with that nurse these days, but Sonal supposed she should be glad. Having someone in her son's life would make him less reliant on her and Abhijeet.

She often allowed herself to think of what it would be like when Bhavan flew the nest. She imagined he would live close and she would visit him, taking him his favourite foods and offering to do his laundry. Sonal shook away the thought. Bhavan was her only son, and only in his twenties. She shouldn't be dreaming of his departure from his family home. She wanted to hold on to him for a little longer.

Sonal sighed, thinking of Bhavan's girlfriend. She was well aware that she could inform Cynthia that one of her members of staff was having relations with her son, but it would only drive Bhavan further away from her, and the poor girl would get the sack. Besides, Bhavan needed support from someone outside the family, and a nurse was better than just anyone. She would know how to deal with Bhavan's moods, his temperament. Sonal would stay quiet for now.

Her son moved swiftly towards the front door. Lately Bhavan had a sense of determination about him, and Sonal had to wonder if the girlfriend was the cause. This change in behaviour scared and impressed her in equal measure. In some respects it felt like he was finally growing up, making his own mark on the world. In other ways it felt dangerous. Dangerous because there was still so much that had been left unsaid between them. Sonal stepped away from the kitchen sink and busied herself with putting away the plates from lunch. She heard the front door slam and called out to her son.

Bhavan walked into the kitchen and sat down at the breakfast bar. Sonal fetched him a glass of cold milk and rubbed his back. 'How have you been?' she asked tentatively.

He didn't respond, so Sonal filled the room with the sound of her voice as she continued to put the dishes away. She told him of her morning, what she and Abhijeet had for lunch, of his father's trip into town where he was meeting an agent, someone who was going to help get his business back on track.

'I read that article again,' Bhavan said eventually.

'Which?' his mother enquired, although she knew exactly what article he was referring to. The boy had become obsessed with a piece written in the local paper about her ex, Jagdish. Sonal stood on the other side of the breakfast bar and refrained from saying anything. 'Let him speak,' she heard Cynthia's advice replay in her mind. 'Give him time. Don't be so quick to interrupt and rescue him.'

Bhavan stared at his mother. 'He died that night,' Bhavan said. 'The night of the show at the centre.'

Sonal nodded. 'Don't interrupt his flow,' she silently told herself.

'I lost you that evening,' Bhavan said. 'You were there with Dad one minute and the next I couldn't find you.'

'Yes,' Sonal said. 'We got stuck talking to Andrew's mother. She's just started sending her son to the centre and we hadn't met in a while, so we started talking.'

'I don't know Andrew,' Bhavan said.

Sonal looked away. 'You don't know everyone at the centre. And some residents must like their privacy.'

'That article says that Jagdish was stabbed.'

'You know these papers,' Sonal said. 'Sometimes they don't have all the facts.'

'And sometimes they do.' Bhavan reached over and retrieved a banana from the fruit bowl. 'If he was stabbed, someone must have been really angry with him.'

'I guess,' Sonal said, not meting her son's eye.

Bhavan watched her. She could feel his eyes on her, and a shiver ran down her spine.

'What was he like?' Bhavan asked. 'When you two were married?'

Sonal shook her head. 'We've been through this,' she said. 'I know you were close to him this last year, but he was a different man now from what he was then.'

'How so? You barely saw him recently or so you've said to me. So how do you know?'

Sonal explained to her son that Jagdish was a rising star back when they were married, that he didn't have much time for her, his kathakali being his number one priority. Of late Bhavan had kept circling around her history with him. He was so eager to know more about the man who had been brutally murdered in his dressing room. Bhavan had grown close to the star. It was natural for him to be confused and curious about his death, but there were only so many times that she could answer the same questions.

'And then you met Dad,' Bhavan said, with a distant look in his eyes.

'That's right,' Sonal said.

'Has it been difficult for you to deal with me these past twenty-four years?' he asked.

'Oh Bhavan,' Sonal said. 'You can't think that way. I longed for a child, and you have been everything to me and more.' Her words came out automatically even though there was some truth in what Bhavan was saying. He had been challenging. He was still challenging, and some days she wondered if he would ever want to forge his own way in this world.

'I wonder if they'll catch his killer,' Bhavan said, peeling the banana. He took a bite and leaned back in his chair, looking at his mother. 'Do you think the police are capable of that?'

'I'm sure they are,' she responded. She didn't think now was the right time to tell her son about the investigator that Kapoor had hired. It would only give him something else to obsess over.

'They haven't spoken to me,' Bhavan said.

'Who? The police?' Sonal asked, drying a glass.

'Yeah,' Bhavan said. 'I knew him. Shouldn't they want to speak to us?'

'I've spoken to them,' Sonal said. 'They probably don't need to speak to you.'

'I'm not a person of interest?'

'No. I don't suppose you are.'

'But if I knew something, I guess I could make contact.'

Sonal put the glass down and looked at her son. 'And do you know something?'

Bhavan laughed. 'Look at you,' he said. 'Why are you so worried? You're safe. I don't know anything, or at least nothing I'd like to share with the cops.'

Chapter Sixteen

Chupplejeep slipped his mobile phone into his pocket. Still no answer from Jagdish's widow, Rupali Sharma. He had stopped at her house earlier to no avail. The woman was blatantly ignoring him.

The investigator watched Pankaj as he left the front room of the Gopaldas's apartment. Since their trip to the Atul Centre this morning, Pankaj had been subdued. He hadn't been enthused about a stay at the retreat like Chupplejeep had expected. If it was one thing Chupplejeep could usually rely on, it was Pankaj's keenness. But he had to appreciate that private investigative work was new to Pankaj. The boy was used to working with a set of rules when he was in the force. Private detection didn't exactly come with a rulebook. Attending events under false pretences was part of his new role, something Pankaj had to embrace.

Chupplejeep could tell that it wasn't just the idea of staying at the Atul Centre under false pretences that was bothering Pankaj. It was the reality of this predicament he had found himself in with Shwetika. Perhaps a small part of Pankaj believed that somewhere like the Atul Centre could help him. And maybe he was worried some uncomfortable truths about his relationship would be exposed.

Chupplejeep would provide a little encouragement later. For now they had work to be getting on with. Not only did they have the murder of the kathakali dancer to solve but the case of the missing sapphire too, and right now they were back at Reena Gopaldas's apartment looking for answers.

'This is Uma. She's worked with the Gopaldases for over a decade,' Pankaj said as the petite woman entered the lounge and sat opposite Chupplejeep. Pankaj offered her some water. Uma gratefully took a sip, watching Chupplejeep in anticipation.

'You're not in any trouble,' Chupplejeep said as Uma sat down. Instantly the woman's shoulders dropped. 'We just want to know a little more about the run-up to Miss Gopaldas's party before the ring went missing and anything you can tell us regarding the piece of jewellery.'

'*Aacha*,' Uma said, fiddling with the hem of her shalwaar. Chupplejeep asked the young maid when she first saw the ring.

'Reena *Bhai* wanted it from the safe,' Uma said apprehensively. She looked around. 'I don't know. I don't want to get anyone in trouble. *I* don't want to get in trouble.'

'Don't worry,' Chupplejeep said, trying to reassure the maid. He reminded her that Reena wasn't in the apartment and of her loyalty to the family, given how long she had worked for the Gopaldases. He ended his little speech with, 'Mr Gopaldas is relying on us so that the stone can be exhibited at the museum.'

Uma was silent.

'Uma,' Chupplejeep said. 'Mr Gopaldas is relying on you.'

'My mother says I am very helpful. I like to be of use.'

'So then, can you tell me about the first time you saw the ring?'

'A long time back. I first saw it a long time back when Reena Bhai's mother wore it for an event.'

'And more recently?' Chupplejeep enquired.

'Last week Reena Bhai asked her father to arrange for the safe to be opened so she could get the piece to wear for her party. Baba wasn't keen. He told her it was going to be exhibited in the museum for everyone to see. She didn't like that, but she brought him round eventually. Reena Bhai likes shiny things. She wanted to show it off to her friends before articles were written about it in the papers. I heard her tell Miss Nita that.'

'And how did Nita respond?' Chupplejeep asked.

'In her usual way. She told Reena Bhai that she didn't need to show off. It was a pointless comment, and Nita should have known it wasn't even worth uttering. Reena Bhai is the ultimate show-off.' Uma laughed and then checked herself, looking around the room again to make sure that Reena hadn't snuck in.

'Was Reena used to getting her way?'

Kingfisher Blues

Uma nodded. 'She was a spoilt child. She only did things for attention. I've watched her grow up. We're similar in age. She has so much and yet she always wants more.'

'Would you say that you are happier than Miss Gopaldas?' Chupplejeep asked.

Uma beamed. 'I'm not sure why she is always wanting more. She is the only child and her parents are great employers. They are kind to me and to all those around them. Maybe Reena Bhai was just born like that. She doesn't have any brothers or sisters. I am one of six. I know how to share. I know how to wait my turn.' Uma took a sip of water. 'I don't like to speak ill of my employers, especially when they are so good to me, but it wouldn't surprise me if...' Uma trailed off.

'If what, Uma?' Chupplejeep asked.

'It isn't a nice thing to say,' Uma said, as if suddenly remembering her manners.

'You can tell us if you have a theory. All good detectives start with one,' Chupplejeep said.

Uma looked sideways and pursed her lips. 'I think Reena Bhai hid the ring for the attention.' Uma gulped her water as if her lips were on fire.

'You think she still has it in her possession?' Pankaj asked.

'The thing is, the next morning, when we were told to clear up after the party, I looked. I searched high and low, and I couldn't find it, and I know all the hiding places in this house. I know where Reena Bhai used to hide her cigarettes and when she used to hide her birth control,' Uma said, whispering the last two words.

'So it isn't in the apartment,' Chupplejeep said.

'It could be on her person.'

'Could be,' Chupplejeep said. It was a possibility, but the possibility was slim. They hadn't patted Reena down at her party, but it was a pretty bold accusation to make by the host if the whole time she had the Kingfisher Sapphire tucked away in her bra, which had been Christabel's suggestion.

'And before the party, did you notice anything out of place? Something that caught your attention?'

Uma shook her head. 'Nothing.' Uma explained that she didn't normally stay for such parties but that Vihaan was often asked to stay to help serve the drinks.

'He's outside, sir,' Pankaj said.

'We'll speak to him next then.'

Uma stood up. 'I'll see you out,' Chupplejeep said. He noticed that as Uma passed Vihaan in the doorway, a look passed between the two, a look that Chupplejeep couldn't quite read.

~

'They didn't tell us much,' Pankaj said as Chupplejeep closed the door behind Vihaan. 'Their stories were almost identical. Almost as if Uma and Vihaan had rehearsed what they were going to say before.'

'And then there was the silent exchange between them,' Chupplejeep said. 'It isn't what they said but more what they didn't.'

'They could be in it together. Would make sense as to why Uma was pointing the finger at Reena Gopaldas,' Pankaj said. 'It was the first Gopaldas party that Vihaan hasn't attended. Did you see him flinch when you mentioned it?'

Pankaj had a point, but it could just be that Vihaan's pride had been dented because Miss Gopaldas didn't trust him to serve her guests.

'They have motive, sir,' Pankaj said. 'Both have worked for the Gopaldases for some time. They have seen Reena get whatever she desires and still be ungrateful. That can't be easy to watch day in and day out.'

Chupplejeep considered this theory but was sceptical of how they could have stolen the ring if they weren't even at the party. It was one thing for one of Reena's guest to befriend Uma and Vihaan and get them to do their dirty work, another for it to work the other way round. Reena's guests were all high flyers, and none of them appeared to be the Robin Hood type. Pankaj was adamant it was a plausible possibility though.

'They could have taken the ring and thrown it down to Uma or Vihaan who could have been waiting in the bushes,' he persisted.

'What bushes?' Chupplejeep asked. 'Remember we were standing in the drive behind the gates, watching the procession. We didn't notice any commotion in the bushes behind us.'

'But we weren't looking. You were busy with the children, and I had my own dilemmas.'

A silence ensued. 'Shwetty has extended her stay with her aunty in Margao. She will be gone longer than expected,' Pankaj said, looking out of the window.

'More time for you to think,' Chupplejeep said. 'Your job or your family, eh?'

'Too much time to think.'

'Time for you to get away, perhaps, and do some detection at the same time. Have you called the centre, yet?'

Pankaj shook his head.

'Come on,' Chupplejeep said. 'Let's go and examine these bushes.'

~

The bushes to the front of the apartment building had been heavily watered by the diligent gardeners, and no evidence of footprints remained. 'Useless,' Chupplejeep said as he tried to extract himself from the leaves of the pink bougainvillea. 'What are you doing?' he called to Pankaj, who was glued to the screen of his phone.

'Sir, along with watching countless *YouTube* videos of Jagdish Sharma's dancing, I've been checking social media with the hashtag KingfisherBlue and also Reena Gopaldas's name. Reena has garnered a lot of attention because of this stolen jewel. In fact the hashtag StolenJewel is trending.

Chupplejeep peered over his colleague's shoulder. 'Isn't that the owner of Mango Books in that photo?'

Pankaj nodded. He's been tagged in this photo of the party, but he hasn't responded.

'What's he doing?'

'He is looking longingly at the ring, sir.'

Chupplejeep took the phone off Pankaj and examined the photo. Daniel Chatterjee was looking at the ring with hunger. He had been cooperative when Chupplejeep had asked him about the Kingfisher Sapphire but showed little interest in the ring. None that Chupplejeep had been able to detect, but this picture told a different story.

Chupplejeep recalled the look that Nita had given Daniel before he was interviewed which told Chupplejeep that the two knew each other. Co-conspirators or lovers? Chupplejeep wasn't sure. Daniel hadn't really answered when he asked the bookstore owner if he knew her. The bookstore owner had appeared genuine with his answers, but when it came to knowing Nita, Chupplejeep wasn't so sure. He explained all this to Pankaj.

'Maybe Nita didn't want her current employer to know she was sleeping with one of her friends,' Pankaj said.

Chupplejeep handed the phone back to Pankaj. 'Take this,' he said. 'Get back to the office. Print all the photos you can find.'

'Sir,' Pankaj said. 'Where are you going?'

'I have a few errands to run,' Chupplejeep said, his eyes turning towards the main road. A black Mercedes had pulled up outside. Reena and Nita emerged from the car.

'I'll have to take the bus,' Pankaj said a little despondently.

Chupplejeep winced. 'Sorry. Here,' he said, handing Pankaj a hundred rupee note. 'Take a rickshaw.'

Pankaj pocketed the money. 'Thanks,' he said, waving to a yellow-and-black autorickshaw. 'I'll see you back at the office.'

Chapter Seventeen

Popatrao closed the door behind the detective and poured himself a large measure of Black Label. This was the last thing he needed, the police breathing down his neck. He downed the contents of his glass and poured himself another. He checked the time. Midday. He was starting late today, but he couldn't help it. He could hardly help himself to liquor in front of the cops.

The hotelier closed his eyes and tried to erase the image he had of the sub-officer pointing his sausage-like finger at him, accusing him of wanting to get rid of Jagdish. The great Jagdish Sharma. Popatrao wished he had never heard of him. Popatrao's cat Lucky sidled up to the hotelier and jumped on his lap. He stroked the feline and instantly felt calmer.

It was Meera's fault. She was the one who had come up with the bright idea of boosting business by getting the kathakali dancer to perform at the failing resort.

'Why did I listen to her?' he asked his cat.

'It will be like in Vegas. Like Celine Dion,' she had cajoled, batting her eyelashes. She knew how much he liked Celine Dion. Titanic would have only been half the movie without her on the soundtrack. He had agreed, reluctantly at first, but then threw himself into it as he did with most things. Darsh had been his first choice, but Meera didn't want second best. 'We don't want just any dancer,' she had chided when Popatrao had told her about the contract. 'We want the great Jagdish Sharma. He'll pull in the crowds.' Jagdish Sharma was to be given the best suite in the hotel, not that he would stay there when he had a perfectly good home in Goa. Jagdish would perform once a week right through from Diwali to the end of the Christmas season.

Popatrao had worn his finest suit when he had visited the dancer in his sprawling home in Calangute. Jagdish's home was better than Popatrao's hotel with its coastal location, infinity pool and imported marble flooring. Popatrao's wife had no interest, so he had taken Meera, who had smiled shyly and giggled at Jagdish's jokes. Jagdish's wife was nowhere to be seen either. Popatrao should have known then what was happening. He should have known better.

He courted Jagdish like a lover for two weeks that September despite the forty-minute drive to and from his hotel. Popatrao took Jagdish to the finest seafood restaurants, paid for expensive imported wines and laughed at his jokes. Meera made herself available for all their meetings.

Meera was usually tied up with work when Popatrao had called her in his times of need – usually late at night when his wife was away. But when they were courting Jagdish, Meera was always available. Any time of the night and day. Popatrao had even called her at midnight once pretending that Jagdish wanted to party. Of course Jagdish had no such intentions, but Meera came running, and Popatrao had his fun even though it was slightly dampened by the fact that Meera hadn't really come to see him.

When it came to signing the contract, Jagdish Sharma had second thoughts. Popatrao had had enough. Much to Meera's annoyance, he had offered the contract to Darsh instead. Darsh was Jagdish's stand-in, but in Popatrao's eyes the boy was better – younger and cheaper. Darsh was about to sign when Meera called. She had managed to convince Jagdish with some promises Popatrao was afraid they couldn't keep. The contract was signed. Meera had squealed with delight and they had celebrated with passion fruit martinis. Even his wife had congratulated Popatrao when she returned from her mother's several days later.

It was then that the problems started. First it was the rats. A hotel guest had spotted one and immediately posted a video on a review site. The rat looked like it was dancing to the *Macarena* and for that reason the video went viral. 'There is no such thing as bad publicity,' Meera said, trying to calm him down that evening. The next day the charters cancelled their package holidays with him.

'We just can't have a hotel with a rat infestation on our books. Nearly all our customers have seen this video. Our customers want refunds, and we can hardly deny them that.'

'It was a one-off incident. The rat in question has been found and dealt with,' Popatrao said, choosing his words carefully; you never knew these days who was an animal activist. No sooner had those words left his lips than another video was posted, this time showing a nest of furless baby rats. Lucky was useless. Only Popatrao would have a cat who was scared of rats. The woman on the other end of the line must have got the notification of this new media at the same time as Popatrao did. She cleared her throat. 'I don't think we have anything more to say on the matter,' she had said flatly.

And that was that. Popatrao went from hero to zero in less than twenty-four hours. His wife packed her bags and went to the States to stay with her sister. Even Lucky had gone missing for some time. 'I'll be back when you've sorted out this mess,' his wife had said as her taxi arrived to take her to the airport. 'I told you there was an issue with rats a long time back. Also that bookings website called. They have to remove one star. Something about not having enough multi-lingual staff.'

Popatrao's jaw dropped. Not only were the charter holidays cancelling, he had now lost a star on the website where he received most of his alternative bookings. He had looked at the sky and cursed the gods.

'Don't worry, baby,' Meera had said. 'You have Jagdish ready to perform. He's not looking at star ratings or rats. He'll be there.'

'He better be,' Popatrao had said. Popatrao had put his arms around Meera. She was the best decision he had ever made, or so he had believed back then. His wife may have been unsupportive, but his lover was there for him. The only problem now was how Popatrao was going to continue to pay the dancer. He had agreed to pay an extortionate amount of money for the residency, and thanks to Meera's promises, the contract stated that the first payment would be made in advance of the first performance and subsequent payments would be made each week if for any reason the show didn't go ahead.

Popatrao had balked at Meera's suggestion at first, but then she had made him promises of her own, promises that had distracted him and made him intentionally forget to consult his lawyer. Idiot.

Popatrao was already in the red; creditors were chasing him. Without his five stars and the holiday guests, he wouldn't be able to pay Jagdish. He couldn't cancel the contract because regardless he would still owe Jagdish money. He knew then that he should have gone with Darsh. The unknown star couldn't command what Jagdish had. Popatrao should never have let Meera persuade him otherwise.

Popatrao was left without a choice.

As if sensing his owner's unsavoury thoughts, Lucky jumped off his lap and out of his office through an open window. Popatrao finished his drink and picked up his phone. He dialled a number. Meera answered on the second ring. 'They're coming for you,' he said.

'Who?' she asked.

'The police.'

There was a sharp intake of breath on the other end of the line. 'You gave them my name?' she asked.

'They already had your name. They want to speak to you, so you listen carefully to what I have to say and do what I tell you, because I know your little secret, and you don't want that to get out.'

Chapter Eighteen

Another knock on the door. 'Come,' Popatrao said as he disconnected the call. He refilled his glass. Chupplejeep entered the room and introduced himself.

'Unbelievable,' Popatrao said. 'I've just had the police here. What does Kapoor want by appointing you?'

It was obvious, but the man in front of him wasn't thinking straight. Chupplejeep could easily see that. 'Answers,' Chupplejeep said.

'And why do you think I'm involved?' Popatrao asked. His hand shook as he lifted his glass to his lips.

Chupplejeep explained that he knew that Jagdish was due to perform at the hotel. He wanted to know more about the connection.

Popatrao looked defeated. He confided in the detective about his failing business. 'I'm on the verge of bankruptcy if you must know,' he said. 'My wife wants to leave me. Even my lover is cheating on me. Why would I want Jagdish dead? He was about the only person who could have saved this place.'

Marissa de Luna

'But you just told me you couldn't afford to pay Jagdish what he was due.'

'I made the first payment,' Popatrao said. 'It was an eye-watering sum.'

'From what I've heard,' Chupplejeep said, 'Jagdish wouldn't have been happy with the state of your hotel and the reviews online. I doubt he would have wanted to perform here. And by my reckoning he would have still wanted to be paid, for his inconvenience. You just said it was in the contract.'

'He had a good team of lawyers,' Popatrao conceded. 'But it didn't come to that.'

'No, because the man died,' Chupplejeep said.

Popatrao threw his glass at the wall. It shattered, and the dregs of his whisky stained the wall. 'Go to hell,' Popatrao said.

Chupplejeep waited before he responded. 'Jagdish wouldn't have performed here with the reputation of Baytown as it is. We both know that. Jagdish had a habit of ruining businesses that didn't give him the attention he felt he deserved or when he didn't get his way. Jagdish wasn't someone you'd want to get on the wrong side of, or so I'm told. And by the sounds of it, you were very much on his wrong side. Were you not worried about what this superstar would do?' Chupplejeep asked the hotelier.

Popatrao stood up. 'Get out,' he said. 'Get out of my hotel.'

'You mentioned a lover,' Chupplejeep said, ignoring Popatrao's request.

Popatrao looked up. He had his attention again. A black-and-white cat jumped onto Popatrao's lap and he stroked it. The action seemed to calm him a little.

'Can you tell me a little more about her?'

The hotelier hesitated then gave the investigator her name. Then he narrowed his eyes and leaned forward. The cat jumped off his lap. 'She was having an affair with him,' he said.

'Who?' Chupplejeep asked.

'Our Mr Sharma, the dancer.'

Chupplejeep asked whether he had any proof, but Popatrao couldn't provide any.

'Once I waited outside his fancy house in Calangute to see if I could catch Meera out, but nothing,' Popatrao said, his nose scrunched like he had smelled something bad. 'Instead I saw a known prostitute visit the house.'

The investigator questioned whether Jagdish had used his suite at Baytown for any extra-marital affairs, but Popatrao shook his head whilst fiddling with a gold chain around his neck. Chupplejeep studied the gaudy necklace, wondering if it had any green semi-precious stones embedded on it that were missing. Anything to put the hotelier at the scene of the crime, because Popatrao certainly had motive. The necklace appeared to be pure gold. It was then that Popatrao excused himself to go to the toilet. The hotelier's eyes lingered on the broken glass as he walked out, but Chupplejeep wasn't sure there was any feeling of regret there.

Chupplejeep stood up and looked around, then he made his way behind Popatrao's desk, carefully moving some of the paperwork so he could get a better look. When he caught a glimpse of Sharma's name he felt a small victory. Taking his phone out of his pocket, he started photographing the contract between Baytown and Jagdish Sharma. It was seventeen pages long. When he was ten pages through, he heard a noise outside Popatrao's office. He couldn't stop now. Chupplejeep flicked the pages and took the photos, his breath held as Popatrao spoke to someone outside. *Please stall him,* Chupplejeep begged silently to whomever it was outside.

And then he was done. Chupplejeep slipped his phone back in his pocket and sat back in his seat, trying to steady his breathing. Popatrao eyed him suspiciously as he took his place behind his desk, his eyes glancing over his paperwork.

'You're still here,' Popatrao said. 'What else do you want?'

Chupplejeep stood up. 'One last question,' he said. 'Where were you on the 12th November? The night Jagdish Sharma was killed?'

~

Chupplejeep opened the door to his office. Unlike Kulkarni, he hadn't bothered to decorate for Diwali. Christabel would soon make him hang up an obligatory star for Christmas and of course there would be a tree and tinsel for the kids.

'For November it's pretty warm outside,' Chupplejeep said to Pankaj, who was at his desk, looking at some printouts. Chupplejeep switched the fan on and stood in front of it. He wiped his face with a handkerchief.

'Global warming,' Pankaj said. 'Where were you, sir?'

'I briefly spoke to Reena and Nita after you left, but they didn't tell me anything new so I went to visit Jagdish's wife Rupali, but yet again she wasn't at home. I gave up and went to do an errand for Christabel, and Baytown wasn't too far away, so I thought I'd stop by,' he said.

'You went to see Popatrao?' Pankaj said.

Chupplejeep nodded. He relayed his conversation with Popatrao to his colleague and then thrust his phone at him. 'Print this,' he said.

'What is it?'

'The agreement between Jagdish and Popatrao.'

'Popatrao gave it to you?'

'It was on the table, and when he went to relieve himself of all that whiskey, I took a few photos.'

Pankaj grinned. 'I'll get onto it right away.'

'Do you think Popatrao is protecting this Meera?' Pankaj asked.

'From something maybe, but perhaps not murder. As far as we're aware she has no motive.'

'We should check out the prostitute Jagdish was seeing,' Pankaj said.

'I already have,' Chupplejeep said. 'On my way back here. Popatrao had her details, which doesn't surprise me. She was with a client at the time of the murder.' Chupplejeep passed the details to Pankaj. 'Check out her alibi and see if it stacks up. From what she said, Jagdish paid well. She had no reason to want him dead.'

'Where was Popatrao at the time of Jagdish's death?' Pankaj asked.

'Ah,' Chupplejeep said. 'Now listen to this. He was at the show, so he had opportunity as well as motive. Stands to reason why the police suspect him. Can you track down the people sitting next to him and see if he left his seat at any time?' Chupplejeep walked to the whiteboard he had set up to help with the investigation. He wrote a few notes under Popatrao's name and added Meera to the board.

'Have you had any luck with getting hold of Jagdish's wife, Rupali Sharma? Those numbers I gave you...'

Pankaj shook his head. 'I've tried the numbers Kapoor gave us but no luck.'

'If we can't get hold of Rupali, we may as well pay Meera a visit,' Chupplejeep said.

'But what about the photos, sir? The ones from Reena's party you asked me to print. Should we go through them now?'

Chupplejeep was about to answer when his phone started to ring.

Chapter Nineteen

Darsh adjusted his headdress and looked towards the seating area. Kapoor sat in the front row, his glasses balanced on his head, notepad in hand.

'Sure you're ready for this?' Kapoor shouted, which immediately irritated Darsh. Of course he was ready. He had been ready since Sonal's visit weeks ago.

'Yaar,' Darsh shouted, getting into a semi-squat position. 'I'm ready.'

'Okay. Go,' Kapoor bellowed, at which point the drums started. Darsh began to move his eyes. Left, right, left, right, up, down.

'Stop,' commanded Kapoor. 'Something's off. Is it the *navarasams*, facial expressions? I think so.'

'It's the makeup,' a voice said from behind Kapoor. Darsh straightened.

'The makeup's fine,' Darsh said.

'I was married to Jadgish for a number of years. I saw his rise to fame, and he was particular about his makeup. He knew it could make or break a performance.

The black around your eyes needs to contrast with a border with the white. You could ask the makeup person to add a border. That would do the trick.'

'Go,' Kapoor said to Darsh. 'Do as Sonal suggests. Get your makeup fixed and return. We must practice if we are opening again next week, and we must open. It isn't an option. I cannot afford to lose any more money here.'

Darsh skulked off to his dressing room. The makeup lady was nowhere to be found. He opened and closed all the drawers but couldn't find anything he needed, not that he was capable of doing his own makeup. That required a skill he didn't have. Darsh kicked the dressing table that had been wedged into the small room. The police had taken what they needed from Jagdish's old dressing room. There was no reason why Darsh couldn't use it. Kapoor had mumbled something about respect. Like he cared. He just wanted to get his theatre back up and running and yet Darsh had to suffer in an undersized dressing room.

'Can I help?' Sonal said, sticking her head around the door.

'Why are you here?' Darsh asked. 'Are you checking up on me?'

'I came to see how you are, and look what a help I have been. Kapoor thought your navarasams were all wrong, but it was just your makeup. A simple fix rather than a difficult one. Here, let me,' she said. Sonal opened the black bag she was carrying and pulled out a tub of gold makeup with a fine brush.

'You took this from my dressing room,' Darsh said.

Sonal ignored him. 'So,' she said, dipping her makeup brush in the pot of gold. 'Have the police been to see you yet?'

'They asked me some basic questions like where I was when the murder happened. Whether I liked Jagdish, if I knew anyone who wanted to hurt Jagdish.'

'And how did you respond?'

'I didn't tell them anything to cast any suspicion, if that's what you are worried about.' Darsh wasn't worried about the police. It was that other fellow that concerned him; the private investigator who had looked at him as if he knew something when Darsh had been caught in Jagdish's dressing room.

'It's worked out very well for you, hasn't it?' Sonal said. 'From understudy to the star of the show.'

Darsh nodded; he couldn't argue with that. Sonal had told him that his hard work would be rewarded and she was right.

'I'm even fixing your makeup for you, see,' she said, turning Darsh on his chair away from her towards the mirror. 'The gold border has done wonders.'

'You were right,' Darsh said, examining the makeup around his eyes.

'I'm always right,' Sonal said. She stared at him in the mirror. 'Have you found the –' she asked.

Darsh raised his hand to stop her. 'I'm still looking,' he said.

Sonal pierced him with her eyes. 'Where are you looking? Because if you haven't found it here it must be someplace else, and you must find it or we'll all be in trouble.'

'All?' Darsh asked. 'This was your idea.'

'You wanted the fame,' Sonal said.

'I didn't realise –' Darsh said.

He was interrupted by a low chuckle. 'We'll both be in trouble,' Sonal said. 'Because if I'm going down, I'm taking you with me.'

Chapter Twenty

'Ah, Abhijeet,' Chupplejeep said, introducing himself and sitting down at the man's table before he had a chance to protest. Earlier, as Pankaj had attempted to show Chupplejeep the pictures he had printed of Reena Gopaldas's party, he had received a call from Kulkarni, who had spotted Abhijeet Johar in a popular bar in Porvorim.

'He's married to Sonal Johar, isn't he?' Kulkarni said. 'Didn't you say you were trying to get hold of him?' Chupplejeep thanked the forensic pathologist and disconnected. Then he headed straight to the bar Kulkarni had mentioned.

'You?' the former manager of the stars said.

'I've been trying to get a hold of you.'

'Why? I've spoken to my wife. I know what you're investigating. I have nothing new to add. I barely knew the man.' Abhijeet spoke well, like he had been educated at one of those hill station boarding schools.

'Weren't you the man responsible for making Jagdish Sharma famous?'

'It was nothing. Just doing my job,' he said, failing to meet the investigator's eyes.

'Did you resent Jagdish's fame at all?' Chupplejeep asked.

'What are you talking about?' Abhijeet responded. 'It's my job to make people famous, and remember, I get a cut. I go on making the money without having to go out there on stage.' Abhijeet wore several gold chains and rings on his fingers. Chupplejeep looked to see if any were missing a small green stone like the one he had found at the scene of the crime.

'So no animosity between the two of you?'

Abhijeet shook his head.

'Even after you took his wife?'

Abhijeet stared at the investigator. 'That was over twenty years ago. It has nothing to do with now. We've all moved on.'

'But Sonal was the one who left Jagdish, right?' Chupplejeep asked. 'A man like Jagdish would have been scorned, no?'

'But he wasn't. Look, this is none of your business.'

'I'm investigating the man's death. This may have happened twenty-odd years ago, but it is very much relevant, as you were all still in each other's lives.'

'He wasn't in my life,' Abhijeet said, and then went on to tell Chupplejeep that while Jagdish was in touch with Sonal and Bhavan, he had very little to do with him. 'If Jagdish was scorned, he should have taken his anger out on me back then. He didn't. You can't possibly connect the two now. What reason did I have to take his life?'

Chupplejeep had to admit the man had a point, but there was something about Abhijeet Johar that he didn't like. The man was hostile and giving him the bare minimum of answers. Jagdish had resurfaced in his wife and son's lives recently, and Chupplejeep didn't think Abhijeet liked this much. Maybe Jagdish was settling an old vendetta; maybe Abhijeet knew this and wanted to stop him.

'Now if you don't mind, Mr Chupplejeep, I was enjoying a quiet drink.'

Chupplejeep stood up. He wasn't going to get much more out of the man. He enquired after Bhavan, but Abhijeet said he was away with friends. Bhavan was proving as elusive as Jagdish's widow.

'He's not at the centre?' Chupplejeep asked.

'Not today,' Abhijeet said, making a show of checking the date, which told Chupplejeep that the man had no idea where his son was.

~

Chupplejeep updated his notes before getting into his car and returning to Kapoor's theatre. He had checked the theatre-owner's alibi, and Kapoor was in the clear. Not only did Kapoor's girlfriend give him a solid alibi, but Jagdish was making Kapoor money, big money. He had no reason to want his shining star dead.

Chupplejeep was due to update Kapoor on his progress, and he also wanted to speak with the staff again, so he had decided to come to the theatre in person. Pankaj had previously visited Kapoor's to speak to the employees who had been on-site for the opening night, and Chupplejeep had some follow-up questions, especially for Darsh.

Darsh was the only person set to benefit from the dancer's death, and two of the staff that were present that day had overheard them argue before the start of the show.

The investigator spoke to the choreographer first, who confirmed that Jagdish often added bhang to his mid-show lassi drink. It was a habit the choreographer confirmed, a habit the dancer functioned perfectly well with. The way the choreographer spoke, it was obvious that most people working in the theatre knew about it. Meaning that any one of them could have tampered with the measure. The bouncer had conveniently run off to the toilet. An unlikely coincidence and the killer was free to do as he wished. Chupplejeep considered this as he made his way to see Darsh.

'Oh,' Darsh said, as he opened the door to the private investigator. 'You're here again.'

'I never asked you where you were during the interval, the night Jagdish Sharma was killed,' Chupplejeep said.

'Who are you exactly? A two-cent bit private investigator. I don't need to answer any of your questions,' he said, slamming the door in Chupplejeep's face.

'But why wouldn't you?' Chupplejeep shouted.

A minute later, Darsh opened the door slowly. 'I was here that night. You know that,' Darsh said. He looked the investigator up and down and then retreated back into the room. Darsh sat down and lit a cigarette. Chupplejeep sat opposite and watched as his suspect's eyes were drawn to a photograph on his dressing table. 'I had to be here. I was the *understudy*, remember. I was contracted to be here even though I got paid a pittance for it.'

'So you were backstage the whole time. Did you see anything strange that evening, anything out of place?' Chupplejeep asked.

Darsh shook his head.

'No comings and goings from Jagdish's dressing room?'

'No,' Darsh said, blowing smoke away from the investigator. 'As an understudy, I didn't have my own dressing room. I had to share with others. Ask them about my whereabouts.'

'Oh I have,' Chupplejeep said.

'So why are you asking me where I was during the interval?' Darsh's eyes were drawn to the photograph again.

'Who's that?' Chupplejeep asked. 'In the photo.'

Darsh picked up the picture and studied it for a moment then handed it to the private investigator. 'Jagdish and his family. Someone must have left it in here.' Darsh put the picture face down on the table. 'You think I had something to do with the man's death, but I didn't. Look at what he left behind. It's a tragedy.'

Chupplejeep picked up the frame and eyed the photograph of the great kathakali dancer. Jagdish Sharma had certainly left behind a legacy for his three daughters. His offspring were tall like him, elegant with good bone structure like their mother. They were young in this picture. Still too young to lose a father, but at least they had each other. The private investigator cleared his throat.

'I've been speaking to some of the staff that work here,' he said placing the frame back on the table. 'Two people claim to have heard shouting coming from Jagdish's dressing room before the performance.'

Darsh stubbed out his cigarette in a small brass ashtray on his dresser. Chupplejeep watched as the dancer considered the question, deciding whether it was best to lie or tell the truth.

'We exchanged a few words,' he said eventually. 'I wouldn't have said we were shouting. Jagdish was loud generally. I was just matching his volume.'

'What was the conversation about?'

'The usual,' Darsh said, looking away. 'I wanted more of a role in the performance. I wanted him to call me on at the end for a joint performance. He was having none of it. He never wanted to help.'

'I see,' Chupplejeep said. 'And you were in your shared dressing room the whole time during the performance and during the interval?' Chupplejeep glanced up and caught Darsh's eye before the dancer looked away.

'Yes,' Darsh said.

'I've heard that you were missing for at least ten minutes.'

'I was taking a leak then,' Darsh said, staring at the investigator. 'Sorry, there are no witnesses to vouch for me.' Darsh stood up, his hands on his hips.

'Jagdish Sharma was killed during the interval,' Chupplejeep said. Chupplejeep thought back to the fingerprint analysis Kulkarni had called him with earlier. Despite Darsh's fingerprints being found at the scene, they were not enough for an arrest, given the number of other fingerprints that had been found. Some had been identified, others hadn't. Jagdish's dressing room wasn't strictly off-limits and so everyone had a reason why they could have been in there.

'I know that, and I know how it looks, but look, most people move around during the interval. You can hardly blame me. Now,' Darsh said, standing up, 'I must ask you to leave. I need to practice.'

Chupplejeep tried his usual tactic of one more question, but it didn't work. Darsh refused to answer any more of the investigator's inquiries. Instead he stood at the door and waited for him to leave.

~

'This doesn't sound promising,' Kapoor said, shifting in his seat. Chupplejeep had given him a brief account of his investigation so far, and Kapoor wasn't impressed. He was a man who wanted results straight away, and Kapoor didn't seem to mind if they were fabricated or not. Chupplejeep tried not to think about the kind of man he was working for.

'It's still early days,' Chupplejeep said, 'and I still have lots of enquiries to make, but it seems there were several people who had reason to want the dancer dead.'

'I hope for your sake it isn't one of my staff,' Kapoor said. 'I can't afford the negative publicity.'

'Most of your staff are in the clear, I imagine. But I still need to do some more investigating where Darsh is concerned.'

Kapoor grunted. 'I can't have one dancer kill another. No one will want to perform in my theatres. These big shots are pricey as it is. If they think their understudies are ready to kill them, there is no chance they will want to dance on my stage. You promised me a good result,' he said.

'I promised you that I would get the truth,' Chupplejeep corrected. 'And when I do, you will be the first to know, if the authorities don't get there before me.'

'You're safe on that account,' Kapoor said.

'I can't get hold of Rupali,' Chupplejeep said. 'Do you know why Jagdish's widow is avoiding me?'

Kapoor shrugged. 'Rupali's just lost the love of her life. I assume she is grieving and doesn't want to be bothered.'

Chupplejeep had to ask if the theatre owner really believed that. It seemed that he did.

'You're the PI,' Kapoor said.

'I'll let you know as soon as I have more information,' said Chupplejeep, but Kapoor ignored him, turning his attention to the mound of paperwork on his desk.

Chapter Twenty-one

Rupali rubbed sun cream on her legs, her bangles clattering as she did so. Despite it being the middle of the day, she could hear the sound of crackers being set off in the village for Diwali. Rupali tried to ignore the noise. She asked the pool boy to adjust the umbrella so that she was in the shade. Her skin was perfect the way it was.

'Rupali rumali,' her best friend said, walking across the lawns towards her and planting a kiss on her cheek. 'I've missed you. How are you holding up?'

'As well as can be expected.' Rupali looked back towards the house. Her mother was standing at the window watching.

'Don't worry,' Meera said, 'she's just keeping an eye on you.'

'And the company I keep.'

Meera took a step back.

Rupali sat up. 'I want to know how you're doing.'

Meera waited till the pool boy left and then removed her sunglasses. She sat down on her friend's sun lounger.

Rupali leaned forward and touched her friend's cheek. 'Always the Rupali rumali, and underneath those sunglasses I can see those red-rimmed eyes. You've been crying. That man.'

'Men,' Meera said. She turned towards Rupali, her watery eyes trying to focus on her. 'What have we done?'

Rupali leaned back. 'What we had to do.'

'The police have been to see me.'

'And?'

'I said what I needed to, but I don't feel good about it. They've been to see Popatrao too,' Meera said.

'Of course they have. They wouldn't be doing their job if they hadn't. Popatrao had a relationship of sorts with Jagdish. It was obvious that he would be questioned.'

'I know,' Meera said. 'It's just one thing talking about it and another it happening. Popatrao wasn't very happy.'

'He wouldn't be.'

'Sometimes when I think about what we did I just...'

'Don't think about it,' Rupali said, reaching out a hand to her friend. Meera took it, and Rupali squeezed her fingers. 'Those cops are relentless now, but they'll soon give up. They have no reason to come after you. This will soon be behind you and Popatrao will be out of your life.' Rupali took a sip of her pomegranate juice. 'They've been back here again today.' Rupali explained to Meera that the police didn't have any update on who killed her husband. 'They must have a lead, but they aren't sharing it with me. They're still working on it, apparently,' she said. 'And they always suspect the wife first, don't they?'

'*Shhh*,' Meera said, looking over Rupali's shoulder and dropping her friend's hand.

'Oh, she's here again,' Rupali's mother said.

'*She* is my friend and a great comfort to me,' Rupali said. She refrained from looking at her mother.

'Of course, dear.' Rupali's mother turned to Meera. 'Sorry. It's just with everything going on I'm a little stressed. And my daughter,' she whispered. 'She's acting like nothing has happened. She needs to be seen to be grieving, don't you think?'

'She is, aunty, Look,' Meera said, taking out a newspaper from her tote bag. 'Here's a picture of Rupali shedding a tear at the theatre where Jagdish was performing.'

Rupali's mother snatched the paper and examined it. She shook her head from side to side. 'Okay, that's something, at least. I just don't want them to cast judgement on my *beta*. She has enough to worry about. I'll leave you two girls to chat.' Rupali's mother handed the newspaper back to Meera. 'That man called again,' she said as she turned towards the house. 'Three times in an hour. You can't ignore him forever.'

'Show me that,' Rupali said, taking the paper from Meera as her mother disappeared into the house. 'Long paragraphs on how talented the great Jagdish Sharma was. Nothing about his constant philandering, his belittling of his wife, his general disdain for anyone he thought was beneath him. They mention that ex-cop in here. That private investigator. He's the one who has been pestering me. It's bordering on harassment, but I have managed to avoid him so far. I suppose Mother is right. I'll have to speak to him soon.'

'Mr Chupplejeep? He went to see Popatrao too.'

Rupali dropped the paper and caught Meera's wrist. 'We need to be careful around him.'

Meera pulled away. 'I know,' she said.

Rupali took a breath. She leaned back in her deckchair and closed her eyes. 'It will all be over soon, Meera. I'm certain of it.'

Meera looked at her friend, hoping she was right.

Chapter Twenty-two

'Here are all the photos,' Pankaj said to Chupplejeep. It was their second attempt at examining the photographs taken at Reena Gopaldas's party after Kulkarni had interrupted them the last time. 'The ones from social media and the ones Reena sent you.'

'Nita didn't have any photos,' Chupplejeep said. 'Something about it being too easy to compare when you have photographs to continually look at. She had encouraged Reena to take fewer photos that night too. Something they are "actively working on", apparently.' Chupplejeep made air quotes.

'I've started following Reena on social media,' Pankaj said. 'She doesn't seem to be taking Nita's advice at all. There are pictures at the spa and at that new expensive restaurant in Panjim. Yesterday they were at the new Taj hotel and later on a yacht.'

'Maybe it's a work in progress,' Chupplejeep said with a laugh as he examined the photos. There were at least twenty, which Pankaj had put in chronological

Kingfisher Blues

order. The first few shots were of people arriving, the ring being shown to the guests and the reactions of those guests. Daniel hadn't been the only one who had been looking longingly at the ring. There was Judith, the woman in the sarong, and a group of women who held their champagne glasses close and looked at the ring from the corner of their eyes. Chupplejeep remembered talking to them after the party, but despite their longing evident in the picture, there wasn't anything that suggested they were to be suspected. Aman Khosla was in several of the photographs too. He was the one who had refused to speak to Chupplejeep after the party and who had made a quick getaway after Pankaj had patted down his pockets.

'Look at Aman,' Chupplejeep said. 'He's in most of the shots, looking at the ring like that fellow in Lord of the Rings.'

Pankaj laughed. 'Not quite, sir. He has hair and a full set of teeth for a start.'

'But he refused to talk to us, and the showing at the museum is fast approaching. We can't waste any more time. Let's go through the guest list for the party that Miss Gopaldas gave us and do a background check on each one. The longer this takes us to solve, the further that ring has a chance to go.

~

The sun was setting by the time Chupplejeep and Pankaj had worked their way through the party guests.

They were still struggling to find a motive with most of the guests having wealth of their own, but three guests stood out.

'Daniel Chatterjee,' Pankaj said. 'He's my number one. He wants the ring for his private collection. I called a friend in Mumbai, and this isn't the first time Daniel has been in the vicinity of something priceless going missing.'

'Tell me more,' Chupplejeep said, and Pankaj did. Two years ago, on a hot summer's day, there had been an exhibition in the Great Hall in Mumbai. There was a band, some dancing even. It was one of *those* events. They were showing some paintings. Small ones; each the size of a postcard. One in particular was valuable because it was an original sketch from an artist who was now deceased. A well-dressed woman walked in, dripping in diamonds. She started making a *tamasha*, fuss, about something or another, and all eyes turned to her.

'And while they were looking at her, this priceless sketch went missing,' Chupplejeep said.

'Daniel Chatterjee was at the party…' Pankaj said.

'…And his sister was the one dripping in diamonds.' Chupplejeep finished Pankaj's sentence for him.

'How did you know?' Pankaj asked.

'I recall the event, now that you mention it. I read about it in the paper. For once, the paper stated all the facts and didn't speculate, but it wasn't hard to put two and two together. I thought Daniel's name was familiar when I first spoke to him but assumed it was because of his connection to Mango Books.'

'There is one of those stores in every state.'

'His sister wasn't at Reena's party.'

'I did a check on her whereabouts when I read about this. She was in Paris.'

'Lucky for some,' Chupplejeep said. He had once dreamed of going to Paris. Sitting in one of those pavement cafés, eating a plate of macarons, the brightly coloured ones that looked like they melted on your tongue. Chupplejeep cleared his throat. 'Just because his sister wasn't at the party, it doesn't mean Daniel wasn't involved. A painting at the Great Hall would have had security. Most likely it was placed behind a glass cabinet. The perpetrator would need a distraction to get away with stealing something like that. Did they catch the culprit?'

'The investigation went on for months. Eventually, they believed the sketch was taken out of the country and they gave up. The fellow who loaned the frame to the gallery died soon after, and his family were not so concerned in pursuing the painting. Either they forgot about it or they had too much money to bother with it.'

Chupplejeep sat in his chair behind his large desk and leaned back. Perhaps the painting had been a burden to the family concerned, too much value for them to manage; maybe it was a source of bad luck, or perhaps it had a history the family would rather forget. Chupplejeep called up a picture of the Kingfisher Sapphire online. He studied the exquisite piece and then scrolled further down the page. It seemed that the hashtag KingfisherBlue was getting some mentions. Like the old sketch that had been stolen from the Great Hall, the Kingfisher Blue Sapphire had history too.

Chupplejeep clicked on a blog post that explained the provenance of the ring. The blogger believed that the stone had been initially owned by Mughal emperor Kanan. The emperor was said to draw great strength from the stone before heading into battle, but while the Mughal was out making conquests, the stone disappeared. Whether it was lost or stolen no one knew, but Emperor Kanan believed losing the stone was his downfall. He was proven right, as after the stone disappeared, the emperor was murdered. Chupplejeep shuddered. He hoped the same fate wouldn't befall the Gopaldases.

The stone was eventually found and made its way to Europe, where it resided with a well-to-do family for years. The ring changed hands twice after that before Mr Gopaldas's father purchased it for his wife in 1940. The article went on to say that the jewel was the people's jewel. Chupplejeep strongly doubted that anything during the reign of the kings and queens back in the 1600s was really for the people. Chupplejeep was hardly a historian, but he was sure that maharajas and maharanis back then were all about megalomania and slavery.

The blue jewel wasn't quite as brilliant or controversial as the Kohinoor diamond, but many people online were saying that the stone going missing was a sign. That the jewel belonged to the people and that it should be returned to the people. Whether that meant the 'people' wanted it permanently on display without ownership or if they wanted it sold to the highest bidder with the proceeds going into schools and new roads Chupplejeep wasn't sure. What he was certain of was that the general public were quite happy that this stone had gone missing. If they couldn't have it, then nobody should.

'Has anyone seen Mr Chatterjee's private collection?' Chupplejeep asked. When Pankaj shook his head, Chupplejeep asked if they could send someone from the force in Mumbai to check it out. As the words left his lips, he knew it would be a pointless exercise. Daniel Chatterjee wasn't stupid. He would have a hidden safe where any stolen goods could be kept. For all Chupplejeep knew, his entire collection could be in a private vault that only he had access to, with a smaller, less impressive collection for friends to view.

'Who else?' asked Chupplejeep. It was getting late and his stomach was rumbling.

'Judith Merryweather,' Pankaj said.

'Interesting name.'

'Sir, the weather is always merry in Goa.'

Chupplejeep laughed. 'Maybe not so in the monsoons.'

'Liquid sunshine, sir,' Pankaj said.

Hardly, thought Chupplejeep. When the rain was lashing down, the gutters were full, water was pouring through the faulty roof into the sitting room and trees were coming down left, right and centre, but he let it go. 'Judith, our sarong wearer.'

'The one that resembled a wrinkled orange. She looked a little out of place at the party, and one of the guests questioned said that Judith has a habit.'

'Drugs?'

'She's been known to take things from people's houses. Not valuable things, but small things for the sake of it.'

'A kleptomaniac. How do we know she hasn't taken anything valuable before?'

'I called the guest who made the accusation. Judith took a small glass ashtray from this woman's house. She has it on video. She didn't say anything to Judith because they're friends and the ashtray was worthless, but now her staff keep an eye on her at her parties.'

'Tell her to send us the footage. Let's take a look. Maybe our sarong wearer has moved on to more valuable items.'

'Sir, Judith doesn't need the money though. She has wealth. She owns that skincare brand. The one with pictures on all the billboards on the way from the airport.'

'*Be You?*'

'That's the one. Shwetty buys their products. They are very costly, and to be honest, sir, I can't see any difference in her skin since she has been using them.'

'Did you tell Shwetty that?' Chupplejeep asked.

'No, sir,' he said. 'I'm learning.'

'Good,' Chupplejeep said. At least the boy could learn from his mistakes. 'Be You is not profitable though. In a matter of weeks they'll be going into administration.' Chupplejeep leaned forward towards his computer and clicked on his mouse. 'See.' He turned the monitor towards his colleague. *Business Scoop* had reported falling profits. 'Unless Be You suddenly gets a cash injection, their business will be wiped away.'

'So Judith has motive. Suddenly her kleptomania skills come in handy. She'd need to sell that sapphire pretty quickly to get the cash though. She or Daniel could have thrown that ring out of the window when we arrived and retrieved it on their way out. There was no police presence that night or early morning, remember. Reena Gopaldas reported the theft to the police, but they have yet to show much interest. There was so much noise and commotion going on from the parade. A stone like that can be removed from its setting in minutes by a jeweller and sold within hours.'

Chupplejeep scratched his chin. 'I'll call my jeweller contact again. See if he's heard anything.' It had been several days since the ring went missing, which meant it could be far from India by now. The chances of retrieving the jewel were slim. Chupplejeep clenched his fists. He liked Mr Gopaldas, and he was determined to get the Kingfisher Sapphire back for him. But right now he wasn't sure how.

Chapter Twenty-three

'Are you hungry?' Chupplejeep asked, checking the time. He could hear fireworks and music as villagers continued their Diwali celebrations. He couldn't face going back into the house whilst the bedtime routine was taking place, but it was past seven, and he was certain Nicholas and Bonita would be in bed. It would be safe to get a snack. 'Come on,' Chupplejeep said to Pankaj, making his way to the kitchen. He stopped next to the bimley tree and looked at the bright green fruit, which had started to swell. The sour fruit was excellent in a hot prawn curry, which he could smell. The fragrance was coming from the neighbouring house. If only there was a prawn curry waiting for him. With any luck there would be an old bit of cheese and some bread. Christabel had made it quite clear that she was no longer going to do all the jobs in the house and that he would have to go to the market to get some food for his dinner. Of course he hadn't, and now he would have to suffer. He looked longingly towards his neighbour's house.

'What?' Pankaj said as Chupplejeep stared into the distance. Chupplejeep explained what he had been thinking.

'Ah,' Pankaj said. 'Sounds like you need Nita in your life. You don't need to compare, remember. I'll save you some money. Be grateful for what you have. Your neighbour has a nice prawn curry, but you have a loving wife and two children.'

Chupplejeep made a face. 'He too has that,' he said. 'I'm glad you mentioned Nita.'

'Because she had motive to take that sapphire too? Perhaps to teach her client a lesson.'

'I'm not sure it's teaching Reena anything. From what I hear, she's capitalising on the loss of her precious jewel. The internet has exploded with theories of what happened to the Kingfisher Sapphire. She must be loving this drama that is centred around her.'

'Another reason to suspect our victim,' Pankaj said.

'Nita doesn't have the wealth that her clients possess. Nita doesn't have the wealth that most of the people at the party took for granted.'

'Except Judith,' said Pankaj. 'And maybe Aman.'

'What do we know about him?'

'Not much, sir. There wasn't much online when I checked. It's like he doesn't have a digital profile.'

'No social media? If he doesn't have an online profile does he even exist?' Chupplejeep asked, imitating Reena Gopaldas.

Pankaj laughed. Chupplejeep took one final look at his neighbour's house and walked towards the kitchen.

~

'Here,' Christabel said as Chupplejeep approached. Chupplejeep had to admit his wife looked pretty worn out. Bathing two children and reading them stories whilst Nicholas and Bonita jumped around the room like monkeys would do that to you. Christabel handed him a paper bag and made a face.

Chupplejeep pulled Christabel towards him and kissed her cheek. 'You're one in a million, you know that?' he said.

'Yes, I do. I saw a cart selling cutlet bread on my way home, and I knew you two would be working late again, especially now that Shwetty is away.'

Pankaj looked to the floor.

'Don't worry,' Christabel said. 'She'll get used to being married to a private investigator. To be honest, I don't think it's worse than being married to a cop.' She handed Pankaj another paper bag. 'Omelette bread for you,' she said.

'Really?' Pankaj shook his head from side to side in appreciation. 'Do you really think that PI work is less risky than being a cop? he asked, his face looking hopeful.

'No,' Christabel said. 'I just said it to make you feel better.'

'She'll be back soon,' Pankaj said, his eyes shifting to the paper bag Christabel had just handed him. 'She wants me to decide.'

'Decide what?' Christabel asked, sitting down. Her eyes brightening at the thought of a bit of gossip.

'Whether I will choose my job or her.'

'Oh,' Christabel said. 'Quite serious then. I thought you looked unwell the other day. Shwetty didn't quite put it to me like that. She just said she had had enough of your hours. And I put my foot in it saying it only gets worse.'

Pankaj flopped down in the chair next to his boss's wife. Chupplejeep handed them each a Kingfisher. 'What do I do?' Pankaj asked Christabel.

~

Christabel, normally full of advice, didn't know what to say. It was tough being married to Arthur, but she would never ask him to give up what he loved doing. She knew if Arthur stopped fighting crime, he would stop completely, and she couldn't imagine a life without Arthur Chupplejeep.

Pankaj was a younger version of Chupplejeep when it came to his work ethic. The boy was a romantic and a dreamer, two qualities Arthur didn't possess, but he wanted to help people. Seeking justice was part of Pankaj's nature. If the boy stopped doing what he loved at his wife's request, he would ultimately resent Shwetika. She was about to open her mouth and say all this when Arthur put down his sandwich.

'You know what you have to do,' Chupplejeep said. He fished in his pocket and pulled out a card. 'Call the number.'

'Now?' asked Pankaj.

'Why not? You're desperate.'

Chapter Twenty-four

Pankaj rubbed his palms together as Cynthia studied him. 'Nervous?' she asked, twisting a lock of brown hair around her fingers.

'I've never done anything like this before,' Pankaj said.

'*Hna*. You said on the phone. I wouldn't normally allow someone like you here at the Atul Centre. You've made it clear that you're investigating one of our residents.'

'We're investigating the death of Jagdish –'

'So why were you here asking after Bhavan Johar?'

'His mother and the deceased –' Pankaj started, but Cynthia didn't let him finish. She rested her ample bosom on the wooden table and clasped her hands together, looking her subject up and down.

'I'm here for personal reasons,' Pankaj said. 'It's true, before I was here with my boss for other matters, but when I saw what work you do here, I wanted to give it a try myself. You have some great reviews on your website.'

Cynthia beamed. 'I've been managing this place for over seven years. I've made it the place it is today. It's exclusive. You can't just walk in. You need to be referred.'

'You made it look so inviting,' Pankaj said, his mouth a little dry. 'When I was here with my superior –'

'That, it is,' said Cynthia. She pursed her lips together. 'Okay. You can stay for two nights.' She looked over to his black nylon holdall. Peon,' she shouted. A man with hunched shoulders scuttled into the room. 'Take Mr Deshpande's bag to room 114.' Cynthia reached into one of the desk drawers and retrieved a key, which she handed to the skinny peon. She turned back to Pankaj. 'Bhavan Johar has checked out. He won't be back for some time, so there is no reason why you can't benefit from our wellness centre. On the telephone you explained the reason for your stay. Is that your only concern?' she asked, pulling out a form from a tray in front of her.

Pankaj nodded. He watched as she ticked a box marked 'marital concerns'. Cynthia lifted her head and caught his eye. She smiled. Pankaj pulled at his collar.

'It's warm in here, no?' she said, adjusting the neckline of her dress without taking her eyes off him. She reached over and switched the fan on. Walking around to the front of the desk, she sat down on its surface and leaned towards her new client.

Kingfisher Blues

Pankaj could smell cinnamon tea on Cynthia's breath. His instinct was to recoil, but he didn't. He was a professional, after all. He had hoped that the Atul Centre would help him with his current predicament with Shwetty, help him pinpoint where he had gone wrong. Perhaps they would tell him what he knew all along, that he needed to stand up for himself and only then would Shwetty give him any respect. The Atul Centre wasn't cheap. Even a two-night option would cost him more than a month's salary, but he wasn't just there for the therapy; he was there to find out a little more about the Johars, and Chupplejeep said the business would cover the costs. Now, as Cynthia sat in front of him, her dress hitched a little higher than it should have been, he wondered what he was getting himself into.

'Don't worry,' Cynthia said, her voice sounding a little raspy. 'We only have you with us for a short time, but that's all you need at the Atul Centre, and after that I'm sure you will see things clearly with your, hmm, wife.'

Pankaj nodded. He hoped bhang wouldn't be used in any of his therapies. It wouldn't be the first retreat in Goa to think they were being innovative by adding the drug to their brownies and smoothies to help their patients see things from a different perspective.

'So first,' Cynthia said, standing up and stepping away from him, 'get yourself settled and have a wander in our gardens. They're beautiful and lush, and you have a keen interest in flora and fauna. I noticed the other day how keen you were to know more about the birds. Ask one of our wellness nurses in blue. They have a wealth of knowledge about the place. Then later today, following your afternoon siesta, we will meet for our first therapy session. You will be nice and fresh then.'

Pankaj stood. 'See you,' he said, wiping the thin film of sweat from his brow. As he headed for the door, Cynthia cleared her throat.

He turned.

'Please don't ask any of our staff or guests about the Johars,' she said. 'I'll be watching you, and if I sense you are here to make *naatak*, trouble, then you will be marched off the premises. You hear? No matter how pretty your face is.' Cynthia touched the binoculars on her desk and stared at him.

Pankaj managed a half smile and turned back to the door.

Chapter Twenty-five

'Sir, we've made a terrible mistake,' Pankaj whispered. He was sitting behind the thick trunk of an old banyan tree. Its large leathery dark green leaves were keeping the sun out, along with prying eyes. Pankaj was certain that Cynthia couldn't see him. Bhaagvan help him if she could. Mobile phones were not allowed on the premises, and he had to hand his over when he had checked in. Chupplejeep had of course given him a spare, and by the looks of it several other residents had the same idea. In the short time he had been at the centre, he had witnessed at least three guests slyly looking at their phones, hidden behind novels and magazines about meditation.

'No, Pankaj, you've been in similar situations. This is personal and professional though, and mixing the two doesn't do anything for your psyche. But remember, this is your advantage. The manager knows full well what your job is, so you have no reason to feel like you are being underhanded.'

'But sir,' Pankaj said, 'I am being underhanded. I am here under false pretences.'

'You want to make a decision for Shwetty, don't you?' Chupplejeep asked.

'Yes, but –'

'No buts,' Chupplejeep commanded. 'Two birds, one stone. You're a PI now. This is what we do. You're lucky it's not so covert this time.'

'Sir…' Pankaj trailed off. He was certain he had heard a branch crack, and something had flickered past the corner of his eye. He disconnected the call and slipped the phone in his pocket. He looked through the aerial roots of the banyan tree that hung down and rooted themselves in the soil. He stood up and carefully crept around the large tree. There was no one there.

Pankaj sat down again at the base of the tree. The sun was high in the sky. It must have been at least thirty-five degrees. Under the large canopy of the banyan it was cooler. He typed out a quick message to Chupplejeep and assured his boss he was fine.

This was what he had signed up for – late nights and undercover operations. Pankaj had been thrilled at the thought of the drama when he had first started working with Chupplejeep. In fact, he had begged Chupplejeep to take him on, despite Chupplejeep's reservations. 'It's a new business and work isn't that consistent,' he had said. 'I can't offer you the security of the force, and I don't want to take that away from you. You're young, not like me.' But you're the best, Pankaj had thought at the time, desperate to work with his old boss again.

Kingfisher Blues

Chupplejeep was right. Pankaj had done similar before, maybe not quite involved in his position as a sub-officer, but nevertheless he had on occasion pretended to be someone else to get the information he needed. So why was he so worried? Was it because Cynthia was ready to pounce on him in more ways than one, or was it because of Shwetty's threats? Had his wife's questioning made him doubt his abilities? He had been a first-class cop. He had been told that on more than one occasion, and even the recently promoted Director General Gosht had once said it, sort of.

Pankaj chewed his bottom lip. For the first time since knowing Shwetika, he was angry with her. If she couldn't handle the profession he had chosen, maybe they shouldn't be together, but in an instant he regretted his thoughts. He loved Shwetika more than anything. He couldn't imagine a life without her.

'Do you love me more than your job?' Pankaj heard Shwetty say. It was true he loved his job, maybe not more than Shwetika, but perhaps the same. Pankaj stopped his thoughts there. He would save those agonising thoughts for therapy.

'So.' Pankaj heard a young woman's voice from behind the tree. He turned and looked through the aerial roots. A woman in blue with a familiar face was staring at him. Pankaj pulled himself up using the tree as a support and stared at the lady, who was smiling at him.

'Hello,' he said

She looked at his pockets. 'You have a phone,' she said. 'It's not allowed at the centre.'

'I don't know what you are talking about,' Pankaj said. He noticed that the woman had almond shaped eyes which smiled at him and softened her angular nose.

The woman laughed. She tucked a few strands of hair that had come loose from her ponytail behind her ear. 'Every second person here has one,' she said. 'Don't worry. I don't think we would have many reservations if we stuck to our no phone policy. The rich can't bear to be away from their devices.'

'You're that nurse,' Pankaj said. 'I saw you the last time I was here chasing after a lady who had spoken badly, used bad language rather, in front of us.'

The nurse smiled. 'My uniform is also a giveaway. Mind?' she said, pulling out a packet of cigarettes.

'Should you?' Pankaj asked, looking towards Cynthia's office.

'No,' the nurse said. 'But you're not going to tell, are you?' She didn't wait for an answer. 'Cynthia wouldn't be best pleased if she heard you had a phone, would she? Because your reasons for being here aren't exactly as you've said.'

'Why I'm here,' Pankaj said, feigning confidence, 'is not your business.'

'But it is,' she said. The nurse looked up and blew a ring of smoke in the direction of the leaves. Her hair came loose again, and she pushed it away. 'You picked a good spot. Here behind this beautiful Indian banyan and behind the rain tree are the only two blind spots. The only two places Cynthia can't peek. It won't be for long though. She'll probably put a camera in that rock before too long. You know that though, because you've done your homework. You're a cop, aren't you?'

Pankaj shook his head.

'Then you look very similar to a young man who helped my elderly mother who was almost knocked down near Panjim market just over a year ago.'

Pankaj considered this information. He had helped an elderly woman near the market last September. She had been badly shaken by the incident, and he had stayed with her until her daughter had arrived. Pankaj gave the woman a half smile.

'Would Cynthia do that?' Pankaj asked, following the nurse's eyes to a large stone that had been placed a few meters behind the tree.

'I wouldn't put it past her. She likes to be all knowing.' The nurse studied Pankaj. 'So why are you really here? You don't fit the standard clientele we have here.'

'And how would you describe your usual clientele?'

The nurse turned and blew a ring of smoke away from Pankaj. 'So,' she said eventually. 'You're not going to tell me why you're really here. I better be off.' The woman stood up, threw her cigarette on the ground and stamped on it. She bent down and picked up the butt, slipping it in her pocket.

Pankaj hastily got to his feet. He needed a friend in here, an ally. 'Wait,' he said. 'I'm here for a few personal reasons but also to find out about Bhavan Johar.'

'Okay,' she said, pulling out another cigarette. 'Now we're getting somewhere. I'm Monica.' She extended her hand. 'I've been here for too long. You don't need to worry about me. I've outstayed my welcome here.'

Pankaj shook Monica's hand as he lowered himself to the ground and leaned against the thick trunk of the tree. 'You don't like it here or they don't like you?' he asked.

Monica didn't respond. She simply blew another ring of smoke away from him.

Pankaj smiled inwardly. 'So tell me,' he said. 'What exactly is this place?'

'Why are you here? Not the Johars,' Monica said. 'The personal reasons.'

Pankaj sighed. Monica smoking her contraband seemed genuine enough. He told her the whole sorry story about Shwetika's ultimatum.

Monica gave him a pitying smile but didn't offer any advice. 'You may not be one of the well-to-do, but you're here for the same reason fifty percent of our residents are here. They're lost or confused. They want an answer to a simple question. They want to step back from life and reflect, recharge. Some are relieved when we ask them to hand over their devices. They want an excuse to disconnect. And Cynthia has a way of making people see what they already know. Because deep down inside us,' Monica said, putting her fingers on her chest, 'we already know the answers to all our problems; we just don't choose to listen.'

'Does Cynthia help her guests with the use of illegal substances?'

'Would you report her if I said yes?'

Pankaj shrugged.

'She always asks for consent first as far as I am aware.' Monica reached into her bag and pulled out another cigarette along with her lighter.

'What about the other fifty percent?' Pankaj asked.

Monica put the cigarette and lighter back in her bag. 'Walk with me,' she said. 'If we're out of sight for too long, our illustrious leader will get suspicious.' Monica started to walk away, and Pankaj hurried behind her.

Chapter Twenty-six

Chupplejeep cast his line and listened to the satisfying plop of the weight as it entered the water. He leaned back in his deckchair and turned to his brother, who was fixing a small prawn onto his hook. Chupplejeep didn't care if he caught any ladyfish. He wasn't much of a fisherman, but his brother was. It felt good to use that term. It had taken him several months to get used to the idea that he had a brother, and even then the word didn't feel right on his tongue, but following the birth of his daughter, he had wholeheartedly embraced it.

'You spoken to Ma recently?' Karan asked.

Chupplejeep shook his head. 'Not since that last time.'

Karan was quiet. They both knew what that last time entailed: their mother asking Chupplejeep if she could help with the babysitting; Chupplejeep point-blank refusing. The suggestion was ludicrous. His parents hadn't looked after him as a child; there was no way he was going to let them near his children without either Christabel's or his presence.

Whilst Chupplejeep had welcomed Karan into his life, his mother and father were a different matter. Chupplejeep had occasionally visited his biological parents at the insistence of Karan and Christabel, but he often left their home with a bitter taste in his mouth. He had tried to forgive Nishok and Camilla for leaving him at an orphanage at two because they believed their son had been cursed, but Chupplejeep found he couldn't. 'Baby steps,' Christabel had said to him, and she was right, but it had been two years now and still he couldn't bring himself to laugh in their company.

The arrival of Nicholas and Bonita had only made things worse. Karan's presence had made Chupplejeep see that family ties were important, but Chupplejeep couldn't imagine leaving either of his children at an orphanage and allowing them to think he was dead.

Chupplejeep glanced out over the water as it lapped the jetty. He wasn't the best father. He wasn't there for Nicholas and Bonita as much as he should have been. He chose to work rather than to listen to their whining. And he gave them all the wrong sorts of food; food that Christabel had labelled unhealthy and full of additives. But Chupplejeep loved them wholeheartedly. Just the thought of his daughter being stranded alone without either of her parents made his eyes well up and his heart give way. When a boy at school told Nicholas he didn't want to play with him and Nicholas came home crying, Chupplejeep knew that Christabel's mother was right when she said a parent was only as happy as their unhappiest child. He was fiercely protective of his two and could see why Jagdish Sharma gave the third degree to any of his daughter's protective suitors. He would do the same for Bonita.

Chupplejeep struggled to forgive his parents because he couldn't understand how they could have done what they did. He had been miserable for years at the orphanage. It had scarred him more than he cared to think about, yet his parents had merrily had another child and raised it, safe in the knowledge that their supposedly cursed son was out of sight and out of mind. 'Forgiveness will come,' Christabel had said. He hoped it was true.

'You gotta love this time of day,' Karan said, adjusting his glasses. 'The fish are getting ready to bite.' He cast his line and sat back with a Kingfisher in hand.

Chupplejeep smiled. His brother had worked hard to get to where he was. After that business two years ago with the wife of the loan shark, Chupplejeep had convinced Karan to seek help for his gambling addictions and Karan had listened. As far as Chupplejeep was concerned, his brother hadn't been seen in any of those water-polluting casino boats that sailed up and down the Mandovi river in the last two years. It was difficult meeting up with his brother and not talking about their parents. But over the last twenty-four months they had got to know each other, and although they didn't have that much in common, they liked each other's company. They could quite happily sit together in silence, and fishing was perfect for that. Plus, it was the one hobby they could both agree on. They occasionally talked about the cricket, but there was no way Chupplejeep was going to feign an interest in fixing up old motorbikes, and Karan didn't exactly share Chupplejeep's love for savoury snacks. Snacking, Chupplejeep had come to realise, was his one true hobby.

'Rissole?' Chupplejeep offered from his metal tiffin.

Karan shook his head. Christabel hadn't packed as many as Chupplejeep would have liked. His wife had probably eaten a handful of the mini prawn-stuffed pancakes herself. He couldn't blame her. They were hard to resist. Chupplejeep was glad his brother had such a small appetite.

Chupplejeep checked his phone to see if Pankaj had sent any more messages. He wondered if he had done the right thing sending his protégé into the Atul Centre. Pankaj was more than capable of being a great private investigator, but since leaving the force he had lost some of his confidence. Chupplejeep had seen this as an opportunity to give his colleague that confidence back, along with resolving some of his own issues with Shwetika and uncovering further detail on Bhavan Johar and his parents.

Cynthia, the woman who ran the Atul Centre, didn't look as if she would bite, but an uneasy feeling rose in the pit of his stomach when he thought about her. Chupplejeep swallowed it down with the remains of his beer.

~

'Look at this,' Monica said, turning to Pankaj as she spoke. 'This is the rain tree. They call it the *Thungumoonji*.' She pointed to the small dull green oval leaves of the large tree.

'That's its name in Tamil,' Pankaj said.

'You know your trees,' Monica said with a smile. Long brown seed cases hung from several of the branches. 'Like me, this tree cannot stand the cold. It only grows in tropical climates. So what do you want to know?'

'About the tree?' Pankaj began to say. 'About the Atul Centre, the guests,' he quickly corrected himself.

'Like I said, this place is for the rich paying for rehab. Some of them are here to rest, some have minor medical treatments and others behavioural problems, like the person you seem to be interested in. These people in the latter group probably need proper medical care, but their parents don't want to acknowledge that they have a problem. This is a better alternative, one that their social circles will accept. And the residents are not held against their will. They like being here, so arguably it is better than somewhere they are forced to go to.'

'They like being here because they can do what they want?' Pankaj asked. 'Surely that doesn't help them.'

Monica shrugged. 'You've got to want to change or you never will,' she said. 'We have some decent therapists here. Cynthia pays well. Our residents feel better for a day or two. They check out. They have another episode and they check back in. It is a continual problem but it turns a profit.'

'Do some of your residents have addictions? Are they involved in substance abuse?'

Monica laughed. She walked on and pointed to another tree. 'This is a halfway house for the rich. It makes their parents think they are doing something – a salve for their conscience.'

'You really don't have any faith in this place,' Pankaj said.

Monica shook her head. 'Okay,' she said. 'It does help some. I'm sure your problems will be fixed, but it's like I said. It helps those that already have the answers within and are willing to see them. Not the others. Some need better help.'

'Does Cynthia advise her clients if they need professional help?'

Monica didn't answer. But Pankaj wasn't here to establish the ethics of the Atul Centre, of which he was slowly starting to see there were none.

'Listen,' Monica said. 'Kids these days they have a say in where they go, even if it is rehab. They all want to come here, because it's an easy ride. Short bursts of rehab aren't really helping them. By their fifth visit their parents should see that; they shouldn't need Cynthia to spell it out for them. Cynthia is a lot of things, but you can't blame her for wanting repeat bookings. Somebody has to pay the bills. Isn't that right?'

'And Bhavan Johar was one of these rich kids that needed professional help?' Pankaj said, trying to steer the conversation.

'Bhavan Johar has an attitude problem, addiction and anger management issues,' Monica said, reaching up and picking a white flower. She handed it to Pankaj and briefly glanced in the direction of the building behind them. Pankaj could feel Cynthia's gaze on them with her binoculars.

'Was he a threat?' he asked.

'To his mother's ex-husband? Why do you ask that?'

'You just said he had anger management issues.'

'He did. But why would Bhavan want to harm his mother's ex-husband? I'm not into kathakali, but the man must have had money if he was famous, and rumour has it the Johars' money is running out, so why would any of them want him dead?' Monica sighed. She gave Pankaj a sideways glance. 'Bhavan had the occasional tantrum. He spends his money on things he shouldn't. His parents are part of the problem. They are the ones who give him the money. He doesn't have a job.'

Pankaj heard a ringing. He checked his pocket, but it wasn't him. He breathed a sigh of relief as Monica reached into her bag and pulled out an Atul Centre branded mobile.

'We are allowed,' Monica said as she answered it. 'Of course. I'll send him up now,' Monica said. She disconnected the call and smiled at Pankaj. 'You're wanted. Cynthia's had a cancellation. She can fit your first therapy session in now.'

'Now?' Pankaj said. 'I haven't had time to prepare.'

'That's the best way. Here, take this,' Monica said, delving into her bag again. She pulled out some chewing gum and handed it to him. 'Gum is allowed.'

Pankaj took the packet and eyed it curiously.

'Aniseed,' Monica said. 'Cynthia can't stand the smell. She'll keep her distance.'

Relief washed over Pankaj. 'That obvious?' he asked.

'Like I said,' Monica said. 'I've been here too long.'

Chapter Twenty-seven

Meera stood in her garden wearing a floral summer dress, a bucket of washing at her feet. She pulled the washing line across and muttered something as she started the task of hanging out the white clothes. Chupplejeep lowered his sunglasses onto his eyes. The brilliant whites were reflecting the sun right back at him.

Every now and again Meera checked her phone that she slipped in and out of her dress pocket. 'Excuse me,' Chupplejeep said, heading towards her. 'Do you have a few minutes?'

Meera stepped back. She handed the investigator a pile of clothes. 'If you don't mind helping,' she said.

Chupplejeep took a handful of wooden pegs from the bag hanging on the line and started his task. If Christabel could see him now, he chuckled to himself, she would have thought the midday sun had gone to his head.

'What do you want to know?' Meera asked as Chupplejeep hung a pair of trousers on the line. The investigator finished his task and pointed to the cane table and chairs at the end of the patio. The seating area was positioned at the rear of the house where a red hibiscus grew amongst the white and orange bougainvillea and tall grasses. Meera sighed and followed him.

'What do you do?' Chupplejeep asked.

Meera stared at him for a moment. 'Interiors,' she said. 'I have my own business. I organise show homes when developers are selling properties. I take on private clients too. Some people want to update their living room or whole house. I can do that. Now, Mr Chupplejeep, are you here for advice on cushions or is it something else that you are after?' Meera fixed him with her gaze.

'I want to know what your relationship is like with Popatrao,' Chupplejeep said, clasping his hands together. He eyed his suspect carefully.

'Popatrao said you went to visit him. Warned me of your arrival.'

'Was it a warning?' Chupplejeep asked. A bead of sweat ran down the side of his face, which he dabbed at with a handkerchief. Meera offered him a drink and momentarily left him to fetch two glasses of water.

'Popatrao's a good man, or at least he tries to be. He can sometimes find it difficult to...' She trailed off, handing him a glass of icy water and sitting back down again. 'Sometimes he doesn't know his own strength. But he's good to me. I can't complain,' Meera said, fiddling with her necklace. Chupplejeep noticed she was wearing several bejewelled bracelets and an intricate necklace. None had any green stones on them like the one found at the crime scene, but that wasn't to say she didn't have a piece with a missing stone in her jewellery box.

'Did he ever hurt you?' he asked.

Meera looked away but shook her head. Chupplejeep had spoken at length with Popatrao. He couldn't imagine someone as meek as Popatrao being abusive, but then it took all sorts.

'I wouldn't want to get on his wrong side is all I am saying,' Meera said, giving the investigator a sideways glance. 'Like most men, he has a temper. I've seen quite a vicious side to him, but I won't go into that right now. I don't want you to think Popatrao had anything to do with Jagdish's death.'

Chupplejeep nodded. He didn't have to wait long before Meera started speaking again.

'He killed a cat once with his bare hands because it made a number two in the beach restaurant at Baytown. I saw it with my own eyes,' Meera said, with a visible shiver. 'Terrible.'

'Did any guests witness this?' Chupplejeep said, making a note. Popatrao seemed fond of the black-and-white cat in his office the other day. He noticed Meera strain her neck to look at the notes he was making.

'Of course not,' Meera said. 'He waited till the restaurant had cleared out.'

'Anything else?' Chupplejeep asked.

'He used to shoot the crows,' she said casually.

'For pinching food?' Chupplejeep asked. Crows were becoming more of a nuisance in Goa lately with their incessant cawing and swooping down on unattended plates of masala fried prawns. Most hoteliers and restaurateurs had combatted the issue by hanging nets from coconut trees to avoid the preying birds. The crows were most definitely irritating, but shooting them was a bit extreme.

'More like for fun,' Meera muttered.

Chupplejeep moved on, asking his interviewee where she had been the night Jagdish had died. Meera said she was home alone. 'Not with Popatrao?' he asked. 'No,' she said quite clearly, but Meera wouldn't meet his eye. He explained that Popatrao had been at the theatre where Jagdish was performing the night he was killed. Meera didn't look surprised at all.

'Didn't you want to accompany him?' Chupplejeep asked.

'I hadn't been feeling well if I remember correctly,' she said, still avoiding the investigator's gaze.

'When did your affair start with Popatrao?' he asked.

Meera made a face. 'You make it sound so vulgar. His wife is never around, and Popatrao needed me,' she said. 'Needs,' she corrected herself. 'I've been with him a little over a year.'

'And you were key in getting Jagdish Sharma to agree to perform at Baytown, Popatrao's hotel, I understand.'

'It was a good idea. It hasn't been done in Goa before, a residency. Kapoor gave it his full approval. It wasn't going to impact on Jagdish's show there. It would have been a success if it hadn't been for the rats.'

'And Popatrao would have money rolling in, giving him the motivation he needed to leave his wife.'

'His wife controls the purse strings,' Meera said, fiddling with her nails, still avoiding Chupplejeep's eye.

'But now he's worse off than before. And he was contracted to pay Jagdish regardless of whether or not the kathakali dancer performed,' Chupplejeep said, recalling what the hotelier had told him and what he had read in the contract he had found in Popatrao's office. 'Had Jagdish Sharma been alive, Popatrao would have been in more financial trouble than he is now. It gives your boyfriend motive.'

Meera looked away again, this time towards the red hibiscus. She pulled off one of the flowers and twirled it between her thumb and forefinger. 'I told him to sign up that Darsh fellow instead. Jagdish's understudy. But Popatrao wanted the best, as usual.'

'Oh,' Chupplejeep said, pausing momentarily. 'I was under the impression you made the introduction between Jagdish and Popatrao.'

'He said that? He's confused. I mentioned getting a dancer to perform weekly at the hotel. I may have suggested kathakali. My mother was fond of that type of dance when I was growing up, and I guess it just stuck with me, so when I was thinking of a way for Baytown to be a cut above the other hotels, it just came into my mind.'

'*Aacha*,' Chupplejeep said. 'So you didn't know Jagdish?'

Meera shook her head. 'Nor did I know the other one, the understudy.'

'I see. And did you have any reason to want the great kathakali dancer dead?'

Meera dropped the flower. 'Me?' she asked. 'Of course not. I just told you I hardly knew the man.'

'Popatrao seemed to think you were having an affair.'

Meera was silent. She stared at Chupplejeep, and he noticed her right eyebrow had started to twitch. Then she laughed. A big bellow of a laugh like Chupplejeep had just told a first-class joke.

'That's ridiculous,' she said. 'With Jagdish? You know why Popatrao's saying that. It's because he's a cheater. The swine. Can you believe it? He's jealous and possessive despite being married. They say cheaters project their behaviours onto others. That's why your Popatrao has said what he has.'

'Interesting theory,' Chupplejeep said.

'Don't belittle me,' Meera said, her eyes fixed on him. 'You cops think you know everything.'

Chupplejeep leaned back. The good thing about being a private investigator was that if he chose, he could tell his suspects what he really thought. There was no need to be diplomatic or keep information concealed, like he had to as a police inspector.

'So you're not having an affair?' he asked.

'He's ruining my reputation,' Meera said. 'I could sue him for that. If he had any money, I would.'

Chupplejeep didn't point out to Meera that she had probably already ruined her reputation by sleeping with a married man. Mistresses always had a warped perception of what was right and wrong.

'Okay then,' Chupplejeep said, standing up. 'I'll let you get back to it. Do you mind if I contact you if I have any further questions?'

Meera flashed him a smile. The first he had seen from her. 'Sure, anytime, Mr Chupplejeep.'

He turned to go but then stopped. He turned back to Meera. 'Do you know Rupali Sharma well?' When Meera looked at him blankly, he added, 'Jagdish's wife?'

'Oh, err,' she hesitated. 'Vaguely. Jagdish spoke about her at many of the meetings he had with Popatrao. The ones I was present for.'

'He must have loved his wife very much to talk about her so much,' Chupplejeep said. He could see Meera clench her jaw. 'Have you spoken to Rupali or seen her recently?' he asked. 'I'm finding it difficult to get hold of her.'

Meera shook her head. 'This is Goa,' she added. 'It isn't that hard to track someone down. You're a private investigator, aren't you? It should be a breeze.'

'Thanks,' Chupplejeep said. 'I'll take my leave.' He walked through the garden gate back to the main road.

Meera stomped into the house. She pulled her mobile phone out of her pocket and called a number. 'He knows,' she spat as the call was answered.

~

Darsh slammed the phone down on his dresser and swore. That woman was forever eating his brains. Now was not the time.

He heard a knock on the door. The person behind it didn't wait for an answer. She barged in like she owned the place as he busied himself with his headdress.

'You okay?' the woman said, waving her clipboard at him.

'Yes, yes,' Darsh said, patting his made-up face with a tissue.

'Thought I heard voices,' the woman said in a gruff tone. 'Better to check after what happened here.'

'I appreciate your concern, but I'm fine.'

'Good,' she said. 'Because you're on. Follow me.'

Darsh took one last look in the mirror, smiled to himself, and then he did as he was told.

'Ready to get famous?' the woman asked. 'Look,' she said, pointing to a gap in the curtains. The theatre was packed.

Darsh steadied his nerves and stepped out onto the stage. 'You were born to do this,' he repeated to himself silently as he took in the crowds, momentarily dazzled by the bright lights before they were lowered. He scanned the crowd for his girlfriend. She was there; despite all the odds, despite the risk of being seen, she had made it. Of course she had disguised her appearance, but he knew it was her. He would know the curve of her body anywhere.

'Ready to be famous?' The words echoed in his head. Of course he was ready. He didn't like doing people's dirty work, but it had been worth it. With Jagdish out of the way, Darsh was going to be the only name people associated with kathakali dancing. He may have hated her, but Sonal knew what she had been talking about when she had propositioned him. Darsh took a step forward and the crowd roared.

Chapter Twenty-eight

Sonal watched them sitting side by side on the sofa. Bhavan wasn't watching the cricket with his father; he was merely pacifying him.

'Look at him,' Abhijeet was shouting at the screen. 'He's not a batsman, *tche*.' Abhijeet opened a packet of Lays, and the spicy tang of tomato chips filled the air.

Bhavan gave his father a sideways glance and went back to scrolling on his phone. 'Pa,' he said. 'This socialite has had a jewel stolen from her house. It's all over the internet, see.'

Abhijeet looked over at Bhavan's phone and raised his eyebrows when his son showed him a picture of the missing ring. Sonal watched them, her heart soaring as Abhijeet ruffled Bhavan's thick hair and went back to watching the game. The image in front of her was so different to the animosity between the two recently. Three weeks ago, when the crystal vase went flying across the room, smashing into a million tiny shards, Sonal was certain that Abhijeet had had enough of this boy. She was certain that he would do something he would later regret. Sonal touched her eye. It was healing well, and the bruising had almost disappeared. The memory of the incident caught her by surprise, and she swallowed the lump that had formed in her throat. Sonal had braced herself for Abhijeet's outburst after this vase throwing-incident, but it never came. Abhijeet had simply looked at his son with disdain and had walked away.

Her husband's reaction had been worse than just losing it with the boy, because Sonal didn't know what he was thinking. As Abhijeet had walked away, leaving her to clean up Bhavan's mess again, her son had glared at his father's retreating figure. 'Weak,' Bhavan had spat, and she wasn't quite sure if her son had been talking about her or Abhijeet. Sonal wasn't quite sure it made a difference anymore. The boy was more out of control than in control these days; only time at the Atul Centre seemed to calm him down.

After the vase-smashing incident, Sonal had let Bhavan hide away at the centre again. Maybe his girlfriend could help. Cynthia had reported that she was trying a new therapy with her son too; something about tapping into his subconscious and trying to calm his fiery soul, or so she said. Sonal let the woman's words wash over her. They had tried everything at that centre, or so it seemed. Their therapies only ever worked for a short period of time. Sonal would have to eventually admit that the Atul Centre was a scam for parents who were desperate and had nowhere else to go. She would have to find a better solution, although she needed money for that. More money.

Bhavan had always been a difficult child. Attention deficit disorder, one doctor had said early on, but two others had said that Bhavan was just spirited. Sonal didn't know who to believe, but her instinct told her something wasn't quite right, and as her boy aged, she noticed Bhavan's behaviour wasn't like his peers. He was withdrawn one moment and hyper the next.

She and Abhijeet had eventually given up with doctors and managed with patience and love. School life had been tough for Bhavan, and it wasn't easy having to move constantly for Abhijeet's job.

Abhijeet loved Bhavan from the very beginning, but he hadn't often shown the boy affection, and Bhavan had found himself competing with Abhijeet's clients for his father's attention. Sonal eventually made it clear to Abhijeet that he needed to press pause on the business and spend time with their son, give Bhavan the love he deserved. Abhijeet reluctantly agreed, Sonal promising she had enough savings put away to support them.

Her plan had worked for a time. Bhavan was calmer with his father around, and as he entered his twenties, they found the Atul Centre gave them some respite. Months turned into years, and the Atul Centre became a crutch that they needed, an expensive one. Abhijeet had lost most of his clients by the time Bhavan was old enough to need him less, and money had become a struggle.

Bhavan couldn't cope without a trip to the centre every now and again though, and now he had a girlfriend there, well, there was more reason for him to visit. If they stopped Bhavan's visits, he would become moody and lash out. Jagdish had tried with Bhavan last year. The help came as a surprise to Sonal, but she agreed reluctantly at first and then wholeheartedly when she saw the effect he was having on her son, but then as she had predicted, that too had fizzled out. Nobody had the kind of patience Bhavan needed.

Six months ago, Bhavan suddenly started displaying aggressive behaviour. Sonal had been certain it was down to drug taking. She had cut the boy's allowance and had started checking his mobile phone. It made no difference, except that checking his phone had made her even more paranoid. She spent many nights trying to decipher his text speak with his friends. Even the simplest of acronyms confused her. She put a stop to her snooping behaviour and instead decided to ask her son directly what the matter was. It wasn't the way things were done in their family. Certainly no one had ever asked her when she was growing up what was wrong when she was upset. They were Indian. No one talked about their feelings, let alone their mental health. You just got on with it, as her mother liked to say.

Sonal had sat down with Bhavan on the pink sofa in the lounge and had asked him if there was a reason for the change in his behaviour.

Her son was silent for a moment. He pulled off the gold ring he wore on his thumb, a nervous habit he had developed since she had given him the piece of jewellery on his eighteenth birthday. The ring had once been her father's, and it filled her with pride that her boy had agreed to wear it. It was said to give the wearer strength to recover, and it had certainly helped her father through some difficult times. Bhavan had stopped fiddling with the ring, slipped it back onto his thumb, looked at her with his red-rimmed eyes and had said two words – 'You know.' He stared at her until she had to look away, shame burning through her. When she gathered the courage to face her son again, she swallowed hard and said exactly what her own mother would have said. 'I don't know what you mean.'

Bhavan didn't take his eyes off hers until she looked away. She stood, wrapping her long plait in her hand. When she turned back to her son, he had gone. They never mentioned it again, and his behaviour deteriorated. Bhavan continued behaving erratically, directing all his anger at her and Abhijeet.

His words came to her in nightmares. 'You know,' he said with that sad look. 'But how do you know?' she wanted to ask. 'How do *you* know?' Instead, she bought her son the bike he had desperately wanted.

Eventually Sonal had no choice but to take matters into her own hands. She had secured funding for her boy's place at the Atul Centre and had made a decision she hoped she would never regret. She couldn't afford to have regrets. She had braced herself, ready to tell the boy what he desperately wanted to know, and then Jagdish died and everything changed.

The day her ex-husband died, Sonal and Abhijeet had been up at the centre for one of their famous performances. Bhavan never wanted them to go to the theatrical events in the vast grounds of the Atul Centre, but they were quite something to watch, and on this occasion he agreed; no doubt his new bike had been the sweetener. 'We don't have to stick with each other,' he said. 'It's better if we don't. More immersive.' Her son had been right. It wasn't long before they all lost each other in the grounds, but Bhavan had sought them out. He followed them around like a teenager for awhile until they had got talking to some friends and they lost each other again.

Sonal had been distracted that night, but she had managed to catch some of the show. Men and women, trained performers dressed sometimes in thick robes and other times in barely anything at all, danced and sang to the tabla and sitar. Sometimes the music was alive and vibrant, other times it was sombre and blue. In that setting, with just the glow of the flame torches that were carefully positioned amongst the gardens, it was quite magical. You could believe you were somewhere else in a far-off land where your problems didn't exist. Cynthia had explained that it was a combination of being amidst nature and the emotive music that had that effect. Cynthia was full of rubbish sometimes, but in this instance, Sonal believed her. No wonder parents of their difficult children swarmed towards these events.

The next morning Bhavan had come home from the centre, surprising them over their breakfast of idli and sambar. His constant scowl that he wore most days had disappeared. Sonal believed they had turned a corner, and she took back all the things she had said about the Atul Centre. Finally, after years, her son had come back to her. She embraced him and felt something shift between them. Abhijeet too had stood up and held them both. They had collectively sighed.

Sonal's phone beeped, waking her from her reverie. She looked at her device and the news article it displayed. Darsh's made-up face pictured in the *Navhind Times* as the new and noteworthy rising kathakali star looked back at her. She had made this happen.

'No ball!' Abhijeet shouted at the screen. Bhavan moved closer to his father, putting his hand in the packet of Lays potato chips Abhijeet was eating.

'Ya, Pa. I saw it,' Bhavan said, placing his phone on the coffee table and watching the game. Sonal smiled. Whatever she had done, it had been worth it.

Chapter Twenty-nine

Chupplejeep rang the bell outside the freshly varnished wooden door. The mansion had recently been whitewashed too after the monsoons. There wasn't a hint of black mould anywhere.

'*Con*?' A woman Chupplejeep assumed to be in her late seventies answered the door.

'Here again, Private Investigator Chupplejeep,' he said. 'I'm here to see Rupali Sharma. Is she in today?'

'Ah,' the woman said, stepping aside.

'I've been trying to get hold of your daughter for some time, but she has been very elusive.' Chupplejeep kept his voice even, even though he was desperately irritated with how Rupali had avoided him.

Rupali's mother ignored this statement about her daughter. 'And what have you found out so far?'

It was a good question. What had Chupplejeep found out to date?

That Jagdish had signed a bad contract with a novice hotelier. The hotelier could have killed the kathakali

Kingfisher Blues

dancer before Jagdish had a chance to put his name in the gutter. In all honesty, Popatrao had done a good job of that himself. Then there was Meera. She could have been Jagdish's lover, but there was no proof, and Popatrao could have just been diverting his attention, the same way Meera was so keen to disclose what an evil man Popatrao was with the story of the cat.

Darsh, the understudy, was the most likely suspect. He was desperate for fame, and now Jagdish was out of the way, he was in the spotlight. Sonal and her family couldn't be ruled out either. There was something not quite right in the way Sonal had been close to her ex-husband despite having a new husband and son. Sonal, Abhijeet and Bhavan were the only three that had an alibi though. Several people had seen them at the Atul Centre the night that Jagdish Sharma was killed, and Pankaj was about to confirm it.

Finally, there was Jagdish's beautiful wife with her good bone structure and blemish-free skin who had avoided him since their first meeting. What was she hiding? 'She could have been a model,' Christabel had said to Chupplejeep this morning as he had left the house. 'She could have been something, but she let her man's career blossom, not hers.' Christabel had given Chupplejeep a look then, and he had quickly left the house wondering if Christabel was drawing a comparison given the sacrifices she was making so that Chupplejeep could fulfil his vocation. It was too difficult to think about, because Chupplejeep wasn't strong enough to be a househusband. Chupplejeep swallowed down his guilt and looked at Rupali's mother. He cleared his throat.

'We're making progress,' he said.

'Hmm,' the older woman said. 'She's there, my daughter. In the sitting room.'

Chupplejeep took a breath. 'Finally,' he muttered to himself as he stepped inside. 'Finally.'

Rupali was wearing a teal sari, sitting in a large wicker chair in between two potted rubber trees, under a fan. She looked regal sipping her fresh mint tea from an ornate glass. The room smelled of citrus fruits, and he noticed a plate of sweet limes cut into quarters on one of the low wooden coffee tables. Rupali turned in Chupplejeep's direction as he entered the room.

'You're here to give me an update,' she said.

'Mind?' Chupplejeep said, sitting in the chair opposite her.

'Sure,' she said. 'Make yourself at home.' A phone rang somewhere in the depths of the house. Chupplejeep heard Rupali's mother answer it.

'Can I ask what you were doing the night of the 12th November?' he asked.

Rupali stared at the investigator. She placed her glass down on the metal table and ran her fingers along her forearms. 'So I'm under suspicion now, is it?' She looked at Chupplejeep from under her lashes.

'I wouldn't be doing my job if I didn't ask the question,' Chupplejeep said.

'It was Jagdish's big night. I was home alone with my mother.'

'You weren't at the theatre?'

Rupali looked away. 'He didn't want me there,' she said. 'Opening night can be...' She trailed off. 'There are usually afterparties. He has to network, you know.'

'I see,' Chupplejeep said. So Rupali knew of her husband's affairs. Apologising in advance, Chupplejeep asked her if she knew of any women her husband had been with, but she balked at the suggestion. He moved on.

'Can you think of anyone who would want to harm your husband?' he asked.

Rupali looked at him blankly.

Chupplejeep gave her a moment to fill the silence as most did. She didn't. 'Did you know much about his deal with Popatrao?' At the mention of the hotelier's name, Rupali's eyes shifted. She leaned forward in her chair towards Chupplejeep.

'Jagdish didn't trust him,' Rupali said.

'Why's that?' Chupplejeep asked.

'He thought that man was going to ruin his reputation. He didn't want to go through with the contract.'

'So Jagdish could pull out then, I imagine.'

Rupali leaned back, picking up her delicate glass of tea. She didn't take a sip, but she held the glass close to her lips. 'Jagdish went to see Popatrao to explain, but I don't think the conversation went as planned.'

'When was this?' Chupplejeep asked.

'The morning of his opening performance at Kapoor's.'

'The day your husband died,' Chupplejeep said as he made a note. 'Do you know what was said?'

Rupali shrugged. 'All I know was that Jagdish was in a foul mood after that meeting.'

'Can I ask why Jagdish signed such a contract when he had the show at Kapoor's lined up? Surely that was making him enough money.'

'Enough money?' Rupali laughed. 'You can never have enough money. Not that we saw a penny from Popatrao. Jagdish had demanded an upfront payment from Popatrao. I overheard him on the phone and the man promised it. But it never reached our account. Maybe that's why Jagdish was so furious.'

'You have sight of all your husband's accounts?' Chupplejeep asked.

Rupali ignored the question. She placed her glass back on the table and reached over to pick up a cigarette. Chupplejeep watched as she lit up. 'So what can you tell me about the case? I want to know who killed my husband. Isn't that why you have been trying to get a hold of me?'

'Ah, so you know about all my failed attempts. Still, you never got back to me.'

'Don't bore me, Mr Chupplejeep. You must have an idea of who did it by now.' Rupali raised her eyebrows at him.

'I can't share anything just yet,' he said. 'I report to Kapoor.'

Rupali laughed. 'So you have nothing. Kapoor would have told me. I think the cops are doing a better job than you. They certainly haven't hounded me like you have.'

'I see you have a stone missing from your bangle,' Chupplejeep said, pointing to Rupali's wrist.

She frowned and moved her cigarette to her other hand, examining her bangles. 'So I do, Mr Chupplejeep,' she said.

'Are those rubies?' he asked.

'And diamonds,' she said. 'An anniversary gift.'

Chupplejeep watched as Rupali Sharma fiddled with her bangles. The bangle with a missing stone contained only red and white gems. The stone missing was likely to be red or white, but it was central and therefore could have been a different colour. It was a similar cut stone to the emerald that had been found at the scene of the crime.

'Could I take a picture of that bangle?' Chupplejeep asked.

Rupali looked at him. 'Why?'

'My wife would like something like that, and I could get it copied for her. Perhaps with semi-precious stones.'

Rupali covered the bangle with her hand. 'I don't think so,' she said. 'There's a jewel thief around, or haven't you heard? I wouldn't want pictures of my jewellery to get out and tempt the thieves.'

Chupplejeep stood up. 'I think I have all I need,' he said. 'I'll make my way out.'

Rupali didn't look up.

'Can I ask one more thing?'

'What?' Rupali said.

'Do you know someone called Meera? She's a friend of Popatrao.'

Rupali squeezed her eyes shut, then she snapped them open. 'In passing,' she said.

'I see,' Chupplejeep said. 'She too said something similar.'

Rupali smiled, her eyes bright. 'There you go then.'

Chupplejeep gave Rupali a small wave and headed towards the door. Rupali's mother was placing the receiver down in the entrance hall. 'You've finished with my daughter?' she asked.

'Yes, yes,' Chupplejeep said. 'Can I ask where you were the night Jagdish died?'

'Yes,' she said wearily. 'I was out all night with friends. I didn't get back till the early hours. I suppose you have to ask everyone that question.'

'I do,' Chupplejeep said. 'So you were not with your daughter that night?'

Rupali's mother's face froze. 'I really must go, Mr Chupplejeep. The staff will vouch for my daughter's presence here that night. The maid here that day has gone for lunch, but if you come back later…'

You'll have paid her enough to lie for your daughter, Chupplejeep thought, finishing the old woman's sentence for her. It was something he would check, but he couldn't give much credence to someone who was paid by Rupali.

'Thank you for your time,' Chupplejeep said as he left the house. His stomach rumbled. Christabel was right, Rupali was beautiful. She could have been a model. She could have been an actress too.

Chapter Thirty

Pankaj's bedroom at the Atul Centre was fine. A king-size four-poster bed stood in the middle of the room, a slipper bath at one end and a balcony at the other. Pankaj wasn't sure how he felt about a bath in the bedroom. Some may have considered it luxurious, but he preferred to have a wash in the privacy of a bathroom. At least the toilet was behind closed doors.

His room, although plush with its low-level lighting and pink marble, didn't have a great view. He stepped out onto the balcony with a cup of freshly brewed green tea, but all he could see was the car park that led to the main entrance, not the lush gardens of the centre. Pankaj leaned against the railings and strained his neck to find the bird that was cawing in the distance. He closed his eyes momentarily to listen to the tune, but instead of hearing the bird's call, he heard the sound of a powerful motorbike. His eyes were drawn to the powerful black-and-silver bike. He squinted his eyes to get a better look. A man was still seated on the bike as one of the nurses hopped off the back. Pankaj was about to look away when the man moved and something caught his eye.

On the gas tank of the black-and-silver bike there was a picture of something, a picture of a red cobra. He was sure that when they had first interviewed Sonal, she said that her son Bhavan had commissioned a red snake to be painted onto the gas tank of his new bike, his black-and-silver bike.

Pankaj put down his tea and raced out of his room towards the entrance of the centre. As he ran, he wondered what he could say to introduce himself without scaring the boy away. Sonal would have warned her son that two private investigators wanted to speak to him regarding the death of Jagdish Sharma, but would Bhavan know to expect a patient at the Atul Centre?

'Hey, hey,' Pankaj said as Bhavan placed his helmet back on and turned on the ignition. Pankaj tried to steady his breath and act casual, like he was planning to take a walk out of the grounds. The nurse who was walking away from Bhavan towards the entrance of the centre stopped and looked back at Pankaj and then at Bhavan. Bhavan and the nurse shared a look, then she shrugged. Pankaj took it as his cue to continue.

'I think I know you,' Pankaj said, despite not being able to see his face. 'I've just checked in here again and…'

Bhavan turned off the ignition. He put his foot on the road to steady himself and studied Pankaj's face. 'Nah, I don't think so,' he said.

'You don't remember,' Pankaj said. 'We were here together last summer and then for the masked show.'

Bhavan fiddled with the gold ring on his thumb before replacing his hands on the handlebars.

'We shared that spliff behind the old banyan tree,' Pankaj tried. He could feel the heat rising under his collar.

Bhavan nodded. 'You were at the show?' he asked.

Pankaj nodded. 'Only for a short time,' he said.

'You should have stayed,' Bhavan said. 'The ending was the best bit.'

'Are you coming in?' Pankaj asked.

'No. I need to get away. Maybe see you when I'm back.'

'When's that?' Pankaj asked, but Bhavan had started the motorbike, and his words were lost as Bhavan revved the engine. Pankaj waved as Bhavan turned his bike and sped off through the gated entrance.

Back in the centre, Pankaj found the nurse he had seen with Bhavan. She was with a patient in the games room. As soon as her patient had left, Pankaj saw his opportunity. 'I know Bhavan,' he said as casually as he could. 'We met here last summer.'

The nurse nodded but didn't say anything.

'He's a great guy,' Pankaj continued. 'He cares about you a lot.' At this the nurse smiled. 'How long have you two been friendly?'

The nurse pursed her lips together, considering his question. She didn't want to engage with him, but Pankaj was banking on the fact that she had manners and didn't want to appear rude. 'A while,' she responded softly.

'He's here often, isn't he? It must be nice for you when he is,' Pankaj tried.

The nurse stood up.

'Sorry,' Pankaj said. 'I know you can't talk about him, not here. Making conversation, that's all. I was here for the recent show with Bhavan and...that business with Jagdish Sharma, you know the kathakali dancer?'

The nurse nodded.

'That business with that dancer happened that night.'

'I saw it in the papers. I didn't look at the dates. We are always so busy when a show happens here. I don't really have time to think. I recall Bhavan talking about it though. He knew the dancer. He was quite upset actually.'

'That night?' Pankaj asked. 'Did he speak to you that night about it?'

The nurse shook her head. 'Couldn't have been. I had lots to do here, so I couldn't catch up with him after the show. And...' The nurse trailed off. 'I was with him actually when he found out. He read it in the newspaper article. Bhavan was in shock at the news. Said that Jagdish was his mother's ex-husband. I've never been interested in Indian dance, so I didn't know just how famous this man was, but to be on the front of the newspapers like that said something. I was worried for Bhavan though. He didn't look right after he read about it.'

Pankaj nodded. How much of this conversation would Bhavan's girlfriend relay to him? He wondered if it would jeopardise any further interview with the boy. 'Bhavan said the ending of the show here was very good,' Pankaj said, moving the conversation away from Jagdish Sharma.

The nurse nodded. 'They always are. Bhavan isn't a big fan of these shows though. Thinks it's forced fun.' Pankaj noticed the nurse's lips turn upwards whenever she mentioned her boyfriend's name.

'He's a good guy, your Bhavan,' he said.

'Yes he is,' she said shyly. 'Yes he is.' The nurse broke into a smile but quickly composed herself. She looked around the empty games room and then took a step closer to Pankaj. She reached out for his arm and in one quick move started to twist it.

'What?' he yelped.

'Listen carefully,' she said as she pulled him towards the double doors.

Chapter Thirty-one

Chupplejeep disconnected the call. He sat behind his desk and twisted one end of his moustache. As suspected, the maid at Rupali's home vouched for her employer's whereabouts the night Jagdish Sharma was killed. Chupplejeep instantly discounted her story. Not only did it sound like the maid was being prompted by someone standing next to her, but she had called him. Not the other way around. He had spoken to Popatrao too, who denied having a visit from Jagdish the morning of the murder, then swore at him and disconnected. Rupali or Popatrao – one of them was lying.

Liars, they were all liars. Rupali Sharma and Meera were friends, that was obvious, and neither of them had an alibi for the night Jagdish had been murdered. They could have been in it together. Rupali was being cheated on; there was certainly motive there, but what was Meera's motive? You wouldn't kill for a friend, would you?

And Popatrao. The contract he had signed with Jagdish was all wrong. To not have a decent termination clause was a basic error; to agree to pay Jagdish regardless of whether the show went ahead or not was business suicide. Jagdish's wife Rupali had said that they hadn't seen a paise of that first payment though. Was Rupali lying? Popatrao was adamant that he had made a payment. A large payment, by the sounds of it. It was what made the hotelier realise that he would be financially crippled if he had to make any more of the payments without any guests actually paying to watch the show.

Chupplejeep stood up and walked over to Pankaj's desk. He had asked Pankaj to look into the contract between Popatrao and Jagdish, but soon after Pankaj had left for the Atul Centre. Chupplejeep was certain the contract contained the bank details of where Jagdish wanted the money paid. He located the document in a red folder and quickly scanned it.

He was right. The bank details were on the form, but it didn't say whose bank account it was. It was more than likely that the account was in Jagdish's sole name given what Rupali had said, but it would be best to check.

The branch details of the bank were written in the contract, so all Chupplejeep needed to do was to find out who the account belonged to. It wouldn't be easy to get that kind of information. More and more these days people were threatening that they couldn't release personal information, following the west and their data protection ways. Chupplejeep would have to find someone at the bank who would lower their ethical standards and tell him what he needed to know. And if memory served him correctly, Christabel's friend Lisa worked in this exact branch. His odds were improving every minute. Chupplejeep picked up his cell phone and dialled a number.

'I thought you were in your office?' Christabel said.

'I am,' said Chupplejeep, bracing himself for a lecture.

'Come here then if you want to ask me something,' she said, disconnecting.

Chupplejeep made a face, but he supposed he could get a snack whilst he was in the kitchen.

~

Chupplejeep had expected Christabel to call Lisa there and then, but apparently there were things to be done first, like Bonita's nappy. Nappy changing was not Chupplejeep's forte, but he needed Christabel to sweet-talk Lisa into telling him who the account holder was, and so the nappy was non-negotiable.

'Your daughter is nearly two,' Christabel said. 'And I can count the number of nappies you have changed on one hand.'

'Yes, yes,' Chupplejeep said. 'But I have been busy with work.'

'Excuses, excuses,' Christabel said. 'I could catch a killer and change a nappy at the same time. You men need to learn to multitask.'

Chupplejeep had opened his mouth to say something but then thought better of it and closed it again. Not only did he change Bonita's nappy, but he also gave her a selection of chopped vegetables while Christabel spoke to Lisa. Half an hour later, his wife emerged from the bedroom, where she had gone to make the call.

'So?' Chupplejeep asked, leaving Bonita in her highchair chewing on a cooked carrot.

'She'll get back to me.'

'Couldn't she just look there and then?' he asked.

'She has a day off today. She's not at the bank.'

'But she doesn't mind finding out?'

'Why would she mind?' Christabel asked.

'You didn't tell her why you were asking, did you?' Lisa had a big mouth. If she knew why this information was important, he was certain the rest of Goa would also know in less than twenty-four hours.

'You think I'm stupid?' Christabel asked. Motherhood had made her a little more spiky than usual. 'I made up something about a payment due for one of Nicholas's classes. I said it sounded suspicious, so I wanted to check it out. She bought it. See, I'm pretty good at this detective work too.'

Chupplejeep planted a kiss on her forehead. 'You are. Let me know as soon as you hear back from her,' he said. He would head back to his office before he was lumbered with any more childcare duties. Chupplejeep picked up a stick of raw carrot and took a bite.

'I have some other information you might be interested in,' Christabel said.

'What's that?' Chupplejeep asked, chewing slowly. The carrot was hard work.

'About that big blue stone you are looking for.'

Chupplejeep swallowed. 'There are a lot of rumours about where the stone could be. Everyone thinks they're a detective these days. The internet is full of theories.'

Christabel raised her eyebrows at her husband. 'Am I just anyone?' she asked.

'Sorry, Christu,' he said, putting his arm around her. 'Tell me, what you have heard.'

'No.' She folded her hands across her chest and exhaled. 'You never take me seriously,' she said after a breath.

'Are you serious?' Chupplejeep asked. 'Of course I do. This isn't just my business. It's our business.'

'Exactly,' said Christabel. 'You should listen to my theories no matter what.'

'I do, always. So tell me, what are you thinking?'

Bonita started coughing, and both parents turned to her. 'Is she okay?' Chupplejeep asked.

Christabel didn't take her eyes off her daughter. 'Coughing is good.'

Bonita spat out a piece of carrot and smiled.

'You better go,' Christabel said. 'You're distracting her.'

'You were going to tell me something,' Chupplejeep said.

'It can wait,' Christabel said.

Chupplejeep did as he was told. He considered whether Christabel had any real information on the stone but then thought again. If Christabel had a lead, she would have told him.

Back in his office, Chupplejeep reviewed his notes following his interviews with Rupali and Meera. Several people had motive to kill the kathakali dancer, but which one of them was it?

A theory was forming in his mind, but there were still too many unknowns. He needed further information on the Johars, and he hoped Pankaj was obtaining it from the Atul Centre. He wanted to talk to his colleague, run his theory past him. Chupplejeep picked up his phone and dialled Pankaj's number, the one he had smuggled into the retreat.

Pankaj's phone rang, but there was no answer.

Chapter Thirty-two

Chupplejeep couldn't remember the last time he had visited Mapusa market. Several women sat in a line, their saris hitched up around their knees, with woven baskets at their feet piled high with bananas and custard apples. There was chatter all around him, and the air was filled with sweet-smelling spices from a hawker frying bhajis in the distance that Chupplejeep had just visited.

'Sir,' came a small voice from behind him. Chupplejeep turned. He looked towards the girl, who was staring at him with dark eyes.

'Sangeeta,' he said with a broad smile. He had interviewed the girl after she had found Jagdish Sharma's body, and he had been impressed with her answers given her age.

'So,' she said, in a similarly abrupt tone like her mother had taken with him. He looked up, searching for the peculiar woman.

'Where's your mother? Mapusa is far from home,' he said, recalling that they lived in Porvorim, at least twenty minutes away by car.

'She's there,' Sangeeta said, pointing in the distance to a woman peering at the stacked watermelons under a makeshift tent. 'I wanted to know if you have any update on who killed the dancer, sir.'

Who doesn't, he thought. 'We're getting there,' Chupplejeep said, not quite believing his words. 'We just need a little more time, and of course I can't say anything at this stage.'

Sangeeta scrunched her nose. 'Oh,' she said. 'My father checked for me online. The police don't seem to know either.'

'You should probably get back to your mother,' Chupplejeep said. 'She'll worry about you if she can't see you.' Although he wasn't quite sure if she would.

Sangeeta nodded but made no attempt to move.

'Is there anything else you want to tell me?' Chupplejeep asked.

Sangeeta didn't say anything but put her hand in the pocket of her dress and pulled something out. She stretched her hand out towards Chupplejeep, and he offered her his open palm. She deposited the contents of her hand in his and pursed her lips. 'I wasn't completely truthful when I said I didn't touch anything in the dancer's dressing room. I took that gold nose ring,' she said, looking away. 'I was going to put it back, but after what happened I just…' She trailed off. 'I've been carrying it with me ever since you came to my house and

Kingfisher Blues

asked me those questions. I should have said something at the time, but…'

'You have now,' Chupplejeep said. 'Think nothing more of it. I will make sure it is returned.'

Sangeeta turned to leave but then turned back. 'I didn't lie about anything else,' she said. 'Promise.' Then she was gone.

Chupplejeep slipped the nose ring into his pocket and turned back towards the fruit-wallas. He put the death of Jagdish Sharma to the back of his mind and focused on the suspect he was after in the Kingfisher Sapphire case.

'Aman Khosla?' he asked one of them. The woman selling papayas and bananas looked friendly, her hair tied in a bun, her teeth well cared for. She protected her head from the fierce sun with a length of her green-and-yellow sari fabric then turned away.

'Ey,' the woman next to her said, 'you want *kellim* or no?'

Chupplejeep took a few notes out of his back pocket and bought a bunch of bananas.

'Sweet limes?' she asked. He shook his head. The woman was missing the lobe of her right ear. She nudged her friend in the ribs with her elbow.

'There,' pointed the fruit-seller in the green-and-yellow sari.

Chupplejeep looked in the direction where the woman was pointing. Beyond the rows of fruit and vegetable sellers, past the men in *lenghas* selling spices, was a row of houses. As Chupplejeep approached, he was accosted by smells of curry pak leaves, jeera and deep red Kashmiri chillies. On closer inspection, the houses were not houses; each of them had a large opening to the front where men in short-sleeved shirts and women in cotton dresses were selling something. One sold liquor, another brightly coloured household plastic buckets hanging from the ceiling, and the third sold a selection of mismatched clothing from foreign brands. He asked the bucket seller if he knew an Aman Khosla. The man grunted at him and pointed to another row of shops further down the street.

These shops were more of the traditional variety with proper shop fronts and glass display cabinets. They all sold jewellery. Chupplejeep felt a slight victory. Perhaps this Aman fellow was the one they were after. Aman had been the only guest at Reena Gopaldas's party who had refused to speak to him. Pankaj had quickly patted down the man's pockets before he had escaped, but it wasn't a thorough search. That being said, none of the guest had been searched thoroughly. How could they? They had no right and their guests knew it.

Chupplejeep walked into the first shop and asked after his suspect. 'Try the shop at the end,' a young woman said, and as a consequence suffered a piercing stare from a woman sitting in the corner with a walking cane. Chupplejeep thanked the young woman and did as he was told. As Chupplejeep entered the shop, an elderly man who Chupplejeep assumed to be the proprietor was explaining the complexities behind a simple-looking piece of jewellery.

'This ring has rubies,' the jeweller said, 'on the inside. It's not flashy, but those stones touch the recipient's skin directly. They transfer the energy from the stone to the wearer, and what's more, it is not showy.' The jeweller stopped his sales pitch and turned to Chupplejeep. 'Can I help?' he asked.

'I'm looking for Aman, Aman Koshla.'

Chupplejeep heard a shuffling in the back room and a door was opened. Chupplejeep didn't wait. He dropped his bunch of bananas and ran around to the rear of the store. He was grateful that the shop was the last in the row and so he didn't have far to run, but Chupplejeep wasn't so grateful for his decision to shovel two onion bhajis into his mouth before entering the market. A hawker selling fresh hot bhajis was always hard to resist. He couldn't be too hard on himself.

Only a minute into the chase and Chupplejeep got a stich. He put his hand on his side and followed.

'Aman,' he shouted between puffs. 'I simply want to talk. We know who you are. We will keep tracking you down until we find you.'

Chupplejeep stopped. He stooped with his hands on his knees. The pain from the stich was too much. He needed to get fit, if not for his job then for his children. But now was not the time to ponder this.

Up ahead, Aman had stopped as well. 'What do you say?' Chupplejeep said, taking in a lungful of air. 'Shall we get a tea somewhere and have a talk? I'm not a cop,' he added.

Marissa de Luna

'What is it you want to know?' Aman said, once they were seated inside a small café selling potato bhaji, samosas and chai.

Chupplejeep asked Aman why he ran while trying to regulate his breathing.

'Why are you so desperate to talk to me?' Aman said, ignoring the question.

'Isn't it obvious? You were at a party where a priceless jewel went missing. We need to find its whereabouts.'

Aman laughed. 'You know where it is.'

'What do you mean?' Chupplejeep said.

'I don't have the jewel and you know it.'

'Is it because you've passed it on? You have connections to jewellers. I've looked you up, and today you were in your grandfather's shop. Is his shop doing okay?'

Aman scowled. 'You leave my grandfather out of this. I stay with him sometimes, that's all. I don't need a tiny shop in Mapusa. If you've Googled me then you know I have a very lucrative import/export business. I wouldn't stoop so low as to take what isn't mine.'

Chupplejeep took a sip of his tea, eyeing up a deep-fried samosa with tamarind chutney placed on a tin plate currently being delivered to the table next to theirs. 'The Kingfisher Sapphire is priceless and a thing of beauty. One could be very rich and still want it. The rich always want to get richer, no?'

Aman sighed. 'I ran because I had someplace to be.'

Chupplejeep leaned back in his chair. 'You don't seem in a hurry now.'

'Not today,' Aman said. 'After the party. I didn't want to just sit around and be questioned by two wannabe detectives. I don't have anything to hide.'

'You didn't think it would look suspicious making a quick exit like that? And today? You ran again.'

'You're a nobody,' Aman said. 'Why the hell should I answer your questions?'

'I *am* a nobody,' Chupplejeep said. 'And still you ran. It doesn't look good. I spoke to Reena yesterday. I asked her about you.'

Aman didn't respond. He just stared into his glass of tea.

'I wanted to know why you refused to talk to us that day. I could tell from speaking to Reena that she holds you in high regard.'

Aman's eyes shifted to Chupplejeep.

'Why were you at her party?' he asked.

'She invited me.'

'You didn't have to go,' Chupplejeep said. When Chupplejeep last spoke to Reena, Nita had explained on Reena's behalf that Aman and Reena used to date but that Reena had broken up with him. Chupplejeep had enquired as to why, but Reena couldn't come up with an answer. Nita could. 'He was very negative,' she said. 'Reena doesn't need that energy in her life.' Chupplejeep had asked why Aman was invited to the party if he brought the mood down. Nita stuttered; Reena looked away. 'He was good to have at parties,' Reena said with a distant look in her eye. 'He made parties fun.' Not so negative after all, Chupplejeep had thought, but he kept that thought to himself.

'It was a bad idea having Aman there,' Nita had said. 'But she didn't listen.' Reena had been quiet during this conversation Nita was having for her. Chupplejeep couldn't help but wonder if Nita was trying to make Reena's life better or worse.

At one point Nita took Reena's hand. 'She's still finding it tough. Aman had been drinking excessively that day. He wasn't nice to be around. Not happy. Lots of negative energy. And then he left without any consideration for what you and your colleague were trying to achieve,' Nita had said. Chupplejeep didn't know about Aman's energy, but he had to agree with Nita on the last point, and it made him uncomfortable. There was something about Nita that unsettled him. It was more than likely that it was her job title. Chupplejeep couldn't help but think that Reena Gopaldas was being taken for a ride.

'Rumour had it that Reena had the hots for Daniel. I wanted to see it for myself,' Aman said, bringing Chupplejeep back to the present.

'And did you?' Chupplejeep asked. It would explain why Reena was so keen to hear how well Nita knew Daniel if she was romantically interested in him.

'I'm pretty certain she wasn't interested and neither was he.' Aman smiled.

'How well do you know Nita? Your ex's social media coach?' Chupplejeep asked.

'Not very,' Aman said. 'She arrived on the scene just before I left. I wouldn't have put it past her to…'

'To what?'

Aman rubbed his chin. 'To have been the instigator behind our breakup. Reena and I were getting on quite well before Nita arrived.'

'Do you blame Nita for the breakup?'

Aman added two teaspoons of sugar to his tea and stirred it, the metal making a clinking sound on the glass. 'Reena's old enough to make her own decisions, and Reena was never really happy, you know. She was looking for something else. She desperately wanted to be seen.'

'Seen by who?'

'Good question. Reena wanted to be loved by the masses. She wanted to be talked about. She knew she had a problem but she couldn't help it. It's why she called this social media coach.'

'Reena found Nita?'

'She heard about her from a friend of a friend, asked to get in touch and that was it. It's like they've been friends for years. I hope that babe helps Reena out after this last debacle.'

'How long were you two dating?' Chupplejeep asked.

'Six months, maybe more. I'm not one of those people that celebrate monthly anniversaries. We met at a mutual friend's yacht party and hit it off.'

'So Reena hosted other parties while you were on the scene.'

'Sure. She loved to host.'

'And were her staff always there? Uma and Vihaan?'

'The man yeah, not Uma, but I'm not surprised he wasn't there for the last party. Uma and Vihaan always had their heads together. Looked like they were scheming. You can't have that with your staff or another *White Tiger* situation could happen. Did you read that book?' Aman asked.

Chupplejeep shook his head. He wasn't a reader, but he had seen the movie. He decided to keep that to himself.

'Where were you when Reena noticed the ring was missing?'

'I was on the balcony. She was somewhere behind me, getting herself a drink, I think. She was talking loudly about this bottle of Dom she had procured. By this point no one was listening to her.'

'But you were,' Chupplejeep said.

Aman was silent.

'Who else was on the balcony? Do you remember?'

'Nita, of course. Reena and she are inseparable. The others I'm not sure. Maybe that woman in the sarong.'

Chupplejeep flicked through his notebook. 'Judith is her name,' he said. 'Nita was doing a crystal meditation at the time on the balcony.'

Aman shook his head. 'No she wasn't, although I'm not sure I know what that entails, but she wasn't sitting cross-legged in a quiet corner with a piece of quartz on her head. Which is what I can imagine a crystal meditation is. No, Nita wouldn't have been that alternative at one of Reena's parties. She certainly wasn't that night. She was drinking with Reena, even though she was on the clock, so to speak.'

'I see,' Chupplejeep said, twisting one end of his moustache. He made a note.

Aman looked up. 'Listen, you know who took the jewel, so why are you here badgering me?' he asked.

'Meaning?' Chupplejeep asked.

'When we first sat down. You didn't say the jewel had been stolen. You said you were trying to locate its whereabouts. We've just been through my relationship with Reena. I've told you what she's like, and no doubt everyone else you've spoken to has said something similar. The hashtag that she has coined, KingfisherBlue, it has sent her rocketing up the social media charts. Provenance of the stone, the beauty of it, the mystery of the disappearance – finally Reena has what she has always wanted: millions of followers all talking about her.' Aman stood up. 'You want to find that rock, go back to see Miss Reena Gopaldas. Or better yet, wait it out; that ring will miraculously appear again. She has to keep producing content for her fans now.'

Aman stood up. He threw down a five hundred rupee note on the table, narrowly missing Chupplejeep's half-full glass of chai before he stormed out of the café.

Chapter Thirty-three

Chupplejeep snuck around to his office and let himself in. He could hear Bonita playing with Christabel somewhere in the cool of the house, and although he was desperate to see them, he needed some mental space to think. He wouldn't be able to do that if Bonita insisted on following him back to his office to sit on his lap and draw all over his notes.

Leaning back in his chair, Chupplejeep placed his notepad in front of him. Every one of Chupplejeep's suspects, from the suave Daniel Chatterjee to the unstable Judith Merryweather, had all said in one way or another that Reena could have hidden the jewel herself. Was there any truth in it? There wasn't often smoke without fire, as he had told Pankaj time and time again.

Chupplejeep twisted one end of his moustache. Or could it be that his suspects were trying to divert his attention away from them, playing on the fact that their host was needy. Daniel, Judith and Aman all had motive. Aman's motive was particularly strong given he had just been jilted by Reena too. All three of them had opportunity to take the gem too.

The private investigator took a red pen and circled Nita's name. The social media coach was certainly not to be excluded from his enquiries either. From what he had seen, the woman was conniving. She was trying to run Reena's life under the pretence of reducing Reena's craving for social media likes, but from what Chupplejeep had seen, so far Nita was having the opposite effect, and if Aman was to be believed, Reena was now thoroughly addicted to her fan base. But where was Nita's motive? Apart from the money, she was failing in her job, and the ring going missing was the cause of this. Did Nita really want that? Reena was a socialite; one word from her and all her friends could be queuing up for Nita's services. Surely that was more lucrative than the sapphire.

Chupplejeep shook his head. Money was always the motive, wasn't it? Money and love. The Kingfisher Sapphire would mean that Nita could retire. Being a social media coach was hardly a vocation.

He flipped to his notes on Vihaan and Uma, the two staff that were noticeably absent for the party. It didn't make sense to Chupplejeep why Vihaan wasn't present to serve drinks and keep an eye out for their host. Aman had referred to them as scheming, and Chupplejeep himself noticed that the two had shared a conspiratory look the last time he was at the house.

Chupplejeep picked up his phone and dialled Reena's number.

~

Turning off the ignition of his Baleno, Chupplejeep watched the small one-storey house from the comfort of his car. It wasn't long before he saw Uma enter the house. Chupplejeep put his hand on the door handle to get out but then refrained. From his previous conversations with Uma, he knew that every afternoon, once she had swept and mopped the floors, ironed Reena's clothes and prepared a simple lunch, she returned home to do the same. Despite being one of six children, Uma, it seemed, was the only child who had stuck around to care for their mother. He imagined the inside of Uma's home. From Chupplejeep's experience of being inside such homes, the floorplan was simple: one room for cooking and sleeping, two rooms if they were lucky, and an outside toilet. The room or rooms would contain a small stove, a bucket for washing and two mats on the floor for sleeping.

Chupplejeep could question her now or he could wait, because he had a suspicion that Uma would see to her mother and leave as soon as she could.

'Some people are not very generous about Uma and Vihaan,' Reena Gopaldas had told the investigator earlier. 'Aman was never keen on them, and even Nita thinks they are shady, and Nita always thinks the best of people.'

'Really?' Chupplejeep wanted to say. Nita thought that Aman, the man who appeared to make Reena happy, was negative. 'What makes your friends think that Uma and Vihaan are up to no good?' he had asked.

There had been a pause on the other end of the line. 'Sometimes they don't turn up for work.'

'They aren't reliable?'

'They turn up eventually. They get the work done, I suppose. But they are not very present, as Nita would say.'

'How do you mean?'

'Their minds are elsewhere,' Reena said.

Chupplejeep had wanted to ask, 'You mean they are not thinking about the silver when they are polishing it?' He refrained.

Reena yawned.

'Do you think they had anything to do with your missing ring?'

'The two of them left while the ring was still on my finger. I was admiring it in the mirror as they were leaving. You know, the full-length mirror in the hall? That one. Uma was trying to get a look at the ring. I could see her eyes darting this way and that. So I held my hand out for her to see. Vihaan had a look too. The ring was simply stunning. It was one of those pieces everyone wanted to admire, even if they never had a chance of owning something like it. Beautiful things are lovely to look at, don't you think?'

Chupplejeep agreed, but it was better if you could afford it. He thought of Uma now quickly cooking and cleaning for her mother after doing the same thing all morning for Reena Gopaldas. Reena couldn't have been paying her much, perhaps just enough for her rent and to put food on the table. Had Uma seen that ring and wanted it for herself?

'Look,' Reena had said, 'I've thought about getting rid of those two, but getting staff these days is difficult. Nobody wants to work properly, and all the hotels are pinching good local maids. Plus, Daddy would never have it.'

'He wouldn't?' Chupplejeep had asked.

'Those two may be lazy now, but they have been very good to my father. Whenever he's in Goa, they make sure they are on time, they make his favourite foods, Vihaan polishes his car. Nothing is too much for them where my father is concerned.'

'Maybe they like your father,' Chupplejeep had said. He couldn't help himself.

Reena was silent for a moment. 'Maybe,' she had said eventually. Chupplejeep was sure Reena would be speed dialling her social media coach after their conversation to justify why she wasn't more popular with the staff than her father.

The door to Uma's house opened. Chupplejeep sat up in his Baleno and watched. The maid had changed into a yellow shalwaar with red embroidered flowers. Her hair was loose around her shoulders as opposed to the tight plait she wore to work. She wore a brown handbag, and she had a spring in her step.

Uma walked towards the centre of the village, which was alive with various shops blaring music and flashing lights to get the attention of passers-by. Chupplejeep followed his suspect at a distance. Uma passed the small café, the Crazy Cuts hair salon, the fruit seller with perfect pyramids of oranges, watermelons and guavas and the small temple that had incense burning, filling the air with a musky aroma. Uma turned down a side street and knocked on the rickety door of a makeshift house painted a vibrant green.

Chupplejeep watched from behind a gulmohur tree, its feathery leaves fluttering in the wind. Several dark brown seed-cases had fallen from the tree. They cracked as Chupplejeep stepped on them. Looking up, Chupplejeep noticed that the door had opened, and he caught a glimpse of the person behind it. He nodded to himself. His suspicions were right.

Walking up to the door, Chupplejeep knocked and waited.

Chapter Thirty-four

Minutes later, Chupplejeep found himself standing in the exact spot Uma had stood moments before. He rapped sharply on the door. At his feet were earthenware tealights to mark the festival of light. They hadn't been lit.

Vihaan opened the door and faced the investigator. 'What are you doing here?' he asked.

Chupplejeep didn't see the point in lying. 'I followed Uma. I know she's here,' he said, craning his head to look behind Vihaan.

'So, what's it to you?' he asked. 'You're not her father.'

'No, I'm not,' Chupplejeep said, 'but I'm investigating the theft of a valuable piece of jewellery, and it's my job to follow any suspicious leads.'

'We've got nothing to do with that,' Uma said, pulling the door open. She looked behind Chupplejeep at the houses opposite. 'You'd better come in,' she said.

The house was small. One room, a stove in one corner and a mat on the floor for sleeping. There was one window that was wide open, allowing some circulation of air in the small space. A fan stood in the corner of the room, but it wasn't plugged in. These days a fan was expensive to run. Electricity prices were going up and up. People who didn't have much money rarely used them. Meanwhile, the five-star hotels were lighting up their vast lawns for Instagrammable pictures.

'Tea?' Uma asked, pointing to the *charpoi,* mat, on the floor.

Chupplejeep nodded and took a seat. Uma served the tea in small glasses, and she and Vihaan sat cross-legged on the floor. Chupplejeep wondered if he would be able to get up when their discussion was over.

'My mother used to work with the Gopaldases,' Uma offered. 'She worked with Gopaldas Senior and his wife for years. She was with them until her eyes went bad. Mr Gopaldas paid for all her medical bills, and there were many. My mother sent me there at a young age to work in return for everything the family were doing to help her. Mr Gopaldas didn't just allow me to work, he also paid me. I didn't tell my mother, and it is my shame, but she would never have allowed me to take his money, not when they were still paying her. Mr Gopaldas knew what I was doing. He suggested I use some of the money I was earing to buy books to learn to read and write. I took his suggestion.'

'You stayed on as a maid?' Chupplejeep asked.

'My mother would never forgive me if I left,' Uma said. 'Plus,' she said with a small smile. Uma looked towards Vihaan, who put his hand on hers.

'Ah,' Chupplejeep said. 'I thought you two were friendly. You want to marry.'

'We do,' Vihaan said. 'But we can't. Reena Bhai has forbidden it.'

'She knows?' Chupplejeep asked. Reena had failed to mention it, but then again Reena didn't think much of her staff. She probably didn't think their relationship was worth mentioning.

'Reena Bhai has seen it happen with her maids in Mumbai. They get big ideas and think they are better than they are. Their work is lazy. I have told her it won't be the case, but she's worried.'

'Worried about what?'

'That we will want a family and leave her. It's difficult to find a good maid, she says.'

Chupplejeep held his tongue. How had he ended up working for someone so indifferent to others' emotions as Reena Gopaldas? When he started his private investigation practice, he truly believed that he would be able to do good, but maybe it was a sign that Reena had lost the Kingfisher Sapphire. Maybe she just didn't deserve it. The internet had come up with the same assumption without having the knowledge of how Reena Gopaldas treated her staff. The Gopaldases couldn't control other people's lives just because of their wealth.

Who was he kidding? Indians were very much aware that the world was not fair. It was how poverty and wealth lived side by side with so little animosity between the two. Uma and Vihaan accepted that Reena would suffer consequences in the cleanliness of her house because of their marriage even when Reena's suffering was futile.

Uma and Vihaan were holding hands. Chupplejeep had previously seen a look pass between them at Reena's apartment. Had it simply been a look shared between lovers or had it been more sinister than that?

It was time to find out.

~

On his way back to his office, Chupplejeep had stopped at Kapoor's to return the gold nose ring that Sangeeta had taken. He had left it with the reliable production assistant, who said she would find out whether it belonged to the theatre or if it was Jagdish's personal jewellery. He believed she would. Now back in his office, Chupplejeep called Pankaj. It was lonely working on his own. Christabel was out with the kids and the house was unusually silent.

'Pick up,' he murmured.

It was supposed to be a research trip, but Chupplejeep knew it was more than that. He didn't pay Pankaj a big wage, he couldn't afford to, and yet the boy had left his position in the force to join his business. The least he could do was to pay for Pankaj to have a little therapy.

This business with Shwetika had worried the private investigator. Understandably, Pankaj's new wife had reservations about the hours her husband was doing for a paltry wage. She had given him an ultimatum. It was a little harsh, but perhaps Shwetika was making sure that she didn't end up resenting her husband.

Chupplejeep wasn't sure that the marriage would last, but who was he to judge. Pankaj was besotted. And it wasn't too long ago that Christabel had presented Chupplejeep with an ultimatum. She wanted marriage, and he had struggled to give it to her for a time. It would have been nice if someone had paid for him to attend a retreat to work through his commitment and abandonment issues. He still blamed his biological parents for that legacy.

The phone rang out. Chupplejeep threw the device on his desk. What was happening at the Atul Centre? Therapy aside, Pankaj was supposed to be working too. Sonal had paid a fair amount to get her son a place there. He couldn't rule out Jagdish's ex-wife as a suspect. He picked up his mobile and tried again.

'Ah,' Chupplejeep said as Pankaj answered on the third ring this time.

'Sir,' Pankaj said. He had a certain lightness to his voice. Maybe all that money was worth it.

'So,' Chupplejeep said. 'What's it like? You haven't answered any of my calls.'

'I thought I'd give in to the experience,' he said. 'I like it here.'

Chupplejeep laughed. 'You sound like you don't want to leave.'

Pankaj was silent.

Chupplejeep cleared his throat. 'Have they been giving you any drugs?' he asked in a low voice.

'No, sir,' Pankaj said.

'And bhang? Some people don't think bhang is a drug, but it is…'

'Sir, I know what bhang is,' said Pankaj. 'And don't worry, I'm due to check out tomorrow and I will. Bhavan is coming back, and so they want me out of here. And speaking of Bhavan…'

'What?' Chupplejeep asked.

Pankaj told him about his brief meeting with the boy and the discussion with his girlfriend. 'There was one point when I was a little worried about her. She's slight, but she had no problem twisting my arm and warning me not to discuss Bhavan with her. She's desperately worried Cynthia will find out about their relationship and fire her. My time here is nearly up, but I've failed to find out anything substantial.'

'Well, we had agreed only two nights,' Chupplejeep said, thinking about the large hole in his account made by this two-night stay.

'I've made a friend though,' Pankaj said. 'Her name is Monica. She may open up and give me some information about the Johars. I'm working on it. She's been telling me things.'

'Like what?'

'Like where to answer my mobile so I won't get caught by Cynthia,' he said. 'Right now I am in the shade of a big rain tree. They have some magnificent trees and plants here. Beautiful butterflies and birds. I can see why the place is healing.'

'Okay,' Chupplejeep said, worried he had lost his only colleague to mother nature. 'Is there anything suspicious going on there? Anything about Sonal and whether she was there the night Jagdish was killed? Or are we looking in the wrong direction?' Chupplejeep looked up at the corkboard that they had installed in his office. His suspects for Jagdish Sharma's murder were mounting.

'I'm working on it, sir.'

'Work a little faster,' Chupplejeep said. He took a breath. 'And you? How are you doing? Apart from wanting to move there permanently.'

'I had my first session yesterday,' Pankaj said. 'It was with Cynthia, and at first I felt uncomfortable. She was asking me all these questions like how I felt in my body when Shwetika put her ultimatum to me. But then her method started to make sense and I actually began to see clearly what the real choice was. Also the aniseed gum Monica gave me helped.'

'Gum? Never mind. The reason for my call is…'

'Oh yes,' Pankaj said excitedly. 'Fill me in on the Kingfisher Sapphire. What have you found out?' Chupplejeep filled him in on Vihaan and Uma's love story and how Reena had told them that the relationship had to stop.

He could hear Pankaj's sharp intake of breath. 'She never, sir,' he said. 'I don't want to say it out loud, but I will. She doesn't deserve the Kingfisher Sapphire. Wasn't the ring originally bought by a ruler to show his love for his wife?'

'Maybe,' Chupplejeep said. All he knew was that it had been stolen, originally. It made sense that the jewel had been purchased for a wife or lover. Chupplejeep knew how these rich Indian families operated. Buying expensive jewels for their wives and daughters-in-law as a show of wealth and love, when really all it was, was an investment, like buying shares or property.

'So Uma and Vihaan took the ring out of spite, revenge even, or because they needed the money,' Pankaj said, breathlessly.

'Hold on,' said Chupplejeep. 'There's no doubt in my mind that the two are very much in love and they won't let Reena spoil their fun, but they have obligations, or at least Uma does, to her mother. And they need money if they are to get away and take their baggage with them.'

'The Kingfisher Sapphire would give them more than they needed.'

'Uma and Vihaan are not cunning, but they're desperate. I can't imagine they want the hassle of selling the Kingfisher Sapphire, especially now that everyone is talking about it.'

'Sir, you could argue that its popularity online has made the stone even more valuable.'

'True,' Chupplejeep said. 'But I don't think they did it.'

'Why?' asked Pankaj.

'Because they committed another crime and are so wracked with guilt they are unable to run away. Let me explain,' Chupplejeep said. He told Pankaj how Uma confessed to having taken a large sum of money from Reena Gopaldas.

'The problem,' Uma had said, 'is that Reena hasn't realised the money has gone missing. You'd think that would make it easier to run away with, but I just can't. We can't,' she had said, looking at Vihaan.

Her boyfriend shook his head. 'Nothing good will come from stolen money.'

'You're right,' Chupplejeep had said. Uma explained that she had taken the money slowly over the last year. Five hundred rupees here, two thousand there. Eventually they had enough to run away and take her elderly mother with them, but when Uma suggested to her mother that they should go somewhere else, her mother refused to leave.

'I've lived here all my life,' she had said to Uma. 'I'm not leaving at the very end of it.' It was then that Uma and Vihaan started having second thoughts.

'Reena Bhai always left her money lying around, especially before Nita was on the scene. It was tempting, and it was easy to take. She never realised, and for a time I thought if she hasn't noticed then does it really matter?'

'But the money wasn't ours. We didn't earn it,' Vihaan had said.

'We've worked for that family for years. We've earned some of it,' Uma had said, staring at her partner.

'But he's right. It was a foolish idea, and now we don't know what to do with it. She must suspect something. It's why she didn't want you at her party.'

'Nothing doing,' Vihaan had said. 'She wanted me at the party. Nita didn't.'

'Why?' Chupplejeep had asked.

'What do we do with the money?' Uma had asked, her hands now on the investigator's forearm. 'Tell us what to do.'

'It's simple,' Chupplejeep had said. He had explained to them how to return the money. 'You don't have to hand it directly to her, but perhaps just leave it in a cupboard, a drawer she doesn't look in often. She will find it and buy herself something nice no doubt, and your conscience will be clear without having to face her wrath.'

'She will report us to the police,' Vihaan had said.

Chupplejeep nodded. If Reena suspected them, she would, but then again, she may just let them go or carry on as if nothing had happened. As Reena said, getting good staff in Goa lately was a problem. A middle-class problem which was a great concern for her. Before Chupplejeep left, he had some more advice for the couple. 'Life is short,' he said. 'When you hand in the money, maybe you should hand in your notice too. I hear good staff are hard to find, so I'm sure you'll find work locally. Some bigger houses want to take on a couple who will look after their house and garden for them.'

Uma and Vihaan had smiled at this; a plan in place without having to come clean about their theft. They looked much lighter than when he had first knocked on their door.

With some effort, Chupplejeep had stood up to leave. He stretched out his legs, and Uma and Vihaan kindly didn't mention it.

'You're serious about finding this blue stone?' Uma had said as Vihaan opened the door for the investigator.

'Of course,' replied Chupplejeep.

'Well, then there is something you should know,' Uma had said.

Vihaan gave his girlfriend a look. He closed the door, and Chupplejeep had returned to the mat.

Chapter Thirty-Five

Rupali Sharma stood in her grey tunic and white linen trousers on the beach, looking towards the sea. It was tranquil at this time of the morning when the fishermen dragged their hauls into the quiet bay. The tourists were not up yet, but they would arrive mid-morning with their music and incessant chatter, disturbing the peace.

Rupali took a lungful of salt-laced sea air and started walking back towards her car. Her mother hated it when she took the car out without a driver, yet she found she was doing it more and more these days. The house she had shared with Jagdish was stifling her. As soon as the locals and the papers had forgotten about the dancer's death, she would sell up and move. Move where? Away from Goa? Goa had originally been their home and then they had moved away, but with Jagdish's new contracts, they had decided to return and settle here for good. Rupali couldn't see herself living in Mumbai or Delhi.

They had done all that and they had been ready to return home, or at least she had.

The girls liked Goa too. Goa was just about hip enough for them to invite their friends back for holidays. Goa gave them the beaches and parties in equal measure; a taste of the exotic without them having to adjust their cultural expectations too much.

Rupali sighed as she sat in her car, turned down her air-conditioning and drove home. It wasn't just the perfect marriage of east and west of Goa that attracted her daughters back here. It was home, and Rupali had a sneaking suspicion that her youngest daughter had met someone out here. Given their father's death and how close he and Tanya had been, she had expected her youngest to fall apart. But after the first few days of keeping to herself in her room Tanya appeared stoic, a resilience Rupali knew only came with the confidence of someone believing wholeheartedly in you.

Tanya was the first to arrive after the news broke. Her youngest had made her own way to the house, unlike her sisters, who demanded a driver be sent for them. She had said she had been on her way to surprise her parents, but Rupali knew better. Her daughter had been on her way to meet her boyfriend. The tell-tale signs of late-night phone calls and constant messaging were there. Rupali hoped this man, whomever he was, was worth it and not one of those underdogs that Tanya had a habit of falling for.

Whoever this man was, though, he was providing a welcome distraction. If it wasn't for Tanya's lover, Rupali was certain that her headstrong, passionate daughter would want to know more about her father's death. Rupali didn't want the questions. She couldn't afford for her daughters to be too inquisitive.

The watchman opened the wrought-iron gates for Rupali, and she drove in. Minutes later she had handed the maid her keys and was back in her sitting room, a fresh mint tea brewing in a glass teapot on a silver tray. Twice the police had interviewed her despite the bottle of whisky she had sent the superintendent. The murder had certainly shaken up their daughters, and two of them were desperate to return to England after the period of mourning was over. This morning she had told them to go. What did formalities matter anymore? It had only ever mattered to her husband and her mother, and one of them was dead.

It was best that her daughters were as far away from this mess as possible. Rupali tried not to blame herself, but how could she not. She had made a decision, that was all. Now she just had to wait. The police were primed; they had been directed to the best of her ability. There was nothing more that she could do.

Rupali had to believe the police would lose interest soon if they hadn't found a suitable candidate for a killer. She certainly wasn't pressuring them to find Jagdish's murderer. It wasn't the police that worried her, though. What worried her was that private investigator. He was the one she had to be wary of, and so did Meera.

Rupali paced around the room. The silks draped on her sofas were slightly faded, and the rug beneath her feet was too beige. She remembered Jagdish had picked it out at a carpet merchant in Mumbai many years ago. The memory brought a smile to her lips, which quickly vanished. As Rupali lifted ornaments and cushions from around the ornate room, she realised she no longer cared for most of these possessions. They no longer reflected the life she wanted to lead. With Jagdish she had been a caged bird. Now she was free.

Almost.

Rupali pursed her lips together. She no longer had to share her house with a man who thought so little of her, of her wants and needs. She had been the one to find their house in Goa. She had loved it then and she still loved it now. Rupali realised that she didn't need to uproot her mother and children and move away from their family home. She had a better idea. Rupali would instruct an interior designer to redo their house, completely revamp it. They had the space. She smiled. She liked having a plan.

She pulled her mobile phone from her black canvas bag and dialled Meera.

'I have a job for you,' she said.

'What now, Rupali rumali? You're always finding me jobs to do. This one can't be as bad as the last, can it?'

There was a silence on the line.

'I need to go,' Rupali said, any softness to her voice gone. 'I'm at home. I shouldn't have called. I'll call later. Okay, bye.' Rupali disconnected before Meera said any more. She slumped down into the red silk of the sofa. Jagdish's favourite spot – she could smell him, that aftershave he used to wear. She had hated the smell of musk, but now she found it strangely comforting. She closed her eyes, thinking about what she had done and what she was about to do. Had she really thought any of it through?

Rupali hadn't thought of her mother, of her daughters, of her husband. She had been selfish. She could see that now. She had believed she deserved a better life, someone who loved her for who she was, someone who saw her as a person, a living, breathing person. But now she wondered if she had made the right decision, or had she just been caught up in lust, infatuation, in a relationship that was detrimental to her being? Rupali wasn't just a wife, she was a mother and a daughter. She had responsibilities. She couldn't just change her course on a whim, and yet she had, effortlessly, without a second thought. Tears streamed down her face. She picked up one of the yellow cushions next to her and put it over her face. Her tears soaked the fabric.

Rupali's phone rang. She glanced at the display, half expecting it to be her mother or Meera calling back, but it wasn't. It was Tanya. Her youngest was never up so early. She answered the call. Her daughter was crying. Rupali's tears began to flow again.

'I miss him, Mum,' her daughter said. 'I really miss him.'

'I do too,' Rupali heard herself say, and for a moment she actually believed it. When her daughter ended the call, Rupali found herself crying loudly, not caring about her maid who was listening at the door. She pounded the cushions with her fists, regretting all her actions over the last fortnight. All of them.

Chapter Thirty-six

Pankaj popped a stick of aniseed gum into his mouth and chewed. The receptionist briefly looked up at him and then turned back to her computer. He was ready for his session with Cynthia. He would even go as far as to say he was excited.

Yesterday's session had been an eye opener. Pankaj had been nervous more than anything. Instead of closing his eyes and concentrating on his breathing like Cynthia had instructed him to, he had peeked through his half-closed lids at her, fearful that his wellness manager, which she had asked him to refer to her as, was taking advantage of him. It wouldn't be the first time that someone almost double his age had tried it on with him. His experience told him to expect the worst from lonely older women.

Cynthia must have sensed his energy, because once he was breathing the way she had wanted him to, big lungfuls of air which he had to hold for four seconds and release for eight, she positioned herself behind the desk.

When she instructed him to open his eyes, he could see that she was some distance from him. She had asked him questions about his childhood, his mother, how he had met Shwetika and what he expected from her.

That was a question. What did he expect from his wife? 'Someone to love and care for him,' he had said, meekly.

And what could Shwetika expect of him? Cynthia had asked. What was reasonable? It was then that Pankaj saw the problem, like one of those light bulb moments in a cartoon. He expected more from his wife than he wanted her to expect from him.

Pankaj had been a little surprised to realise that he was the one who wasn't being fair to his wife. No wonder she had given him an ultimatum. He told all this to Cynthia. He expected her to agree. But she didn't say anything, leaving Pankaj feeling a little empty. Cynthia had left him alone with his thoughts for a full ten minutes and then rubbed some essential oils on his temples.

'Is it right to make someone choose?' she had said eventually.

'Who are you referring to?' Pankaj had asked, the question making him feel uneasy, and if he had to identify the dominant feeling he would say a little bit incensed. A feeling he wasn't very familiar with. It didn't sit well with him. 'Are you referring to me, making my wife choose?'

'Choose what?' Cynthia had asked.

'A miserable husband or a happy one?' he had said, breathing out some of his anger.

'You're giving Shwetika all the power and at the same time making her powerless. Imagine the burden she must feel. She tells you to stop working and she knows that it will kill you. She tells you to carry on but she won't have a family with you and it does the same. And where does it leave her? She must want a family too, a husband that is home at a decent hour, don't you think?'

'She knew what my job entailed when we met,' he had protested.

'And now you have left the force your salary has halved,' Cynthia had said. 'I think you said that in your questionnaire.'

Pankaj had looked to the ground.

'Lots of risk, not much reward. Must be worrying for a new wife,'

'It's worrying for me too. And she is making me choose. You can't put this all on me.'

'I'm not doing anything,' Cynthia had said. 'I'm simply asking the questions, and you only have two days here, so let's be quick about it.'

Pankaj had balled his hands into fists by his sides. 'Shwetika shouldn't make me pick between my career and a family. Our relationship is as good as over if I'm made to choose. If I want a family and no career, I will feel like I have failed myself.' Pankaj chewed his fingernails. A silence ensued. Pankaj hadn't expected to say all that. He hadn't been sure that he really felt that way, but now the words were out, he could feel the conviction of them.

When the session was over, Pankaj had felt lighter.

When he had entered Cynthia's treatment room yesterday, she had told him that the room was a safe place. Somewhere he could speak his mind free from any feelings of repercussions. 'These rooms don't have ears,' she had said with a deep laugh that had made him wonder if her sessions were being recorded and broadcast on the dark web somewhere.

The door to Cynthia's office opened, and Pankaj was called inside. He went in readily. And despite the gum he was merrily chewing, he wasn't afraid of Cynthia anymore. Last night he had a fitful sleep, but he had woken with a conviction of what he needed to do. The thought of it left him with a knot in his stomach, but he had to be strong and follow through with what he knew was right.

'So how do you feel?' Cynthia asked when Pankaj was seated in the chair facing her desk.

'Good,' he said. 'Our therapy yesterday made me see sense.'

Cynthia laughed again. 'That wasn't therapy,' she said. 'It was simply some breathing work and a conversation. Most people don't know how to breathe. Everyone should practice some daily *pranayama*. Half our problems would be solved if we just did the right breaths at the right time. These days we want everything quickly. We are so impatient even for our breathing. You need to inhale slowly and exhale slowly, always. Will you remember that?'

Pankaj felt a little deflated at Cynthia's dismissal of what he believed to be an intense therapy session yesterday. Still, he nodded.

'You don't need therapy,' Cynthia said. 'Well, let me rephrase that. We all need therapy. We were all brought up by people who were testing out their parenting skills. First children are affected the most. You know when a child is born a mother is born too. The child is learning, she is learning. It has an effect. I'm surprised there are not more damaged people out there. Listen,' Cynthia said, leaning in a little conspiratorially. 'Ultimately, we all face little and big traumas, and some get affected more than others because some are more sensitive. Look, perhaps if you had the money, I would charge you for a few more "therapy" sessions,' she said, making air quotes. 'But take it from me, you don't need that. You need to look into your heart and think with your head and make a decision.'

'That I need to leave Shwetika,' Pankaj said, the knot in his stomach tightening. 'After our session yesterday,' he said, avoiding the use of the therapy word again, 'I realised that perhaps we are not suitable for one another. Before, I was blinded by what I thought was love. I couldn't see past Shwetika. I thought I needed to follow her every command. At the same time, because of my intense love for her, I expected too much from her.'

'Have you had a conversation explaining all this to your wife?' Cynthia asked.

Pankaj shook his head.

'Do you love her?'

'With all my heart,' Pankaj said, the knot inside loosening. Whenever he thought of his wife, a warm feeling spread across his chest.

'So before you make any rash decisions, have that conversation. Tell her how you feel. Don't be so worried about hurting her feelings, because in not being honest, you will break her down, and I'm not speaking as a therapist, I'm speaking as a woman.'

'I think you're right,' Pankaj said. Last night, before his head hit the pillow, he had considered giving it all up. Not just Shwetika but his job as well. Taking a sabbatical from life. When Shwetika had given him her ultimatum, Pankaj was sure that giving up investigative work would break him, but last night, as he weighed up his options, his thoughts had turned to his other passion. His guilty pleasure which he had never given a second thought to. Now he wondered if he could make a career of it, a part-time one at least. Or maybe something he could try for a year.

He closed his eyes and could see a vision of a nursery, his fingers muddy as he planted new seeds. Manifestation, is what another wellbeing nurse had told him yesterday. 'Manifest your dreams and they will come true.' He had tried manifesting a plate of *brinjal* curry later in the evening, but it hadn't worked. Instead, he had been served a plate of *aloo palak,* potato and spinach, instead of his beloved aubergine.

Pankaj had always loved nature. He could see himself running a small plants emporium, and it had always been a secret dream of his, but previously whenever he thought about it, it felt wrong. He had responsibilities to Shwetika. He had to provide for her. Arguably he would make the same money with his own little business as working for Chupplejeep though.

Chupplejeep. The dream quickly dissipated. He couldn't let his boss down. Chupplejeep relied on him now. Chupplejeep and Pankaj; they had always been a team.

With Pankaj's newfound confidence, instead of worrying about how Shwetika and Chupplejeep would react, he decided to ask them. The thought of losing either one from his life pained him, but maybe if they discussed it, they could come up with a solution together. This put a smile on his face. 'I'm glad I came here,' Pankaj said. 'Even if it was just for a chat and some breathing work. It was a pretty insightful chat.' Pankaj stood up. He held out his hand and Cynthia shook it. The Atul Centre certainly charged a lot, but maybe it was justified.

'Why are you chewing that awful-smelling gum?' Cynthia asked. 'All my male patients seem to chew it. The smell is nauseating.' Cynthia looked Pankaj up and down. 'You need to leave by noon tomorrow. You've got your money's worth, and you managed to do some snooping here at the same time.'

Pankaj gave his wellness manager a quizzical look.

'Don't think I haven't seen you chatting to Monica. Now go,' Cynthia commanded.

Pankaj stood to leave, feeling strangely empowered, not just about his situation with Shwetika but about life in general. He straightened his back and felt a foot taller.

'Thank you,' he said. 'I think I'll spend the rest of the day by the pool before I check out tomorrow.'

'By noon,' Cynthia said.

Pankaj put his hand on the door handle and stepped over the threshold.

'And remember to breathe,' she called after him.

Chapter Thirty-seven

'So I hear you're going,' Monica said to Pankaj, who was sitting at the bottom of the rain tree. 'Cynthia said you had planned to spend your last day by the pool, but I knew I'd find you here.'

'I tried the pool,' Pankaj said. 'But I found I couldn't just sit and do nothing.'

'So instead you're making notes on your phone,' she said, looking over his shoulder. Pankaj slipped his phone back into his pocket. 'I see,' Monica said. 'You still have a case to solve.'

'And the Johars were here the night of the 12th November?' Pankaj asked.

'You've already asked that,' Monica said. 'I checked the visitor book and asked around, as I am sure you have, and yes, they were here.'

Pankaj nodded. Monica stood behind the tree and pulled out a cigarette from her bag. She lit it and blew a ring of smoke towards the leaves of the tree.

'What's Bhavan like?' Pankaj said. 'You said he had anger management issues.'

'I don't deal with him exclusively. I don't deal with him much at all. He's one of our more challenging patients,' Monica said.

'As in?'

'He gets angry and then he's quite hard to control. When he wants to do something, he does it, and he doesn't like it if you get in his way.'

'Does anything in particular set him off?' Pankaj asked. He wondered if asking Monica if Bhavan was capable of murder was a step too far.

Monica pursed her lips together. 'I don't think so. He just likes getting his way, and he doesn't have much empathy. I saw him throw a stone at a pretty little bird one day. Hit it just under its ribs.' Monica winced at the memory. 'And he has a thing with one of the nurses here. It can be awkward.'

'Isn't it a little unethical for her to be seeing one of her patients?'

'It's unethical for me to be talking so openly to you about Bhavan Johar when I know you are investigating the death of Jagdish Sharma and think he's somehow connected. This is Bhavan's safe space, and I am breaking his trust with the centre.' Monica turned away, visibly irritated.

Pankaj took a breath. He didn't want to push Monica away. He wasn't going to be at the centre much longer, and he needed her. No one else was going to help him.

Kingfisher Blues

He had already tried speaking to Bhavan's girlfriend and that had ended badly.

'But he was here that night?' Pankaj said. 'Bhavan?'

Monica nodded. Pankaj considered Bhavan as a suspect. Even if Bhavan had behavioural problems, why would he lash out at Jagdish Sharma? If Bhavan was enjoying a show with his parents, it was unlikely that he would have escaped to murder his mother's ex-husband. And didn't his girlfriend say he was visibly shaken when he discovered Jagdish had been murdered after reading an article in a local paper? Pankaj shook his head. There was no motive for Bhavan to kill Jagdish. In fact, the opposite was true, if Sonal Johar was to be believed. Jagdish had been helping Bhavan with his behavioural issues.

'I hear you're having another show tomorrow night,' Pankaj said. A few of the guests had been talking about it earlier in the day. It was another masked performance in the vast grounds of the centre. 'It's a shame I can't stay to watch it.'

'There'll be dozens of people here, and with the masks, no one would know if you were here,' Monica said.

'Cynthia has made it quite clear that I am to leave at noon,' Pankaj said. 'And I'm sure your security…'

'Like I said,' Monica said, stubbing out her cigarette on the trunk of the tree. 'No one would notice if you came back.'

'How would I get in?' Pankaj asked.

Monica's eyes drifted to a slim wrought-iron gate at the end of the premises. She looked around. 'CB29083,' she whispered.

'Why are you helping me?' Pankaj said, making a note of the code. 'Not that I'm not grateful, it's just…'

'You took half an hour out of your busy day to help my mother when she was hurt outside the market,' Monica said. 'My mother often talks about the young man who helped her that day and wishes she could pay him back for his kindness. Now she can consider that debt paid.'

~

'Any news?' Chupplejeep asked Christabel as she walked into the kitchen, Bonita on her left hip. Chupplejeep rubbed his lower back. It had been a long evening following a suspect to a hotel where he had to wait for two hours before the suspect left again. Another half hour until another person of interest also left the hotel, telling him everything he wanted to know.

'There is always news, my love,' Christabel said. 'Nicholas needs to practice his letters and Bonita's bowel movements –'

'Not that,' Chupplejeep said. 'The other thing?'

'Don't you want to know what is going on with your kids?' she asked.

Chupplejeep stepped towards his wife and put his arm around her and his daughter. Bonita reached out her small chubby hand towards him.

Kingfisher Blues

'Take her,' Christabel said, passing their daughter to him. 'I'll check my messages. Lisa did reply…' she said, her words trailing off as she disappeared down the hall.

'Here,' she said a moment later, taking Bonita back and jiggling her on her hip as their daughter cried out for her father.

Chupplejeep pulled up Christabel's messages and scanned through a conversation about some Bollywood actor and his supposed affairs until he caught sight of a discussion about bank details. Christabel had asked Lisa to check the account details he had discovered in the contract between Popatrao and Jagdish on the pretence that she was asked to pay money into it for a course for Nicholas.

'What course is this?' Lisa had asked. It was obvious that Lisa was suspicious of what her friend had been asking, because her next question was whether Arthur had put her up to this.

Christabel had a fine response, saying that her husband was too busy to help with paying for Nicholas's meditation classes. It stung Chupplejeep to read that, because he knew it to be true. He made a mental note to try harder with getting involved with the kids and their interests as soon as Jagdish Sharma's killer had been caught.

Chupplejeep had grown up without a father figure and he was resentful. The last thing he wanted to be was an absent father, yet he was very much becoming that. Chupplejeep had to change his ways. He had recently heard on the radio that children either grew up wanting to be like their father or nothing like their father. He did not want the latter for himself or his children.

Chupplejeep glanced back at the messages. 'It's an old account,' Lisa had written. 'The bank account holder is the Atul Centre…' Chupplejeep closed his eyes momentarily. Had he read that correctly? He reread the message, ignoring all Lisa's commentary on what the centre did. 'Is that where Nicholas is doing his course?' Lisa had asked.

Chupplejeep handed his wife's phone back. Why would Jagdish want to make a payment to the Atul Centre directly? He had been right to suspect the Johars and the centre. He hoped Pankaj was going to come back laden with information. Spending the money on the retreat for his colleague could have been the best money he had spent on this case to date.

'Is that it?' Christabel asked. 'No thank you even?'

'Thank you,' he called after her.

'Are you going to help with bath time today?' Christabel asked as he disappeared into the distance.

Chupplejeep stopped. He thought about it. It would be a good start to being a more present father. But the link between the Atul Centre, Popatrao, the Johars and Jagdish Sharma was the best lead he had. It needed further exploration, and it couldn't wait. Or could it? He heard Bonita wailing as the bath tap was turned on. He continued towards his office but stopped a few steps later. His parents had failed him. He wasn't going to fail his daughter or his wife. Chupplejeep took a breath, turned on his heel and headed towards the bathroom.

Chapter Thirty-eight

'My maids have done a bunk,' Reena said as she opened the door to Chupplejeep. 'Can you believe it?'

Chupplejeep's heart sank. He had expected Uma and Vihaan to deposit the stolen money at the house and hand in their notice, not just leave without a trace.

'They didn't just leave,' Nita said from behind Reena. 'They gave notice but asked if they could go immediately. It was for the best.'

'I can't stay here now,' Reena said. 'Who'll do all the work? I'm going back to Mumbai.'

'I see,' Chupplejeep said. He stepped into the apartment filled with freshly cut flowers in various vases. Nita was bending over a pink rose, taking in its fragrance.

'Don't you love the smell of roses?' Nita asked.

Chupplejeep nodded. They must have been excellent quality roses because their fresh fragrance filled the air.

'Can you believe that those two want to marry? Good luck to them,' Reena said, ignoring the conversation about the blooms. 'Finding that cash in my wardrobe this morning was a sign – a sign that I should just eat out when I'm in Goa. I can't be bothered to find another maid who can clean and cook.' Reena's gaze shifted towards Chupplejeep. 'Maids these days have so many requirements. If they cook, they expect not to clean. If they clean, they want extra to cook. *Oof.*'

'Terrible of these people to want to have some control over their lives, no?' Chupplejeep said.

'Absolutely,' Reena said, missing the point. 'So, tell me, have you found my ring? What will Daddy say? He said that you were the best, but maybe…'

'I'm here to speak to Nita,' Chupplejeep said.

Nita straightened. Her eyes peered out at him from under her fringe. 'Me? Again?'

'You didn't want Vihaan at Reena's party. Is that right?'

Nita shook her head to adjust her fringe and get a better view. 'I can't recall saying that.'

'Did you ask him to leave?'

'I don't think I did. Did he tell you otherwise?' She paused a moment. 'Your silence speaks volumes. You think I had something to do with the ring going missing, don't you?' she asked, holding Chupplejeep's gaze.

'When I spoke to Uma, she was certain that it was you and not Reena who didn't want Vihaan at the party, and she gave me a reason as to why.'

'Well, don't keep me in suspense. Enlighten me, please,' Nita said. Her eyes turned towards a potted money plant in the corner of the living room.

Kingfisher Blues

Chupplejeep's eyes moved from Nita to Reena and back again. 'Uma and Vihaan suspected you of trying to mislead Reena. They've both worked for the Gopaldases for some time. They accept their position, but they didn't want to see their employer being taken advantage of,' Chupplejeep said, recalling Uma's words. He turned to Reena. 'Uma remembered how kind your father was to her mother not just while she was working for him, but after that, when her mother had to leave your employment.'

Nita tilted her head back and laughed. 'Can you believe it?' she said, her eyes on Reena. 'They thought I was trying to mislead you.' Nita must have seen a flicker of hesitation in Reena's eyes, the same one Chupplejeep had seen, because she quickly reminded Reena that she was paying her for services and that she was doing exactly what had been asked of her.

'I told Reena not to host a party wearing that ring. I told her not to post any photos of it. Ask her, she'll tell you. People want to be envied, but with envy comes something else, something much darker.' Nita gravitated towards the potted plant. When Reena was silent, she looked to her client. 'Oh Reena,' she said. 'Look at you. Look at what that ring has done to you. Maybe you are better off without it.' Nita made her way to Reena and put her arm around Reena's shoulders. Turning to Chupplejeep, she said, 'You can't possibly believe Uma and Vihaan over me. And in any event, what does it prove? I didn't want those two at the party. Why should they be there? They were scheming, and they have just proved it by leaving Reena like this.'

Nita turned to Reena. 'You're better off without the ring.'

'You're right,' Reena said, brightening. 'The loss of the ring has made other things possible.' Nita shook her head. 'Because of the missing ring, I now have a following. I'm an influencer. Brands are contacting me asking me to use their products and put them up on social media. I'm getting daily deliveries of goods.'

'Was that always your intention? To have a career like this?' Chupplejeep asked. 'Because in that case you would have been better off working with a content creator rather than a social media coach, who was supposed to get you away from social media, if I'm not mistaken. It appears to me, Reena, that you are ready to compare more than ever. I would agree with Uma and Vihaan that your social media coach hasn't done what she promised to do.'

Nita scowled. 'I can only do so much,' she said. 'And besides, if Uma and Vihaan are pointing the finger at me, let me point it back at them. They are the only ones around here that have suddenly disappeared. I am still here, and I'll be here for Reena as long as she needs me.'

Nita was right about Uma and Vihaan, he couldn't deny that. Chupplejeep's gut told him the two members of staff were innocent, but what if his gut had been wrong? He was always telling Pankaj to back up his gut feelings with evidence. But what evidence did he have? Nothing.

From what Reena had said, Uma and Vihaan had returned the money. Was it because they had taken his advice, or because their loot was bigger and in the shape of the Kingfisher Sapphire? Now Uma and Vihaan were gone, it would be incredibly difficult to get them back. But not impossible, he told himself.

~

'Finally,' Chupplejeep said as Pankaj walked through the door. He stood up and embraced his colleague. 'I missed you.' The words were out before he could stop himself.

Pankaj grinned. 'I missed you too, sir.'

'So? How was it? Did the sessions help you and your dilemma?'

'Sir, that place did wonders for me. I too thought it was all a con, but that Cynthia, she really does know what she's doing.'

'So, you've made a decision?' Chupplejeep asked.

'Sort of,' Pankaj said. 'I need to discuss it with Shwetty first, and you.'

'Me?' Chupplejeep asked.

'Let's not talk about it now,' Pankaj said, and Chupplejeep had to wonder what miracle Cynthia had performed on his colleague at the Atul Centre. Usually you couldn't get Pankaj to stop talking about his personal quandaries.

'Okay,' Chupplejeep said. 'I was going to get you a cup of tea first, but let's get back to the case. Did you find out anything about the Johars? Because interestingly I have found a connection between Jagdish and the Atul Centre, and I think it could be the link that will lead us to our murderer.'

'How so?' Pankaj asked.

'The bank details in the contract between Jagdish Sharma and Baytown were not Mr Sharma's personal bank details. His wife Rupali said she didn't know of any money being paid despite the promise of an upfront payment. The reason for this was because Jagdish had directed Popatrao to pay the Atul Centre directly.'

'Was he planning a stay there?' Pankaj asked.

'I doubt it,' Chupplejeep said. 'I asked Popatrao, but he was none the wiser. He just said that Jagdish was certain that he wanted the money paid there.'

'Did Popatrao ask how you knew?'

Chupplejeep shook his head. 'I think the man has bigger things to worry about.'

'Like his hotel ratings?'

'An ex-colleague tells me that he is prime suspect in the murder of our kathakali dancer.'

'Do we need to take a closer look at him?' Pankaj asked.

'We need to take a closer look at everyone,' Chupplejeep said, 'but right now I'm not too worried, especially if the police have him in their sights. Sonal's son attended the centre, and Bhavan and Jagdish had become close of late. You said yourself that the Johars were running out of money. Right now, we need to explore this connection.'

'Abhijeet lost a lot of contracts when he started taking time off to care for his son,' Pankaj said. 'He never managed to regain the trust of his clients again. His earning potential was limited, and as far as I can tell, Sonal was using her savings to pay for their lifestyle. Her father had left her some land, and she has been slowly selling it off. Rumour has it there's nothing left.'

'So Jagdish stepped in to pay for the boy's treatment,' Chupplejeep said.

'Without the money from Jagdish, Sonal would need to find the cash elsewhere. She couldn't afford to want him dead. So does that take her off our list of suspects?'

'Possibly.'

'And Abhijeet, sir? Does that make him more of a suspect or less of one?' Pankaj asked. 'His pride being dented could be enough of a motive.'

'And Bhavan,' Chupplejeep said.

'Bhavan's girlfriend said he was pretty upset when he found out Jagdish had died. She said that he found out when he was with her. He saw it in a newspaper.'

'A newspaper? Is Sonal so intent on protecting her son that she didn't tell him when her ex-husband had been murdered? We need to speak to the Johars again. Bhavan may be able to tell us what Sonal isn't,' Chupplejeep said.

'Bhavan's arriving at the centre today,' Pankaj said. He smiled. 'I already have a plan.' Pankaj relayed to Chupplejeep his conversation with Monica. 'She's given me the code to the back gate, and it's a masked event. I could slip in unnoticed and speak to Bhavan.'

'You think you can get him to talk?' Chupplejeep asked.

'I can certainly try.'

Chupplejeep nodded. 'It's worth a shot. His parents are too protective of him to let us talk to him, and the centre is unlikely to help. Let's see what tonight brings. Won't Shwetika mind that you are out again when you have only just got back?'

'She's still away,' Pankaj said a little despondently.

'Is everything okay?' Chupplejeep asked.

'She wants a couple more days. I thought I had it all figured out when I left the centre. I had some really good sessions there, but I'm not so sure now. Talking about the case again, it's made me realise…'

'Where your heart is,' Chupplejeep said.

'I love her,' Pankaj said.

'I don't doubt that. Sorry, I didn't mean…never mind,' Chupplejeep said. 'When you love someone, it isn't that simple, is it?'

Pankaj seated himself behind his desk.

'Listen, for now you can afford to forget about it,' Chupplejeep said. 'We have work to do. We've got most of the day before the event at the centre tonight, and Christabel is making a tasty lunch.'

CHAPTER THIRTY-NINE

Chupplejeep rubbed his belly. 'That was a good lunch,' he said to Pankaj, whose nose was stuck in Jagdish Sharma's case file. Pankaj momentarily lifted his head and nodded his agreement. Christabel had outdone herself with her latest batch of *soropatel*. It had been a treat, and on the spur of the moment they had invited his brother Karan over to enjoy the spicy pork curry with them.

Karan was becoming a regular in their house, and it felt good that finally Chupplejeep had some family to invite over on a whim. Karan had even enjoyed playing football with Nicholas in the garden afterwards, and Bonita had laughed at their play. A warm feeling spread across Chupplejeep's chest. It had taken the investigator several years and hours of rumination to get to where he was, but he was content with the result. He had two beautiful children, a loving wife and now a brother.

Two days ago, Karan had called him to tell him about a date he had had, and Chupplejeep's heart sang when he realised he was the first person Karan had confided in. 'Brother,' Karan had said when he had answered the phone. Chupplejeep beamed at the title. Next Sunday Chupplejeep would invite his parents over too. As Christabel had advised, he had to take baby steps when it came to Nishok and Camilla, and whilst he found it hard to completely forget what they had done to him, he knew there was a place in his heart for him to forgive.

Chupplejeep picked up the red Gopaldas folder. The case of the Kingfisher Sapphire had stalled. They had too many suspects – at least four that had reason to want the jewel, and an unreliable victim. Chupplejeep glanced through his file notes and then turned towards the window. The outlook was bleak. Beyond the grille there was an old bimley tree and the gable end of his neighbour's house. Pankaj was right: an office somewhere other than at home would be nice. Somewhere where he had a decent view. Town would be a better alternative. At least in town he could people watch when he needed to rest his brain.

In the distance he heard Bonita crying. His daughter wasn't having a great day. Just this morning she had fallen and grazed her knee, and she had made the same whining noise she was making now. Had she fallen again?

'Don't cry,' Chupplejeep had said earlier as Bonita curled her bottom lip and looked at her grazed knee.

'Whose benefit are you saying that for?' Christabel had asked.

Chupplejeep stared at his wife, unsure of what to say. Anyone would have thought he had sworn at his daughter the way Christabel had chided him.

'Her benefit,' he had said, pointing at his daughter, who had been scooped up by her mother. Bonita had buried her head in Christabel's shoulder.

'It's for your benefit because you don't want to see her cry. She's hurt herself; let her cry.'

'Okay,' Chupplejeep had said, not quite sure where he had gone wrong but conceding defeat in any case. Christabel was not in the mood to be argued with, and somewhere in the recesses of his mind, he could see that she had a point.

'I'll leave you to it,' he said. His daughter had turned to look at him, her tears almost dry.

'Be happy,' he said, smiling to her. The moment the words left his mouth he realised he had said something very wrong.

'Toxic positivity,' Christabel had said with a scowl. 'Take your toxic positivity back to your office and read those parenting books I gave you.' Chupplejeep didn't dare ask what toxic positivity meant, but he had glanced at a book Christabel had left for him on his bedside table, written by Alani Ali. The name rang a bell, but he couldn't place it.

Now he turned to Pankaj, who was intently looking at his laptop. He enquired what his colleague was doing, noticing that Jagdish's file had been put to one side.

'Going through the photos under the hashtag KingfisherBlue for the hundredth time,' Pankaj said. 'I missed a few days while I was at the centre.'

'Anything new?'

Pankaj shook his head and explained that it was just more of the same, but fewer posts, suggesting people were losing interest in the story.

'Do you know what toxic positivity is?' Chupplejeep asked.

'It's when you refuse to let people experience their emotions. You just want them to be happy. If you continue to do it, people end up suppressing their real feelings and then twenty years later it all comes out.'

Chupplejeep eyed his colleague. 'How do you know about this?'

Pankaj shrugged. 'It's all over social media, the press. I thought with having children you'd know all –'

'Okay,' Chupplejeep said, holding up his hand. 'Thanks for the explanation. Do you think that Nita was a little toxic in her positivity with Reena?'

Pankaj turned away from his computer and removed the glasses he had recently started wearing for screen use. 'She wanted Reena to only see the positive even after her ring went missing. She told her that she didn't need material possessions. She didn't let her just experience the loss. You could be right.'

'But was it as simple as toxic positivity or is there another reason why Nita wants Reena to think that losing the ring was a good thing? If Nita is a social media coach, you'd think that she too knows about toxic positivity, but it appears she is no wiser than me.'

'Maybe toxic positivity and social media coaching are mutually exclusive, sir?'

'Or maybe not,' Chupplejeep said, thinking about the book Christabel had given him. He put the author's name, Alani Ali, into a search engine on the web browser on his phone. The name was so familiar. Had he worked with her before? Maybe a picture of the author would tell him what he wanted to know. 'I would think that if you are trying to get your client to be positive, you would or should know all about the consequences of toxic positivity. Is Nita qualified?' he asked.

'In what?'

'Good question. I don't suppose there's a diploma in social media therapy. Or maybe there is. But this toxic positivity has got me thinking. Like Uma and Vihaan said, I don't think Nita has Reena's best interests at heart. Reena believes that her popularity has stemmed from the disappearance of that ring. But it wasn't her ring to lose. It was her mother's.' Chupplejeep twisted one end of his moustache. 'Find out Nita's history.'

'We've already looked at all that, sir. She came from Hyderabad and started her business in Mumbai two years ago. Before that there is very little about her. I asked my contacts in the force. No one has heard of her.'

'Try her other name,' Chupplejeep said, his eyes glued to his phone.

'Her other name?' Pankaj asked.

Chupplejeep knew now why that name Alani Ali was so familiar. It wasn't just the book that Christabel had given him to read on toxic positivity. 'Remember when we interviewed Daniel, he mentioned an Alani Ali. Said she was an author whose book he had tried publishing but that it had failed. He was talking about Nita. He was cryptic at the time, and I thought he was trying to divert our attention, or perhaps show me that he was human by having failed at something, but in hindsight I think he was trying to tell us something.'

'Why didn't he just come out and say it?' Pankaj asked.

'Daniel was responsible for the author's book which never succeeded. Maybe he thought it was a double betrayal of sorts. That night the ring was stolen, Nita gave Daniel a look as he agreed to be the first person we interviewed.'

'I recall you saying that it was a look of warning.'

'A look of keeping secrets,' Chupplejeep said.

'We thought they may have been romantically involved.'

'But it was more than that. Daniel knew exactly who Nita was. He knew her history.'

'Nita never wanted the ring to be photographed. And come to think of it, there are no photos of Nita in Reena's social media.'

Chupplejeep picked up his mobile and made a call. 'Christabel,' he said. 'Do you have a moment? Can you come to my office?'

Kingfisher Blues

Pankaj pulled his laptop towards him. 'Look,' he said seconds later. 'I typed Alani Ali into the search engine and see.' Both Pankaj and Chupplejeep leaned in to take a closer look.

'What?' Christabel asked as she walked in carrying Bonita on her hip.

'That book you gave me to read. What do you know about the woman who wrote it?'

'Which one? I've given you so many.'

'The gentle mothering one about toxic positivity. Alani Ali is her name.'

Christabel beamed. 'I wondered when you were going to ask me about her, especially after all that "be happy" nonsense you were saying to your daughter when she had clearly hurt herself this morning.'

'I'm not interested in the theory,' Chupplejeep said.

Christabel's smile turned into a frown. 'So Arthur, why have you called me here then?' she asked. 'Don't you think I have better things to do? I can't afford to run around all day playing detective.'

Chupplejeep straightened. 'We are not playing detective,' he said. 'This is my job, and Gopaldas is paying generously to get his stone back.'

'Oh, the stone, again. Now I see why you are interested in that author,' Christabel said.

'Why is that?'

'I told you the other day,' Christabel said. 'This Alani woman walked into my friend's brother's jewellery store and asked to go to the back room. She had dark glasses on and a scarf around her neck, so my friend wasn't sure who it was, but she heard her say Alani Ali and it piqued her interest. The woman showed the man a ring and asked for a price. This jeweller lives without internet. He hadn't heard of the stolen stone, but Elvina was in the shop. She recognised the name. You see, Elvina is the one who lent me Alani's book. She was a big fan of hers when her children were small.'

'You didn't tell me that,' Chupplejeep protested. 'You told me you heard a theory or something like that.'

'Oh yes, now I remember, you weren't interested. You said everyone has a theory. Frankly, Elvina isn't that accurate in her stories, and she didn't know much about the stolen ring the woman had brought in. I made that connection myself.'

'B-but Christabel, if it was important, you should have said.'

'How do I know what's important? You shouldn't have made me feel so foolish. And Bonita was choking, remember? The jewel didn't seem so important then.'

'Did your friend's brother buy it?' Chupplejeep asked.

Christabel laughed. 'He was going to, apparently, but then Alani never came back. But who knows, maybe Elvina made the whole story up. You know what she's like. I'm going,' Christabel said. 'This one needs to have her snack.' Bonita reached for her father. Chupplejeep embraced her and then handed her back to her mother. 'Come on then, little one,' Christabel said, putting Bonita on the floor and leading her out of the room.

'What does it say about her?' Chupplejeep asked, turning back to Pankaj.

Pankaj began to read quietly to himself at first, then he spoke. 'Alani Ali had been a parenting guru. She had published a book, but like Daniel told you, it didn't do well. Parents didn't want to take advice from someone who didn't have any children. They were also not ready for her gentle parenting views. It says here that Alani had a typical Indian childhood where she was told not to embarrass her parents and punished for stepping out of line, misbehaving and generally being a kid. Her parents were very much of the children should be seen and not heard mentality. Alani wanted to show parents that there was a different way to raise children.'

'So Alani doesn't make any money from her parenting book, the Hydrebadi mothers are not interested in what she has to say…'

'So she moves to Mumbai and reinvents herself as a social media coach.'

'Her website boasts of success with changing behaviours of well-known Bollywood actors and actresses,' Pankaj said, jabbing his finger at the screen. 'Although Alani or Nita can't name them, as discretion is key in her line of work.'

'Of course it is,' Chupplejeep said. 'No one can check the credibility of her statement either.'

'Why change her name though. If she wanted to transition from parenting coach to a behavioural one, why not keep the same name? It's not like she did anything wrong.'

Chupplejeep twisted one end of his moustache. 'Maybe she wanted to project something different with this new setup of hers, like a branding thing.'

'Like some authors. They have different pen names for different genres that they write,' Pankaj said.

'Exactly like that. Go back,' Chupplejeep said, pointing at the screen. 'Go back to the page you were on about Alani Ali. What other results are there?'

Pankaj clicked on the back button and waited for the page to load. Halfway down the search page was an article written by a blogger who claimed to have been conned by Alani Ali.

'Click on that,' Chupplejeep said. 'Now we're on to something. And get ready.' He took his car keys from his desk. 'I need to make some calls, then we are going to pay our social media coach another visit.'

Chapter Forty

Chupplejeep took a guess that Nita would be at Reena's place, but when they buzzed up to her apartment, neither of the women were there. No one answered the door, suggesting that Reena hadn't managed to hire any new staff as yet.

'Do we wait or do we go looking?' Pankaj asked. 'We're not in any rush, are we, sir?' Pankaj checked the time on his phone.

'You still have time before the party tonight,' Chupplejeep said.

'It's not that, sir,' Pankaj said. 'I messaged Shwetty, but she isn't responding. She's supposed to be back tomorrow night.'

'You think she might stay away longer?' Chupplejeep asked. 'Pass me your phone; I need to send a message.'

Pankaj handed over the device. Chupplejeep typed something in and pressed send. 'Here,' he said, handing it back.

Pankaj put the phone back in his pocket. 'I don't think Shwetty can stay away any longer. She has work.'

It didn't take long for the old Pankaj to resurface then, Chupplejeep thought to himself with a small smile. Chupplejeep didn't know what decision Pankaj had made, but it would be a shame if the boy left the world of private investigation when he was so good at it. At the same time, Chupplejeep understood Pankaj's predicament. He could easily return to the force. The hours still wouldn't be better, but the pay, he supposed, would be.

'There,' Pankaj said, pointing to the café across the road.

Chupplejeep followed Pankaj's gaze. Nita and Reena were sitting at a table. Two buses went past, dangerously leaning to one side with their heavy loads. One narrowly missed a scooter carrying a family of four; a little girl in a pink-and-white frilly dress was standing in the front between her father's arms as he rode the two-wheeler. A boy of about ten was squashed in-between his father and mother. Chupplejeep waited for another bus to pass before he and Pankaj crossed the road.

As they reached Reena's table, the social media coach saw them and her face fell. 'You again,' she said, shifting her gaze down towards her smoothie. One of the waiters was pulling down Diwali lanterns and tasselled garlands from the coconut trees.

'I have some news,' Chupplejeep said, turning his eyes back to Reena. 'I know where your ring is.'

Kingfisher Blues

Reena looked away. She touched the glass in front of her before looking up at the investigator. 'Really?' she asked. 'I suppose I could do with giving my fans an update.'

'A few days ago you were desperate for news of the missing ring. Now you don't seem bothered. Why?' Chupplejeep asked.

'My father's acting crazy,' Reena said. 'With all the coverage and people talking about the provenance of the ring, he believes we should return the stone to the people or something like that, for free. Can you believe it? What's the point? He thinks we have enough money and we don't need any more. He wants to gift it to the Chhatrapati Shivaji Maharaj Vastu Sanghralaya.'

'Your father's a decent man,' Chupplejeep said.

'So now it's irrelevant if the ring is returned to me or not,' Reena said. 'That's why your news isn't having the desired effect.'

'Well,' Chupplejeep said. 'Like you said, you can update your fans. And I think they'd be in awe of you if you told them your father was donating it back to the people.'

'That's true,' she said. She pulled her phone out of a pink patent leather bag.

'Don't you want to know where the ring is?'

'Of course,' she said.

'Would it surprise you to know that out of all the suspects I interviewed whilst searching for this ring, nearly all of them suggested you hid the ring for the attention, Miss Gopaldas?'

'That's crazy,' Reena said, still not meeting his eye.

'It made sense. The missing ring has finally bought you the fame you crave. But this social media crowd, or should I say your followers, are fickle. They're quite bored with the story now, am I right?'

'You think I took it? I should never have hired you,' Reena said. 'Wait till my father hears about your accusation. You're fired.' Reena stood and stared at the investigator; he stared right back. In one quick move, Reena picked up her smoothie and poured what remained of her drink over Chupplejeep.

Chupplejeep looked at her incredulously. Customers in the café were staring. Some were laughing. He grabbed a fistful of napkins from the dispenser and wiped away the thick pink liquid before it trickled down his neck. Pankaj motioned for a waiter to fetch a wet towel.

Nita, who had watched the scene play out, stood. 'I think you better leave,' she said. 'I'll take it from here.'

Chupplejeep was tempted to follow her instructions. He desperately wanted a shower, but he had been hired not by Reena but her father, and he liked the old man. He wasn't going to let this thief get away with it.

'You still haven't asked me where the ring is,' Chupplejeep said.

'I think you've made it clear –' Nita started, but the investigator cut her off.

'Oh no,' he said. 'I haven't made anything clear yet. I was just getting started.' The waiter appeared with two towels, and Chupplejeep cleaned himself as best he could. The smell of guava clung to him.

'So where is it?' Reena asked. 'Where's the ring? You want to search me again?'

'I think you should ask your friend,' Chupplejeep said.

'What friend?' Reena asked.

Chupplejeep motioned to Nita and Reena laughed.

'Accusing Nita is as ridiculous as accusing me. Nita was with me the whole time. She didn't take it. She's against material possessions.'

'Is she?' Chupplejeep asked, making a show of looking at what appeared to be a designer handbag on Nita's lap.

'Nita doesn't need money or possessions to prove her success. She's one of those people who is just content, aren't you, Nee? It's what we are all striving to be like.'

Nita didn't say anything. Her eyes flitted from Chupplejeep to Pankaj from under her heavy fringe. 'I don't think Nita has told you everything.'

'I'm not listening to this,' Reena said as she shared a look with Nita. She started to walk away but Pankaj blocked her way.

'I think you'll want to hear what Mr Chupplejeep has to say.'

The two women sat back down. After a moment's silence, Chupplejeep spoke. 'Has she told you her name isn't Nita Das?'

Reena looked at her friend and back at Chupplejeep. 'I've seen Nita's passport. We travelled together from Mumbai.'

Nita leaned back in her chair and smiled.

'That may be so,' Chupplejeep said, 'but your friend has had another alias.' He turned to Nita. 'Do you want to tell her or should I?'

When Nita didn't say anything, Chupplejeep spoke. 'Alani Ali, does that ring a bell?'

'I have no idea what you're talking about,' Nita said.

'Reena, take out your phone and put that name into any search engine, see what you can find out,' Chupplejeep said.

Reena glanced over at her friend. She didn't reach for her phone on the table in front of her. Nita looked away.

'What you'll find is that Nita was actually calling herself Alani Ali a decade ago in Hyderabad. She wrote a parenting book, and it didn't do well.'

'Where's the crime in that?' Nita asked. 'So what? I made up the name Alani Ali. Nita's my real name. Alani was a lifetime ago. I don't recognise her anymore.'

'Alani was accused of something back then, something that precipitated the name change, I imagine. She did an interview with a blogger when she was trying to get publicity for her book. The blogger was quite wealthy, and after that interview, a piece of the blogger's jewellery went missing.'

'It's all lies,' Nita said. 'That woman was crazy. She was just after free stuff the whole time. She didn't even have any followers.'

'I thought it didn't matter how many followers someone had,' Pankaj said.

Kingfisher Blues

'Google her,' Chupplejeep said, giving Reena the blogger's name. Reena put her hand on her device and then picked it up. She unlocked the screen and started tapping away, her fake nails making a *click-click* sound as she did so.

'You'll see,' Nita said. 'No charges were pressed. That woman was deluded.'

'No charges were pressed because you disappeared, or rather Alani did, until she turned up at a jeweller's a few days back.' Chupplejeep eyed the two women. Reena was sitting very still, her eyes glued to her screen. Christabel's friend hadn't seen Alani or at least couldn't identify her with her scarf and dark glasses. Had Reena been in on it with Nita? Had she used her friend's alias to try and sell her own ring? Chupplejeep watched Reena carefully then made his decision.

Chupplejeep turned to Nita. 'I think you saw your opportunity when you met Reena, or should I say targeted her. Not only could you swindle her out of money on a regular basis, but when she produced the Kingfisher Sapphire, you knew you had hit the jackpot.'

'What rubbish,' Nita said. 'Targeted? Reena called me. I didn't approach her first.'

'It's true, Mr Chupplejeep,' said Reena. 'I sought her services out. She couldn't have targeted me, like you say. Your theory is all wrong.' Reena put a manicured fingernail to her mouth.

'If I recall correctly, your ex-lover Aman told me that a friend of yours recommended her. She had done wonders for her, am I right?'

Reena nodded slowly.

'Go back to your friend and ask her how she found Nita. I'm willing to bet my fee that Nita worked tirelessly for your friend and maybe a friend of a friend too, in order to attract your attention.'

'Nonsense,' Nita said, avoiding Chupplejeep and Reena's eyes. 'And on top of this ludicrous accusation, you are also accusing me of stealing the Kingfisher Sapphire. You searched me. I didn't have it on me.'

'You made sure Vihaan and Uma, who were on to your deceptions, were not there the night of the party. I believe you took the ring. We all know it was loose on Reena's finger. You stayed close to your employer, and I have a witness who says you were close to Reena when she discovered her ring had disappeared. You were not, as you initially told us, doing a crystal meditation.'

Nita sneered.

'Reena had had a few drinks. She was talking animatedly about an expensive bottle of champagne. You, Nita, put your hand in hers and slipped the Kingfisher Sapphire off Reena's finger. It disappeared into the folds of your dress and then you put it somewhere, somewhere in the apartment you knew we wouldn't search. You've spent enough time in Reena's home to know exactly where it could be hidden, undetected. Then later, on another visit, you removed the ring and took it back to your hotel.'

'Great story, Mr Chupplejeep, but you can't prove any of it,' Nita said. She took a cigarette from her handbag and lit it.

'I have a witness who said you tried to sell him the jewel not long after it went missing,' Chupplejeep said.

'People will say anything for a bit of attention,' Nita said. She gave Reena a sideways glance. 'It will be his word against mine.'

Chupplejeep nodded. 'You didn't sell it to him though, and I think I know why.'

Nita shifted her gaze away from her cigarette towards the investigator. 'Why?' she asked.

'You got a better offer. One you couldn't refuse.'

Nita hesitated. She put her handbag under her arm and stood up.

'I wouldn't go anywhere if I were you,' Chupplejeep said.

Nita stared at something behind Chupplejeep.

Chupplejeep turned towards the entrance of the café. 'Ah,' he said to the man approaching. The man turned back towards the road.

'Don't run off,' Chupplejeep shouted after him. 'I know where you live, remember.'

Daniel Chatterjee stopped. A moment later he headed towards their table.

'Your purchaser is here, Alani,' Chupplejeep said.

Chapter Forty-one

'That was pretty amazing, sir,' Pankaj said. 'How did you know?'

'Good detective work and a little bit of gut instinct,' Chupplejeep said. 'It did cross my mind that Reena and Nita were working together at one point, but apart from the social media popularity, Reena didn't have much to gain with the stone going missing, and she certainly wouldn't have wanted to sell the gem. She doesn't need the money.'

'I called Elvina's brother, the jeweller. He may not have the internet, but he has quite a lot of emotional intelligence and impeccable hearing. He was making a deal with Alani when her phone rang. It was a man she referred to as Dan. Then she failed to turn up to sell the ring. Dan is short for Daniel. We both know that Dan and Nita knew each other in a past life. We both know that Dan collects priceless articles.

'Daniel realised what his old friend Alani had done, and he couldn't resist having a piece like that in his collection. Daniel wouldn't have stolen it, but when he found out that someone had done the dirty work for him, he was ready to buy it. Alani or Nita tried a few jewellers, but she was nervous because the Kingfisher Sapphire was becoming famous on social media. Her coaching of Reena hadn't gone to plan, and nothing could stop Miss Gopaldas from posting about the loss of her jewel. The ring was becoming too hot to handle, so to speak. Daniel reached out to Nita at the right time. He knew Nita's history. He knew that she had stolen jewellery before. He made her an offer she couldn't refuse, and she was about to accept, but something told me she was holding off. She had probably asked for more money, and Daniel, knowing he was the only one she could sell to, was refusing to pay.'

'So you sent him a message from my phone pretending to be Alani and said you were ready to make a deal.'

'I took a risk and it paid off.'

'How did you know Nita would have the ring in her bag?' Pankaj asked.

'It was far too precious to leave in her hotel room. She had to take it everywhere with her. And her handbag was on her lap the entire time we were speaking to her. It was too valuable for her to lose.'

'It did look stunning, sir. You could get lost looking into that deep blue stone. It was smart calling the police too. They'll get the credit in the papers for getting the jewel back, no doubt.'

Chupplejeep looked at his phone. 'Mr Gopaldas has already wired over our fee,' he said. 'Reena must have told him.'

'What will Reena do without Nita now?' Pankaj asked.

Chupplejeep laughed. 'She'll be better off without her, don't you think?'

Pankaj nodded.

'Come on,' Chupplejeep said. 'Get in the car. Our work isn't done yet.'

'Sir, it feels like we should have a break,' Pankaj said. 'After what just happened, and I have the party tonight…'

'First a shower,' Chupplejeep said, sniffing his shirt. It still reeked of guava. He checked his phone. He had three missed calls from Kulkarni. 'We have time before the party, and we still have work to do.'

Chapter Forty-two

Freshly showered and changed, Chupplejeep made his way back to his office, where Pankaj was sipping on a freshly brewed tea. He handed a cup to Chupplejeep just as the investigator's phone rang.

'Mr Chupplejeep,' Kapoor said, his voice booming down the phone. 'Are you avoiding me?'

Chupplejeep protested. He had been calling Kapoor with regular updates, but the man never listened.

'I hear the police are getting nowhere also. You know what they are going to do, don't you? They're going to set someone up to take the fall. They are going to set up –'

'Your new star, Darsh,' Chupplejeep said, finishing Kapoor's sentence for him.

'Are you saying he's the one who did it, because he assures me that he didn't.'

'Darsh was backstage. He had the perfect opportunity and the motive. He's been waiting for his chance to shine and now look at him,' Chupplejeep said.

'He's great,' Kapoor said. He went on to tell Chupplejeep that Darsh had more potential than Jagdish. 'Darsh is young. He's attracting a bigger crowd, a younger crowd. I thought kathakali was lost to the young. They want all this modern dance, but Darsh is bringing the youth back in.' Chupplejeep could hear the emotion in Kapoor's voice. When he had first met the theatre owner, Chupplejeep hadn't realised just how passionate the man was about the art of kathakali. He had believed Kapoor just wanted to make as much money as he could, but perhaps there was more to it than that.

'Jagdish was full of himself,' Kapoor continued. 'You couldn't tell him anything, but Darsh, he listens. We've paid for a choreographer, one of the best in India. Jagdish was a star, but I think Darsh is going to be a superstar, and we can't afford to lose him. I'll get him a solicitor if I need to, the best in town.'

'What was Darsh looking for in Jagdish's dressing room?' Chupplejeep asked. 'The day after Jagdish was found murdered, I was in Jagdish's dressing room and Darsh came in frantically looking for something. He told me it was makeup, but I don't believe it.'

'What do you think it was?' Kapoor asked.

Kapoor wasn't able to give Chupplejeep any more information. Darsh had motive, opportunity and no alibi. He had fought with Jagdish the night of his performance.

It was time to pay Darsh another visit.

~

Darsh opened the door and turned, walking back into the penthouse suite of the five-star hotel he was staying at, close to Kapoor's theatre.

'Very nice,' Chupplejeep said, as he followed the kathakali dancer into the living room area. It overlooked the Mandovi river. A cruise boat was going past as the sun began to set.

'Kapoor called,' Darsh said. 'Says you have questions.' Darsh walked over to the open-plan kitchen and retrieved a bottle and a glass. He offered the investigator a drink.

Chupplejeep declined. He noticed Darsh slowly turn over a framed photograph on the kitchen worktop amongst the brightly coloured Diwali greeting cards and distinctive boxes of unopened halwa from the local *mithaiwalla*, sweet seller. 'The cops have you as their number one suspect,' Chupplejeep said. 'Why do you think that is?'

When Darsh shrugged, Chupplejeep explained why he had taken their interest.

'So what if I don't have an alibi? So what if we were heard arguing? I explained all that. It isn't me they should be looking at.'

'So who should they be looking at?' Chupplejeep asked.

'Kapoor said you wanted to know what I was looking for in Jagdish's dressing room the day you were in there, hiding.'

'I wasn't hiding. I was examining the crime scene,' Chupplejeep said.

'I'd been asked to retrieve something from there, by someone. That's all that I was doing.'

'You didn't spike your colleague's drink?'

'What?' Darsh asked, forcefully pushing a clay oil lamp aside on the worktop.

'Jagdish's lassi was laced with bhang the night he was killed.'

'He did that himself. Ask anyone,' Darsh said.

'Oh I did,' Chupplejeep said, putting the oil lamp back in its place. 'Jagdish used bhang but always the same amount. But the amount found in his drink would have definitely made him lose focus, I'm told. Not what a kathakali dancer needs on his opening night.'

'He had a strong tolerance,' Darsh said.

'I see,' Chupplejeep said. 'So what had you been asked to retrieve from Jagdish's dressing room?'

'I can't say,' Darsh said.

'Can you tell us who had instructed you?' Pankaj asked.

Darsh shook his head.

'You're not giving us much to go on,' said Chupplejeep. 'Who's to say you're not lying to us. No one can back up your story.'

Darsh poured himself a large measure of Black Label. He swallowed it down. 'I can't tell you,' he said.

'And why's that?' Chupplejeep asked.

He could see Darsh's hand start to tremble. 'Because if I do, she might kill me too.'

Chapter Forty-three

'Did you find what you were looking for?' Pankaj asked as Chupplejeep got back into the Baleno after returning to the theatre.

'I think so,' he said. 'I took a photo on my phone.'

'Will Kapoor tell Darsh you were in his dressing room just now?' Pankaj asked.

'I hope so. I'm sure he's on the phone to the dancer as we speak. Darsh was keen for me not to see the photograph he had in his hotel suite, and I wanted to know who was in it. I assumed that if he had a framed photo of a loved one in his hotel, chances were he would have one in his dressing room.'

'And you found it?'

'It wasn't for everyone to see. It was tucked behind a few papers in his dressing table drawer.'

'Why the secrecy?'

'Because the photo is of his lover,' Chupplejeep said.

'Don't tell me it was Jagdish's wife. That would certainly give him motive.'

'Close,' Chupplejeep said. 'Kapoor was called away, so I couldn't ask him, but the face is familiar. I've seen her before, or at least pictures of her. The woman in the photo looks just like Rupali.'

'Her sister?' Pankaj asked.

'Her daughter,' Chupplejeep said. 'One of them.'

'That's why he didn't want us to see it. Jagdish was protective of his girls. Maybe he forbade them to see each other and Darsh couldn't stand it, so he attacked Jagdish the night he was killed. It gives Darsh another motive in addition to stardom.'

'One more stop before the party then,' Pankaj said.

Chupplejeep smiled.

~

'The police don't think it's Darsh,' Chupplejeep said as he put his phone in his pocket and started the engine. Having been denied entry, they had been sitting in his car outside Rupali Sharma's house, the *diyas*, oil lamps, twinkling around the entrance. Chupplejeep was sure that the women were in, but he was also sure that Darsh had called his lover and had warned her. Chupplejeep manoeuvred the car to the main road towards the Atul Centre.

If Rupali hadn't known about her daughter's affair with the kathakali dancer, she did now.

'That was our old friend Manju,' Chupplejeep said. He had been fond of their administrative assistant who had worked his way up and was now a sub-officer. It was handy to know a sub-officer in the force who didn't mind sharing a snippet or two of information here and there.

Pankaj asked what Manju had said, his eyes lighting up at the mention of the young man with wild curly hair and a gappy smile.

'The police still think it's Popatrao. Kulkarni had been mistaken and so had Kapoor, but thanks to that tip-off, we have solved one more piece of the puzzle.'

'Did Manju say why the police still think it is Popatrao, sir?' Pankaj asked.

'Popatrao doesn't have an alibi. He was at the theatre that night, and he was in a contract with Jagdish he couldn't afford.'

'Do you think there's any truth in it or is someone trying to frame the hotelier?'

'Why do you ask that?' Chupplejeep said, curious to know how well he had trained Pankaj.

'Popatrao's the type you could easily set up, sir. He isn't the brightest. He was playing away from home, and he believed his girlfriend to be having an affair. You said Meera didn't take kindly to the accusation that she was sleeping around. So as I see it, there were two people that could land him in it, so to speak.'

'I don't know if it is a good thing or not that we are starting to think the same,' Chupplejeep said. 'Meera and Popatrao's wife have reason to want him punished, but somehow I don't think his wife is to blame for this. As far as I can tell, she has her own life, busy with friends and family. As long as Popatrao pays the bills, she is none the wiser. The question is whether Meera was working with anyone else?'

'What do you mean, sir?'

'While you were at the Atul Centre, I had to do some stakeouts on my own,' Chupplejeep said.

'And?'

'I need to gather my thoughts on this, and we have run out of time. Today has been eventful and it isn't over yet,' Chupplejeep said, pulling up outside the rear entrance to the Atul Centre. They could hear the low beat of the tabla and a sitar playing from the grounds. There was an atmospheric buzz from behind the wall, people chatting and golden lights flickering.

Pankaj opened the door to the Baleno.

'I'll be back to pick you up in an hour unless you call before.'

Pankaj took the mask that they had purchased on their way from a Tibetan market and adjusted it on his face. While Chupplejeep had gone home for a shower after the smoothie incident, Pankaj had taken the opportunity to go home to change too. He had chosen black jeans and a black t-shirt. It wasn't much of an outfit, but he supposed it would complement his brightly coloured mask.

Pankaj punched the code that Monica had given him into the keypad and the slim gate opened with a soft click, barely audible above the noise from the guests behind the wall, then he slipped inside.

Before Chupplejeep could pull out from where he had parked, his phone began to ring. Chupplejeep answered and heard a frightened voice on the other end of the line.

'Help,' the voice said. 'Help me, please.'

~

Popatrao was sitting in the dark when Chupplejeep entered his office. 'They think it's me,' he said, his voice hoarse. 'The cops actually think it's me and they have evidence. But you have to believe me. It isn't true. I didn't do this. I admit I didn't like the man. He was taking me for all I had, but look, even without all that, I have nothing. My business has failed, my wife doesn't want to know me and even my lover, my Meera is ignoring my calls. She thinks I did it too.' Popatrao put his head in his hands.

'You were at the show when Jagdish was killed, so you had opportunity,' Chupplejeep said.

Popatrao's eyes widened. 'I was there, yes. I told you that. I didn't hide that fact. My girlfriend asked Jagdish for tickets and then on the night she stood me up. I was there on my own, but people sitting next to me will vouch for me. They will tell you that I was there all night, or at least until they cancelled the show that evening.'

'Oh, we've asked,' Chupplejeep said. Chupplejeep had only just managed to track down the couple who had been siting next to Popatrao. They confirmed that Popatrao had an empty seat next to him, but they couldn't say if he had been in his seat all night. They had been too preoccupied by the show and the drama that had followed. The woman had helpfully said that she had asked the man for a tissue when her drink spilled and he had given her a handkerchief. The woman had laughed then, because who, these days, carries a handkerchief. Everyone of a certain age, Chupplejeep had wanted to say.

Instead he asked, 'Do you recall what time this was?' to which she helpfully said it was during the interval before the curtains were expected to go up. If the woman was correct about that, there was very little chance that Popatrao could have left his seat to go backstage and murder Jagdish and return calm and collected to be back in his seat within the fifteen-minute time allocation. In Chupplejeep's eyes, Popatrao was off the hook.

'Your Meera. How well does she know Rupali?' Chupplejeep asked, thinking of his recent stakeout. The Baleno in its shade of midnight blue was perfect to follow someone unsuspecting. He had followed her to a hotel on two occasions to meet her lover. Chupplejeep told the hotelier his suspicions.

Popatrao sighed. 'You think my Meera was having an affair with Jagdish's wife, Rupali?' He tried to force a laugh. 'No, boss, you have it all wrong. Nothing doing.'

'Did Meera ever mention that she was hanging out with Rupali?'

'No, never,' Popatrao said, looking away. 'And I would've known because she would have mentioned it when we were trying to wow Jagdish to perform at the hotel.'

'Which was all her idea?'

'Meera did mention Rupali once,' Popatrao mumbled. Chupplejeep enquired in what context this was.

'It was when she was asleep,' Popatrao said. 'She said something about a Rupali rumali.'

'Rumali? As in the roti?' Chupplejeep asked. Now was not the time to be thinking of food, but he couldn't help but think about some chicken hot from the tandoor with a rumali roti on the side.

Popatrao nodded. 'You wouldn't have a pet name like that for someone you didn't know,' he said sadly. 'I asked her about it when she woke the next morning. Meera said that I must have been the one dreaming. I believed her. I believed everything she said.'

'Meera was the one who encouraged you to hire Jagdish for a residency at your hotel,' Chupplejeep reminded the hotelier again.

Popatrao swallowed. He shook his head. 'That's just a coincidence. Not for one minute do I think Meera and Rupali were plotting to get Jagdish to perform at this hotel. What would be the reason for it?'

'Who do you think tipped off the police about your involvement, the fact you were at the show at the time of Jagdish's death?'

Popatrao's jaw dropped open. 'To be the scapegoat,' he said, answering his own question that he had posed to Chupplejeep just moments ago. 'For them to point the finger at me so they could get away with…'

'With murder? Could be,' Chupplejeep mused. 'Maybe Meera and Rupali plotted to kill Jagdish and put you away so that they were both free to be together. By now I've realised the type of man Jagdish was. He wouldn't have let his wife divorce him so easily. Performing at your hotel would be another free evening that Rupali and Meera could meet.'

'Jagdish was fiercely protective of his family, that much I know,' Popatrao said.

'His wife is certainly beautiful,' Chupplejeep said.

'And his daughters. He was particular with who they went out with so much so they were relieved when he agreed they could move to England. At least there he couldn't keep tabs on them like he did here.'

'How do you know all this?' Chupplejeep asked.

'Meera,' Popatrao said, spitting his ex-lover's name out. 'I never asked her how she knew, but now I know.'

'Were any of his daughters involved with men here?' Chupplejeep asked casually, given what he had recently discovered about Darsh.

Popatrao scratched his chin. 'Yes, yes,' he said. 'That Tanya, Jagdish's youngest daughter, was there on opening night. Her parents didn't know she was in Goa because she wasn't here to see her father. She was here to see that Darsh. Jagdish thought she was still in the UK. I knew this because he had told me all his daughters were abroad. That's why I was surprised to see her at the theatre that night.

'When the news of her father's death broke, Tanya must have rushed home, but I suppose she could have told her mother she caught an earlier flight. Youngsters these days have all the answers, and with mobile phones it's so easy to say you're in one place when in fact you are in another. I've seen Tanya before with Darsh; that's how I knew her face. Darsh was the dancer I wanted at my hotel. If I hadn't listened to Meera, I would never have signed Jagdish. I didn't realise Meera had an ulterior motive.'

Popatrao put his head in his hands. 'I suspected Meera of cheating on me, but I didn't know with who or if I was just being paranoid. When I see her again, I'm going to make her life a living –'

'You may be off my suspect list,' Chupplejeep said, interrupting the hotelier, 'but you're still a suspect with the police. If I were you, I'd stay well away from Meera and Rupali.'

'Can you tell the police all this?' Popatrao said, his eyes pleading. 'To clear my name.'

'When I find out who killed Jagdish, the police will get all my notes.'

~

Chupplejeep checked the time as he put his key in the ignition. He would be early for Pankaj, but that wasn't a problem. There was nothing on his phone from his colleague, but that didn't mean anything.

As he drove towards the centre, the investigator considered what Popatrao had said. Not only were

Rupali and Meera now prime suspects, but Jagdish's understudy, Darsh, had risen to the top of the list.

It was all starting to fall into place. The argument heard between Darsh and Jagdish before the show wasn't about Darsh wanting to feature in Jagdish's performance. Chupplejeep had been foolish to have readily accepted that version of the truth. The argument between Darsh and Jagdish was about Jagdish's daughter, Tanya, and Darsh's relationship with her. If Jagdish opposed their love then Darsh would have wanted him out of the way.

Darsh had disappeared from his shared dressing room ten minutes before the interval. He was already backstage, and it would have given him enough time to murder Jagdish and return to his dressing room. There was no doubt in Chupplejeep's mind that Darsh had already spiked Jagdish's drink – to make the great Jagdish Sharma drowsy, ensuring the dancer's first performance on opening night was a failure. Jagdish must have tasted it, which was why he had only drunk half of the yoghurty mixture. Darsh would have had a change of clothes at the theatre too. The opportunity was perfect, and he had a strong motive. Not only would Jagdish's death catapult Darsh's career, but he would get to be with Jagdish's daughter as well. Chupplejeep put his foot on the pedal and sped towards the Atul Centre.

Chapter Forty-four

The event at the Centre was busy. Pankaj pulled the strings at the back of his mask to prevent it from slipping. The last thing he wanted was for Cynthia to spot him and kick him out. She had specifically told him to leave. Attending felt like a betrayal, especially as she had been so helpful with his personal problems. Despite Pankaj's reservations, he had to attend this event. It was his duty. It was his job.

Bhavan and Jagdish Sharma had been close, so there was a chance that the boy could shed some light on who wanted the kathakali dancer dead. Sonal and Abhijeet had done their best to hinder their chances of speaking to Bhavan, and Pankaj had to question whether they were protecting their son or if they were afraid, afraid of something he would say.

Pankaj picked up a glass of something sparkling. 'Alcohol?' Pankaj asked the waiter who was holding the tray. Pankaj couldn't afford to drink on the job. His tolerance to alcohol was limited as it was. One drink and he could easily give himself away without intending to.

The waiter shook his head. 'Not here,' he said. Then in a low whisper he added, 'If you go and ask the man with the blue bird mask, he may be able to help.'

Pankaj didn't expect anything less from the Atul Centre. No wonder the event was crowded. Some people in the centre were trying to fight addiction. Did the man in the blue mask know who he could serve without setting them back weeks of therapy?

'The show's about to start, sir,' the waiter said. The sound of chatter and laughter was all around him, the smoky smell of the tandoor somewhere in the distance mixed with the smell of citronella to keep the mosquitos away.

Pankaj craned his neck to see the crowd part. An area in the middle of the garden had been cleared. A man seated with the tablas and a woman with a sitar began to play. The delicate sound of the strings and the rhythmic tapping on the drums had a soothing effect. Behind the players there was a beautiful painted scene showing the birds of Goa. The kingfisher was painted in vibrant blue and orange in the middle of the scene, and Pankaj couldn't resist a smile. They had solved the case of the disappearance of the Kingfisher Sapphire and been paid handsomely for it. Chupplejeep had mentioned a new office and a pay rise. A pay rise would help when he spoke to Shwetika, but it wouldn't be enough for his wife. If they were to have children, she wanted someone she could rely on, someone who was going to come home in time for dinner, some days if not all.

As Pankaj had left the centre this morning, he had been certain of his next steps with his wife, of what he would say to Shwetika, but after the thrill of finding that beautiful blue stone and speaking to Kapoor, Pankaj was having second thoughts.

Pankaj shook his feelings away. He was working. He couldn't afford to be distracted with emotions and impending decisions. He took a sip of the sparkling grape juice and pushed his way through the crowd. A woman in a purple-and-gold mask was standing next to a lantana bush, and Pankaj made his way over to her.

'Monica,' he whispered. 'I'm here.'

The woman was silent, and for a moment Pankaj thought he had got the wrong person. Monica had told him she would be in a purple-and-gold owl mask, but had he remembered correctly? Monica had also told him what mask Cynthia would be wearing: an orange-and-black toucan mask. Had he mixed up the two? Monica and Cynthia had two completely different body shapes, but they were of similar height, and Pankaj was standing so close to the woman in the purple-and-gold mask he couldn't make out whether the woman was petite or not.

'Ah,' the owl said after what felt like an eternity. 'You made it. The code worked. Cynthia had wanted to change it, but I told her we'd do it tomorrow.'

'I'm grateful,' Pankaj said.

Pankaj watched as the performers entered the clearing. Their outfits were simple. White cotton three-quarter-length trousers and wrap-around jackets with a simple cotton black belt. They too were wearing masks, but their masks were anything but simple. Their ornate masks were gold and black with intricate designs and beaks in different shapes and sizes. Their movements were well practiced, as the performance appeared so effortless. Pankaj was mesmerised as the actors and dancers wandered around the makeshift stage pretending to be birds swooping down to peck at imaginary insects, ruffling their pretend feathers and stretching their wings to the sounds of the drums. Several dancers dressed in black entered. They walked in a line. What were they supposed to be? Ants? Insects? The delicate music stopped. It was replaced by something loud and menacing. One by one the birds picked them off. The crowd was stunned into silence. Pankaj too felt as if he couldn't talk. The piece was dramatic and emotive without a word being uttered.

Minutes later the music stopped and the actors left. The man with the tablas and woman with the sitar started playing their respective instruments again, and the crowd resumed their talking. The audience began to shift.

'Is that it?' Pankaj asked. 'Is everyone going?' The show was over, and Pankaj hadn't managed to speak to his suspect yet. He cursed himself for being so absorbed in the performance and not looking for Bhavan.

Monica laughed. 'We're moving to the next stage. You haven't been before, I keep forgetting. We have residents who have long since checked out, but they pay to come back for the shows. We have sold out the last five shows. Residents and their families get priority tickets. You were lucky I told you how to get in.'

Pankaj looked at the crowd, trying to imagine what mask Bhavan would be wearing, but he had no idea. 'I'm looking for Bhavan,' he said. 'I want to speak to him.'

'Oh yes,' said Monica. 'The murder of the kathakali dancer. How could I forget?'

'Are his family with him tonight?' Pankaj asked. He had only met the man once and he had been wearing his helmet the whole time. The gold signet ring he wore on his thumb was memorable, but that was about it.

'He's over there,' Monica said. She motioned towards the rain tree that the crowd was walking past. The audience stopped. They had reached the second clearing. Lanterns and fire torches were placed strategically around a circular space reserved for the actors. There was no painted backdrop here, just the lushness of the trees that surrounded the space.

Pankaj looked towards the rain tree. A man was standing with his back towards them, a cigarette in his hand. The show started again. This time the actors were trees, dressed again in simple clothes with masks in the shape of leaves and branches of various trees.

'It's stiffened lace,' Monica said, sensing his awe. This time Pankaj didn't wait to watch the performance. Instead he thanked Monica and made his way towards the rain tree.

~

Pankaj could smell the woody scent of tobacco as he approached. Bhavan was oblivious to his presence, lost in thought. It would have been better if Chupplejeep had come with him. He too could have purchased a mask and slipped into the crowd undetected. Pankaj spotted Cynthia in her orange-and-black toucan mask. She was chatting with someone in the grounds as they watched the show. Cynthia didn't seem to be in the least bit interested in intruders. But why would she? In the history of the Atul Centre, no one had leaked any untoward stories to the press about the place. And why would they? The Atul Centre delivered. Pankaj had experienced that firsthand. The beauty of the place was that it didn't promise the best doctors, or a quick fix. It simply provided a place for people to rest. Where people with whatever problems they had could escape for a while, pretend they were normal – whatever normal was. The Atul Centre wasn't a rehabilitation retreat or a medical facility. In fact, from what Pankaj could see and the gathering around the man in the blue mask serving liquor, this centre was encouraging its inhabitants to break the rules.

'What?' Bhavan said without turning.

Pankaj cleared his throat. He should have been the one to speak first. Now he was on the back foot. He shook off his doubt. 'It's me,' he said. 'We spoke in the car park the other day. You were dropping off your girlfriend.'

Kingfisher Blues

Bhavan took a step back. 'She told me you were asking her questions,' he said.

'Just making conversation,' Pankaj said, hoping his girlfriend hadn't mentioned their conversation about Jagdish Sharma. Given how upsetting Bhavan had found it, he hoped the nurse had kept silent. 'It can get pretty boring at the centre.'

Bhavan was silent for a moment and then nodded. 'You came back for the show,' he said.

'Well,' Pankaj said. 'Last time I was only here a short while, and you said I ought to stay till the end, that the end is the best part.'

Bhavan laughed. He stared at Pankaj. It was unclear what he could see of Pankaj's face with his mask on. 'We didn't meet here before,' Bhavan said, slipping the solid gold ring off his thumb and replacing it. 'You were lying. What is it you want?'

Pankaj lifted his palms up. 'Not lying, maybe just a case of the wrong person,' he said. He studied Bhavan's eyes, his hands and the way he moved. There was a familiarity there, but he couldn't quite place it.

'If we knew each other, you'd know that I don't like people much. I don't speak to many people around here.' Bhavan's speech was monotone and detached.

'I see,' said Pankaj, feeling a little on edge at Bhavan's rancour. He stood in silence, wondering if Bhavan was playing him. Monica had never mentioned the boy's aversion to people. Was that because it was untrue, or had she simply failed to mention it? Pankaj decided to ignore Bhavan's request to be alone. He clenched his fists in his pockets and hardened his resolve.

'I wanted to stay to the end at the last show, but my mother wasn't well,' Pankaj said.

Bhavan blew cigarette smoke into the air. He turned towards the clearing in the distance. 'You didn't miss much,' he said eventually. 'They do the same crap every time. Different themes. This time it's birds and trees, last time it was water and wind. I don't see what the fuss is about. I was joking when I said you should stay to the end.'

'Why are you here again then?' Pankaj asked. When Bhavan didn't answer, Pankaj continued. 'Something familiar,' he said. 'There's comfort in that.'

'What are you? A shrink?' Bhavan asked. 'My folks are always keen to see it.'

'Are your parents here tonight?' Pankaj asked.

Bhavan shook his head. 'They have to pay to come, and something tells me they can't afford to keep paying to watch people dressed like birds pick off the little insects.'

'It's expensive,' Pankaj said.

Bhavan scratched at his face under the mask. 'These stupid masks. This one isn't even mine. It was just in my room,' he said. 'What's the point of them? I get why the actors want to wear them, but why us? We are told to be ourselves in order to heal.' Bhavan mimicked Cynthia and had her down to a tee. The boy had spent a lot of time with her.

'Maybe by wearing a mask you can be who you truly are. Say things you wouldn't ordinarily say. So in effect they allow you to express your true feelings.'

'Sure you don't work here?' Bhavan asked with a laugh.

'How long have you been coming here?' Pankaj asked.

'Long enough.' Bhavan took another drag on his cigarette then stubbed it out on the thick trunk of the tree and let the butt drop to the ground. He scratched under his mask again. 'Oh to hell with this,' he said, pulling the silver sparrow mask from his face and throwing it to the ground. Pankaj looked around. He could see Cynthia staring in his direction. Had she noticed him? Noticed that he was not a paying guest? Did she think he was harassing one of her clients, one that she had specifically told Pankaj to stay away from? He wouldn't put it past her. That woman was quite perceptive.

Pankaj turned to Bhavan. He stared at the boy's face. Bhavan shifted his gaze, looked towards the light, and with that angle, Pankaj saw it. The crowd erupted into applause. Pankaj coughed to hide his shock. 'T-the last time there was a show here, someone was killed,' Pankaj said, stammering slightly. He wasn't sure if it was the right thing to say, but his time at the centre was running out. Cynthia was talking to a burly waiter. The waiter looked in their direction and then started walking towards them.

'What, here?' Bhavan said.

Pankaj shook his head. 'At Kapoor's theatre. A kathakali dancer.'

Bhavan stared at Pankaj, his dark eyes menacing. 'Who exactly are you?' he said. 'You didn't give me your name.'

'Pankaj,' he said. 'And you are?'

Bhavan didn't respond. The waiter was heading for them.

'What about that kathakali dancer?' Bhavan asked.

Pankaj eyed the slim wrought-iron gate he had entered the party through. If someone could slip in, someone could easily have slipped out – any one of the Johars. 'There's a rumour that someone here snuck out of the show and went to the theatre that night,' Pankaj said.

Bhavan didn't take his eyes off Pankaj. He took a step closer to the investigator and then without warning ripped Pankaj's mask from his face. Pankaj leaned back. Noticing the waiter coming for them, Bhavan started walking away. Pankaj followed.

'Stay back,' Bhavan barked. 'Stay away.'

Pankaj considered the request, but with the waiter close behind, he didn't have much of an option. He held back a little but followed Bhavan to the coded gate Pankaj had entered through just an hour ago.

Bhavan jabbed his fingers at the keypad. Seconds later he had exited the party. Pankaj followed at a reasonable distance. Pankaj found Chupplejeep's car parked a couple of meters away from the gate. He opened the door of the Baleno and took a breath.

'You're shaking,' Chupplejeep said. 'Did you speak to Bhavan? What happened?'

Pankaj pointed at the silhouette that was walking in the distance away from the centre. 'Follow him,' he said. 'Follow that man.'

Chapter Forty-five

'So you're telling me Bhavan is some relation to Jagdish,' Chupplejeep said.

'When he turned towards the crowd, I saw it,' Pankaj said. 'And the eyes. I've seen so many YouTube videos of Jagdish dancing, his quick eye movements, his mannerisms. I couldn't place it at the time, but when I saw the similarity between Bhavan and Jagdish, I realised that the two have the same dark eyes, that same look that I've seen countless times in Jagdish's videos.' Pankaj went on to describe Bhavan's reaction when he asked him about Jagdish's death.

'We would have found out by now if Jagdish and Bhavan were related. Someone would have said something,' Chupplejeep said.

'Who? Sonal has done everything to keep us away from her beloved boy. There's a reason for that.'

Chupplejeep started the car and followed the figure, who was now several metres in front of them. Bhavan turned the corner and started to descend the hill through the trees.

'We can't lose him,' Pankaj said.

'Don't worry,' Chupplejeep said. 'I know where he's headed. On the way back from Popatrao's I saw an expensive-looking bike parked in an outhouse. It sounded similar to the one Sonal had described. I think Bhavan goes to the centre to keep his parents happy, but he likes to know that he can escape when he wants to.'

'He knows the code for the back gate too. The residents are not supposed to know it. Monica told me,' Pankaj said. 'That way Bhavan can come and go freely. And with a bike parked nearby, Bhavan can get wherever he wants. Sir, are you thinking what I'm thinking?'

There was a silence between the two investigators. 'Hang on,' Pankaj said. 'Bhavan's girlfriend was with him when he found out that Jagdish was dead. He read it in a newspaper. She said he was really upset.'

'Bhavan may have already known about Jagdish's death and put on a performance to get more attention from his girlfriend. We couldn't think of a viable motive before, but now…'

And what was Sonal's role in all this? Had she known whose child she was carrying? Abhijeet must have known Bhavan was Jagdish's boy, unless he couldn't see the resemblance. Sometimes the mind had its own way of protecting itself. They were in Goa though. And people made it their pastime to point out the obvious to others, especially if they knew it could cause some kind of anguish.

The investigator turned a corner and slowed. He switched off the car headlights and waited a moment. It wasn't long before a black-and-silver bike shot out of the outhouse and sped towards the river. Bhavan was heading home.

'Maybe Abhijeet has been angry for years,' Pankaj said. 'He can't take his temper out on his son, but he can take it out on Sonal.'

'It explains the black eye we saw her with that day at the Shake Shack,' Chupplejeep said as he sped up to catch up with Bhavan's bike. 'It was an unlikely story that she slipped getting out of the bath.'

'And what did he dole out to Jagdish?' Pankaj questioned.

Chupplejeep put his foot on the accelerator and followed Bhavan through the winding backroads. The boy rode well, familiar with these smaller mud tracks. You'd have to be in the pitch black of the night. If Bhavan was Jagdish's, son it explained why Jagdish was paying for the boy's stay at the Atul Centre.

Bhavan and Abhijeet had motive to kill Jagdish. But what about Darsh? Until Pankaj came out of the Atul Centre demanding that Chupplejeep follow Bhavan Johar, he was convinced that Darsh had been the one to kill Jagdish. Chupplejeep explained his theory to Pankaj.

'Darsh killed for love?' said Pankaj, a little unconvinced. Chupplejeep had to agree. Killing Tanya's father would mean risking losing Tanya too. Because who would love someone who murdered their own flesh and blood? Eloping with Jagdish's youngest daughter would have been a better alternative.

Bhavan's black-and-silver bike came to a stop outside the Johar house. The house was small and well maintained. Chupplejeep could see that Sonal had taken great care with the small shrubs with purple flowers to the front, planted next to the pink bougainvillea and frangipani tree. Beautiful flowers and plants like that needed watering every evening. He turned off the ignition to the Baleno and watched. There was a whitewashed wall behind the planting at the front of the house, with a wrought-iron gate fitted into an archway. A paper star hung above. Bhavan pushed through the gate. He pounded on the door.

'Where's your key?' Sonal said, opening the door. 'And why are you back from the centre? You only just got there. They'll still charge us.'

Bhavan didn't respond, he just walked past her. Chupplejeep and Pankaj strained to get a better look, but they couldn't see much, just the back of Sonal's head as she closed the front door. The light from within extinguished.

'Come,' Chupplejeep whispered.

The investigator gently pushed open the gate and walked around the side of the house. The garden had low-level lighting dotted around the shrubs, and navigating the path was easy. Pankaj followed, stopping behind Chupplejeep, who had found a window. It was closed, despite it being a warm night, but nevertheless it was better than nothing. Chupplejeep squatted underneath and shuffled to the other side. He stood up and stretched his legs out. He looked at Pankaj and put a finger to his lips.

For a moment thy could just hear the sound of the cicadas then there was shouting from within the house. Chupplejeep couldn't make out what was being said. He could identify two voices, maybe three, Sonal's and Bhavan's, possibly Abhijeet.

The sound of breaking glass was heard, and Pankaj took a step back. Chupplejeep frowned at his colleague. 'Quiet,' he whispered.

'I don't think they're going to hear us, sir,' Pankaj said. 'Not with all that noise they're making. Should we go in? They sound like they could be doing damage to one another.'

'You never told me,' Bhavan screamed. 'Never.'

'How dare you,' said a man's voice. 'After everything I've done. After everything your mother has done.' Another crash was heard. This time not the breaking of glass or china. It sounded as if a chair had been picked up and brought down on another piece of furniture.

A moment later the house was plunged into darkness. Chupplejeep looked around. The neighbours too had lost electricity. It wasn't uncommon for this to happen in Goa. It was just bad timing. A moment later an engine whirred and a few lights in the house came back on. The generator had kicked in. The house was eerily silent for a few minutes. Then the shouting began again. Chupplejeep tried to prise open the window, but it was no good. The voices from inside the house were getting louder and louder. Sonal cried out in despair. Images flashed through Chupplejeep's mind. Abhijeet with Bhavan in a chokehold; Bhavan holding a knife to his father's neck.

'Come on,' Chupplejeep said to Pankaj, walking towards the front door. This time he didn't bother to lower his voice to a whisper.

'Where are we going, sir?' Pankaj asked.

'It's time we confronted the Johars before anything terrible happens,' Chupplejeep said.

Pankaj nodded, right before they heard the shot.

Chapter Forty-six

Chupplejeep put his weight against the front door of the Johars' house and pushed. It didn't budge. He stood back and kicked with all his force. Nothing. Chupplejeep ran up the path from the front gate and ran back towards the door, dreading what would happen when he reached it, but before he could get there, Pankaj motioned for him to stop. He had found a key under a flowerpot. Opening the door, the two investigators stepped inside.

It was dark. The generator had only powered a couple of lights. Chupplejeep pulled out his pocket torch, a gift from Nicholas last Christmas. He was about to call out when they heard a screeching sound, like a chair being pulled against a stone floor.

Chupplejeep pointed in the direction of the noise and started making his way towards it. The pair stood at the entrance to the living room. They could hear talking from behind two obscure glazed double doors. There was a gap between the doors, and Chupplejeep could see through. Two grandfather chairs were in opposite corners of the room; a wooden seat with thick cushions was against one wall; a sofa had been placed in the middle of the room. Its back was towards Chupplejeep and Pankaj. Sonal and Abhijeet were seated on the sofa looking towards their son, who was sitting in a wooden chair opposite them with a large flat screen television behind him. None of them looked injured. Had the shot been made simply to scare, or had it just been a poor shot?

Bhavan looked up. He would have seen the shadowy figures at the door. Chupplejeep pushed the door open. Bhavan was holding a gun. He was shaking.

'You're here,' Bhavan said, but his look of fear was slowly dissipating. It was turning into something else. The boy looked straight at Pankaj, ignoring Chupplejeep.

'Bhavan,' Sonal said, her voice warning him of something.

'Maybe now we will get the truth,' Bhavan said to his mother. He shifted his body weight, and the hand holding the gun flopped about carelessly. 'I saw your expression earlier at the show,' Bhavan said to Pankaj. 'Bet you thought I missed it, but I didn't. I see it all the time now. The way people look at me.' Bhavan stopped waving the gun around and looked at his mother with watery eyes. 'I asked her,' he said. 'I asked my mother if Abhijeet was my father, and you know what she said?'

'He's your father,' Sonal said. 'He raised you from when you were born. He has given up everything for you. His career, his –'

'His career?' Bhavan laughed. 'He was Jagdish's manager. Jagdish dropped him when he found out about your affair.'

'Bhavan, take it easy,' Abhijeet pleaded with his son.

'Go to hell,' Bhavan said.

'I know you're upset about Jagdish. I know his death has affected you,' Sonal said.

'Put the weapon down,' Chupplejeep said, his arms outstretched, his palms facing up – a sign of surrender that he had practiced countless times on the force.

'Who are you?' Bhavan asked, as if seeing Chupplejeep for the first time. 'Of course.' Bhavan didn't wait for an answer. 'Ah, the two investigators. I didn't know you were one of them.' Bhavan stared at Pankaj. 'You tried to question me in the car park that day. You asked my girl about me, too. You've been trying to speak to me for some time, haven't you? My mother did her best to keep you away. I heard her whispering over the phone to Cynthia how terrible it would be for me if I was subjected to questioning, any questioning; she said that it would set me back in my recovery. Cynthia didn't quite agree, but nevertheless she has to listen to her clients, no? Good old Cynthia. Look at them,' Bhavan said to his mother. 'They're not even cops. What were you afraid I would tell them? And where are the cops? The cops haven't been to the Atul Centre at all. Whereas this one' – Bhavan pointed his gun back at Pankaj – 'he checked in. You PIs must have a lot of cash to go to such lengths to go digging like that.'

'The cops haven't been at the centre because they're doing their job, a proper job, unlike these two men,' Sonal said.

Bhavan ignored Sonal. 'My mother has my birth certificate, but she didn't want to share it. I don't know why, because it clearly says that this man here is my father.' Bhavan waved the gun in the direction of Abhijeet.

'Was it because of the lie?' he asked his mother. Bhavan didn't wait for a response. 'What I don't understand, dear father, is how you put up with her and me all this time. Knowing full well that I was nothing to do with you.'

'I love your mother,' Abhijeet said. His large frame appeared small under the threat of the gun. 'I love you. I always have. It didn't matter.'

'So you're admitting it, finally. That you're not my biological father? I'm glad you two turned up,' Bhavan said to Chupplejeep and Pankaj. 'Now we're getting somewhere.'

Abhijeet shared a look with Sonal.

'Still you want to play this game,' Bhavan said. 'But let's not waste the time of these two fellows. They have come all the way today, and Pankaj, you must have paid for the show at the Atul Centre, and now you have missed half of it. We must give you another show here.' Bhavan stood up and turned. Chupplejeep took a step forward, but Bhavan spun on his heel to face him. 'Stop right there,' he commanded. 'Go back to your place.' He waited until Chupplejeep had taken a couple of steps back and then turned again to the chest of drawers underneath the television set. 'Here it is,' he proclaimed, pulling out a piece of paper. 'My birth certificate, but not just that. With this document was an important piece of paper. Results from a paternity test; my paternity.

'Do you know how I have this?' he asked.

'Let me tell them,' Sonal said.

'Be my guest,' Bhavan said.

'Just over a year ago I arranged to meet Jagdish to tell him about Bhavan. We hadn't spoken in years, and it was time to confess. Until then Jagdish had been in the dark about Bhavan. He believed, or at least he allowed himself to believe, that Bhavan wasn't his. Jagdish had never wanted children with me, and when he found out about my affair with Abhijeet, we split up.

'Soon after he dropped Abhijeet as his manager. It was expected. Abhijeet and I married and then for various reasons Abhijeet decided to work less.' Sonal briefly looked at her son. 'Money was tight, but we managed for years. We have lived off my inheritance for the large part of the last twenty years. My father would have been ashamed of me selling all his land, but I had little choice. And then…'

'You started to run out of cash.' Chupplejeep finished her sentence for her.

'I had no choice but to reach out to Jagdish,' Sonal said.

'Jagdish listened to my story. More than twenty years have passed since we were together.'

'Twenty-four,' Bhavan said. 'Twenty-four years, surely. If I was conceived around about the time he ditched you.'

'Jagdish had only met Bhavan a handful of times when Bhavan was younger, and he didn't think the boy looked like him,' Sonal continued. 'If you had met Jagdish, you would know why. He didn't see other people. Just himself. I didn't want to ask for financial help, but I had no choice. Abhijeet is struggling to build up a client base after all these years, and we needed the money.

'I showed Jagdish the paternity test. I gathered my own samples and sent them off to this company for a result I knew to be true. I showed him pictures of Bhavan, now in his twenties. At first he didn't believe it, but then it made sense. He said he wanted to spend time with Bhavan, and that's what they did.'

'They grew close,' Chupplejeep said, turning towards Bhavan. Bhavan wiped away a tear with the back of his hand.

'Jagdish liked Bhavan. He wanted to help. Once Jagdish had time to adjust, I asked him for money,' Sonal said.

'He took the job at Popatrao's hotel with the monies being paid directly to the centre,' Chupplejeep said.

'He didn't want anyone to know what he was doing. This way the money didn't need to come out of his account,' Sonal said.

Chupplejeep considered what Sonal was saying. They had only known each other a short time, but it was clear that Bhavan had had some affection for his biological father. Chupplejeep hadn't ever met the great Jagdish, but he had heard enough about him to know that the feelings Bhavan had for his biological father were not reciprocated by Jagdish.

Chupplejeep turned back to Sonal. What he was about to say was going to break Bhavan's heart, if it wasn't sufficiently broken already. 'You blackmailed him,' Chupplejeep said, looking at Bhavan's mother. 'You said to Jagdish that if he didn't pay up you would go to his wife, the press. You threatened to tell everyone that he had always known about Bhavan but chose to disown him because of his problems.'

Sonal shook her head. 'It's not true.'

'Is that what you did, Mum?' Bhavan asked. 'Is it?' He turned to Chupplejeep. 'She's a liar. You can't trust what she says.'

Sonal looked towards Bhavan. 'Give me the gun,' she said. 'It's time.'

Bhavan laughed. 'No way. This is how I get you to tell me what I need to know. Did you blackmail Jagdish to pay for my therapy, or should I say your time-out from your crazy son?'

'He would have done it,' Sonal said. 'Jagdish would have paid willingly, but he was worried.'

'About what?' Bhavan asked.

'His daughters. He was so protective of them, and of course he didn't want them to see him in a bad light. Jagdish didn't want his daughters finding out and so…' She trailed off.

Kingfisher Blues

'And so you had to force his hand,' Chupplejeep said.

Sonal looked towards the investigator. 'On the night of the 12th November, I was at the show with my family. I slipped out of the event. I made my way to Kapoor's theatre using Bhavan's bike and I killed Jagdish.'

'Baby,' Abijeet said. 'Don't do this. You can't –'

'Why?' Chupplejeep asked Sonal. 'Why would you kill him? Jagdish was paying for Bhavan's treatment at the Atul Centre, which isn't cheap. With Jagdish out of the picture, you don't benefit in any way. I've checked the details of the will.' It had been a hard task to check, but a few payments here and there and one intern at the law firm dealing with Jagdish's will sent him a copy of the kathakali dancer's will.

'You didn't kill Jagdish,' Chupplejeep said. 'You blackmailed Jagdish, definitely. You took the paternity test results to him sometime before he was killed, before he had signed the contract with Popatrao. This is what you asked Darsh to find in Jagdish's dressing room after Jagdish had been murdered. Did you promise the dancer fame if he found it? You're smart enough to make him believe that if you so wished.

'Darsh's new fame has nothing to do with you though. You were just using him, making him believe that you were capable of making him great when in reality you had no say at all. But you needed that piece of paper because the paternity test result is what linked you and your son, your husband even, to Jagdish. It gave not one but all three of you motive for murder.'

Chupplejeep shook his head. 'But no,' he said. 'You didn't kill Jagdish. You needed him. Bhavan, on the other hand, was angry. He had been at the show at the Atul Centre with you, but at some point you lost each other. Bhavan slipped away, through the back gate. He has the code. We witnessed that tonight. He took his bike, the new one that you had given him which was hidden nearby, and made his way to Kapoor's theatre. He waited, watched a bit of the dancing and then approached Jagdish in his dressing room during the interval. Jagdish and Bhavan had built up a relationship, and Bhavan enjoyed Jagdish's company, but it didn't take long for Bhavan to realise they were related. Bhavan recognised who his biological father was, and he was desperate to know why Jagdish had rejected him all those years ago.

'Bhavan went to Jagdish's dressing room on the opening night at Kapoor's theatre to ask him. Jagdish laughed, said he had put his career first. Maybe he denied knowing. Bhavan lost it. He couldn't control his anger, especially when he knew that only two years after Bhavan had been born Jagdish would go on to have children. Three daughters in quick succession which he doted on, cared for and gave everything for. The rejection was too much.' Chupplejeep could imagine how Bhavan had felt. He too had been rejected as a child where Karan, his brother, had been loved. The same way Jagdish had loved his three daughters and had denied his son.

Kingfisher Blues

There was no reason, not a rational one at least, as to why Chupplejeep's biological parents had disowned him, and yet his life was dramatically different because of it. Chupplejeep had carried a burden of not being good enough his entire life. Christabel had done much to relieve him of his encumbrance, and being a father had made Chupplejeep want to be a better person, to rid himself of this unnecessary baggage. But he couldn't deny it completely. It was part of his fabric, and he knew he would die with that same feeling of inadequacy. Not because of anything he had done, but because of a poor decision his parents made years ago.

He looked at Bhavan, saw the plain gold ring on his right thumb. It was familiar, something he had seen before. Despite the ring's simplicity, there was something about that style of ring, if he remembered correctly. But what was it? He couldn't recall. Chupplejeep put the thought aside. The hurt Bhavan must have felt at his biological father's rejection was evident. Chupplejeep understood. Bhavan was the result of his parents' poor decision making, but whilst Chupplejeep had put his energies into making something of himself, Bhavan had stalled. He had put his energies into taking revenge. And revenge never felt good.

'Bhavan found the paternity test results and birth certificate in the dressing room right before he took the knife, Jagdish's knife. You confronted your biological father,' Chupplejeep said, focusing on Bhavan. 'Jagdish had those test results in his possession, so he knew you were his son. Jagdish would have argued that he had only just found out, but you didn't listen. You argued, you couldn't see straight, didn't want to listen to the lies, especially after you had grown close to him of late. You felt betrayed. Another betrayal.'

'You're wearing a gold ring, Bhavan,' Chupplejeep said, the memory from his brief interaction with Aman Khosla's uncle coming back to him. 'Let me guess: if you take it off, inside the ring will be several emeralds. There is a belief that you must wear stones touching your skin to feel their benefits. The emerald is said to help with regeneration and recovery and will help with your behaviour problems. That's why your mother gifted that ring to you. With the stones being on the inside, they wouldn't be too ostentatious either. You slip that ring on and off your thumb, don't you? A nervous habit, perhaps. I think if you remove your ring now, you will see that one of the stones is missing. Do you know how I know?'

Bhavan looked at Chupplejeep blankly. 'Because one of those stones was found at the crime scene,' Chupplejeep said.

'Your husband is right,' Chupplejeep continued, looking at Sonal. 'You can't protect Bhavan anymore. He made his decision the night he took another person's life. I think you've known what your son is capable of; you've always known.'

Chapter Forty-seven

Chupplejeep touched his eye in the same place he had seen Sonal's bruise the first time he had met her. Sonal instinctively touched her face, the bruise long gone.

'I know you want to protect your son, but you can't protect him forever,' Chupplejeep said.

Bhavan was laughing now, laughing and crying. Tears were streaming down his face. Chupplejeep stepped towards him.

'Back off,' he screamed and Chupplejeep obliged.

'You,' Bhavan said, looking at Pankaj through bleary eyes. 'You came into the centre. You talked to me. You singled me out. You.' His eyes pierced through Pankaj. 'You. I killed my father, but I'm not going to jail.' Bhavan raised his gun. He pointed it at Chupplejeep first and then towards Pankaj.

Chupplejeep once again put his hands up. He could feel Pankaj's fear behind him. Sonal and Abhijeet were pleading with their son to put the gun down, but Bhavan silenced them with a menacing look. The gun wavered towards them and then back again to Pankaj. Bhavan's hands were shaking. Fear and anguish were heavy in his eyes.

'Do as your parents ask,' Chupplejeep started. 'They've always been there for you. They want to help. Put the weapon down and we can talk about next steps. There are always options. Don't assume the worst will happen.'

Bhavan looked at his mother again. 'You wanted me to suffer. That night, I asked Jagdish why he didn't love me and look after me as a son. He said that you never told him, and you've just admitted it.'

Sonal was silent.

'You have integrity though, don't you? That's what you are always saying to your friends on the phone. That you have integrity. So you would have at least told me, your son, who his real father was, even if you didn't tell him.'

Abhijeet put his arm in front of Sonal as Bhavan pointed the gun at her. Bhavan's eyes darted from Abhijeet to Sonal to Chupplejeep. Finally, they rested on Pankaj. Chupplejeep shifted slightly to protect his colleague. He glanced at his colleague, to reassure him more than anything. He saw Pankaj's fear, and he shifted again to act as a barrier between Bhavan, who was increasingly unstable, and Pankaj, the man he thought of as a son.

There was a moment's silence and then Chupplejeep heard a shot.

Chapter Forty-eight

Pankaj passed Rupali as he entered the ward. He walked up to Chupplejeep's bed and put a hand on his shoulder. 'Are you in pain?' he asked.

'What do you think?' Chupplejeep said with a wince. 'Visitors are helping though.'

'You were lucky he only got your leg, sir.'

'Lucky indeed,' said Chupplejeep with a laugh. 'Bhavan was a terrible shot.'

'I know what you did,' Pankaj said, looking directly at his boss. 'You put yourself between the gunman and me. You saved me. You even managed to restrain Bhavan and call the cops after you'd been hit. Sir, you're incredible.'

'If Bhavan had aimed for you, he would have got the grandfather chair,' Chupplejeep said.

The two men laughed. Pankaj squeezed his boss's shoulder. 'What was that all about, sir?' Pankaj asked, looking in the direction that Rupali had just left.

'She came to tell me her side of the story.'

Pankaj pulled up a chair and leaned towards his boss. 'Did Meera tip off the police suggesting Popatrao had something to do with Jagdish's death?' he whispered. 'Did they engineer Popatrao to be at the theatre that night, the night Jagdish was killed?'

'Coincidence at first. Meera had wanted Popatrao to be at the show, but she also realised if Popatrao was there and so was Jagdish, she could meet Rupali quite safely at home, as Rupali had made it quite clear to Jagdish that she wouldn't attend. It was just another opening night in her eyes, and the love between them had long gone. After the event, when Jagdish was murdered, the two schemed to frame Popatrao. Meera had told Rupali that Popatrao was a brute, and Rupali, blinded by love, believed her. It also worked to her advantage as Jagdish was now out of the picture and no lengthy divorce was required. Rupali was finally free, and she couldn't quite believe it. The man was dead, and she didn't have to get her hands dirty. She didn't put it that way, but I could read between the lines. Meera and Rupali thought they could set up Popatrao and get him arrested and out of the way.'

'But Popatrao wasn't controlling. He couldn't have controlled someone like Meera. He's not capable.'

Chupplejeep shrugged. 'Meera initially claimed that Popatrao was obsessed with her, and it was the only thing she could think of to get away from him. She said she was certain that if she left him for Rupali, he would have made trouble for her and her lover.'

'Unlikely,' Pankaj said.

Chupplejeep nodded. 'She was questioned further, and it turns out Popatrao was blackmailing her.'

'About what?'

'Popatrao knew more about his lover than he let on. Turns out she had a history as a lady of the night. It was some time ago, and it's how she got the capital she needed to start her interiors business. She wasn't proud of her early career, and she was desperate for no one to find out. Popatrao had previously threatened to tell friends and acquaintances about her past whenever she threatened to leave him. Meera couldn't afford for Rupali to find out about it.'

'Scheming,' Pankaj said. 'Do you think Rupali will stay with her?'

'Not if Rupali's mother has any say,' Chupplejeep said. He laughed and then winced, reaching for his elevated leg that was in a cast. 'The family are packing their bags as we speak. Rupali's mother thinks they all need a break from Goa.'

'Did Rupali say anything about Darsh and her daughter?' Pankaj asked.

Chupplejeep nodded. Rupali had told him that her youngest was in love with Darsh. Jagdish had found out about their relationship the night he died. Darsh had a terrible argument with him before the performance, said some things he later regretted, especially when Jagdish was killed later that night.

'As we suspected.'

Chupplejeep nodded. Darsh was certain the finger would be pointed at him, and he was scared of Jagdish's ex-wife, who had promised him fame for retrieving her son's paternity test results from the dancer's dressing room. On Sonal's instructions, Darsh had been the one to increase the quantity of bhang in Jagdish's lassi so that he would lose a little focus. He has been feeling guilty ever since. Darsh couldn't have predicted the consequences of his actions. Chupplejeep couldn't see why Sonal had put Darsh up to this. Spite, perhaps.

Darsh regretted his actions. He confessed all this to Tanya. Rupali hadn't seemed bothered by her future son-in-law's confession. It would take more than bhang for her late husband to have lost focus, she had said with a laugh. "The man was immune to the stuff. And Darsh, he knows better now." Chupplejeep repeated his conversation with Rupali to Pankaj. 'Rupali also confirmed that Darsh was with her daughter at the time that Jagdish was killed.'

'During the interval?' Pankaj asked.

'Tanya had been at the show. Jagdish never liked Darsh, Rupali said, but she also said that Jagdish never liked anyone. Rupali and her mother have given Tanya and Darsh their blessings in Jagdish's absence.'

'And the bouncer, sir?' Pankaj asked.

'Bouncer?' Chupplejeep said.

'The one who was supposed to be outside Jagdish's dressing room but was in the toilet after eating cutlet bread?'

Chupplejeep smiled. The boy had a good memory. 'I originally believed that someone had tampered with his food.'

'There are no such things as coincidences,' Pankaj said, spouting back one of Chupplejeep's usual phrases.

'But sometimes there are. Like in this instance.'

'Well, sir, one can never quite trust a cutlet bread from one of those carts.'

Chupplejeep nodded, and even though Pankaj was right, his tummy rumbled.

'Kapoor sent his regards, sir,' Pankaj said. 'He said he knew you'd get there before the cops did. He's happy with the result. The name of his theatre is untarnished.'

Chupplejeep's eyes focused on a vase filled with orange flowers. 'He sent those flowers too.'

~

Chupplejeep took a breath. It had been an intense day yesterday, ending in an injury which could have been fatal. Christabel had been by his side since he had been brought in. Only now that Pankaj was with him had his wife taken a break. Christabel's mother had been looking after the children at home. From his hospital bed, he could hear Mrs Saldanha tutting.

Chupplejeep wasn't a spiritual person, but he saw his injury as a sign. His children were young; they wouldn't be young forever. Christabel had been looking after them tirelessly with little or no help from him. He was always preoccupied with one case or another. It was time he helped out, and more than that, he wanted to spend time with his children, get to know them better, create a bond. It pained him to admit it, but maybe it was time for a break. Not a long break, maybe a year or so. They could live off the little savings they had.

Chupplejeep turned to Pankaj and explained his thoughts. 'It's going to be some time before I'm out of here, and after that, bed rest. Christabel will have me shipped off if I take on any new cases too,' Chupplejeep continued, afraid of the silence. 'I don't know where this leaves you. Of course I'd support you if you want to carry on the business without me. I'll –'

'Before the incident,' Pankaj said, interrupting, 'I had my own dilemmas, if you remember.'

'Of course,' Chupplejeep said. 'How could I forget?'

'Well, sir, if getting shot isn't a good enough excuse, I don't know what is.'

'Me getting shot probably hasn't helped your situation with Shwetty either, I imagine. It just proves that you're in a high-risk job and getting paid very little for it. I'm sorry.'

'It's not your fault, sir,' Pankaj said. 'Even before you got shot, after my time at the centre, I was starting to think…'

'That being a private investigator isn't for you?' Chupplejeep asked, a lump forming in his throat.

Pankaj shook his head. 'I love seeking justice, sir, but I need some space to decide, and this gives me the opportunity to do it. I've always wanted to have my own nursery and so—'

'Children?' Chupplejeep asked. 'You're going to look after other people's children?' He looked horrified.

Pankaj laughed. 'Not children, sir, plants. I'm going to open my own nursery growing and selling plants.'

Chupplejeep laughed. 'Thank goodness. I was going to say, looking after children is much harder than getting shot.' Chupplejeep reached for Pankaj's hand. 'It's a good decision,' he said, giving the boy's hand a squeeze. 'And is Shwetika in favour of your new venture?'

'Shwetty wasn't keen at first. But she can see the benefits.'

'Reasonable hours, same pay.'

'Something like that, sir.'

'So no more ultimatums?'

Pankaj shook his head. 'We're going to start thinking about a family,' Pankaj said, his lips turning upwards.

Chapter Forty-nine

Christabel tucked the sheets in around Arthur and kissed him on the forehead the way he had done to her so many times. It was her turn to look after him. The pain in his leg was easing, but recovery wouldn't be quick. The doctors had warned her that there would be muscle wastage, and he would need months of physio. Christabel didn't mind because the love of her life was alive. She hoped it wasn't delirium, but Arthur said he was taking some time off too. She wasn't sure how they would manage financially, but she would find a way. She was resourceful. She had proven that in the quick adoption of Nicholas, saving him from years in and out of foster homes.

Christabel pulled the curtains to, turned off the light and momentarily closed her eyes, imagining family days out and Arthur getting the children ready in the morning. She couldn't help but smile at the thought of having some help around the house. 'Sleep well,' she whispered to her husband before closing the door behind her.

With the children in bed as well, she decided to catch up on her favourite soap opera. It was rare that she got time to herself these days. Her heart sang as she thought of an uninterrupted hour in front of the television. But no sooner had she sat down than there was a knocking at the front door. At first she thought she had imagined it, it was so faint, but it grew louder. She checked her watch. It was eight o'clock; not an unreasonable time for a friend or neighbour to ask how her husband was doing, she supposed. Christabel stood up and padded over to the door.

She opened it to an unfamiliar face. A tall, well-dressed man holding a briefcase stood at the door. 'Sorry to call so late,' he said with a slight accent. 'I would like to see your husband, Private Investigator Arthur Chupplejeep, if its isn't too much of a bother.'

Ordinarily, Christabel would have let the gentleman in, offered him a cup of tea and woken up Arthur, but it was late, and her husband had only recently been shot. Plus, Arthur had been certain that he wasn't going to take on any new cases for a while, so he wouldn't be cross if she turned this client away.

'Word hasn't got out yet, but my husband is taking a break at the moment. He isn't taking on any new cases,' she said, feeling a little victorious.

The man looked crestfallen. Christabel opened the door a little more. 'Come in. You look like you have travelled some way,' she said. 'Would you like a cup of tea?'

'That would be most kind,' the man said. He stepped over the threshold and removed his hat. She could see now that the man was older than he first appeared. She offered him a seat while she boiled the kettle.

'That is a shame,' the man said as she handed him a cup and sat opposite him. 'And I'm sorry to have disturbed you so late. It's just that I'm desperate. I have no one else to go to.'

Christabel sighed. She hated seeing people in despair, especially old people. 'Tomorrow, when my husband wakes, I can ask him to recommend another company. I'm sure he'll be able to find you someone.'

'Would you?' the man asked, hope in his eyes.

Christabel nodded.

'Your husband comes highly recommended. I really was hoping… But I suppose it is impossible.'

Nothing is impossible, Christabel heard herself say as she had told her children time and time again. But she couldn't ask Chupplejeep to help this man from his sickbed. She looked at the gentleman and his well-kept appearance. Was that all it was, an appearance? What could he possibly need help with? Something, she mused. Everyone had problems they needed help with, no matter what their status or social standing. She wanted to ask him what his concern was, what he needed her husband's help with, but she held her tongue. She couldn't ask him if she couldn't help him. Christabel excused herself to quickly check on the sleeping children. When she returned to the sitting room, the man was finishing his tea.

The evening was cool, and the crickets were making a trilling noise from the scrubland to the rear of their house.

'I do hope your husband can find someone suitable to help me,' the man said, rising to his feet. 'You've been most kind offering me a seat and a cup of tea. There will be a lot of people in need of your husband's services, and they'll have to wait till he is recovered.'

Christabel empathised with him. She would ask Arthur to recommend someone but not describe to him the anguish in this old man's face, because then she was sure Arthur would be desperate to take on his case. She could hear him say, 'I can handle this. Pankaj can do all the legwork.' No, that just wouldn't do. Her husband needed to rest or he wouldn't ever fully recover.

The man started walking towards the door then stopped. He turned to Christabel. 'What about you?' he said. 'Could *you* take this on?'

'Well, I…' Christabel said. She thought back to all the times she had been a sounding board for Arthur. When he told her his wild and often correct theories and she had added her thoughts. He had always been appreciative of her comments, and lately he had been seeking her out, asking for her views. Plus, she had recently helped him with the case of the missing Kingfisher Sapphire by telling him about the jeweller who had been approached with the ring. And she had been the one to find out that the hotelier was paying the Atul Centre, linking the kathakali dancer directly to his killer.

A smile started to form on her lips, but she quickly suppressed it. What was she thinking – of course she couldn't take on a case of her own. But of course Pankaj could help her if he had the time in-between planting seedlings and if he could refrain from telling Arthur everything and getting her husband's blood pressure up. But that would be a tall ask. And what about the kids? How could she forget them in all of this? There was no way she could be a detective and mother two young children. Bonita wasn't yet two. But hadn't she recently said to Arthur that she could catch a killer and change a diaper at the same time? She had been convinced that it was true. Mothers were capable of anything they put their minds to. Plus, Arthur had assured her he wanted to spend more time with the children during his sabbatical, and then there was the money. That would come in handy.

She cast her eyes over the tall, well-dressed gentleman. Straightening her back, she looked him in the eye. 'What is your good name?' she asked.

'Ryan,' he said. 'Ryan Pinto.'

Christabel held out her hand. 'Ryan Pinto, pleased to meet you.' She offered him a seat. 'I think I may be able to be of some assistance.'

Acknowledgements

I would like to say a big thank you to my family and friends for their continual support. In particular, James, Sophie and Nathan for their patience with me as Kingfisher Blues took shape. A massive thank-you goes to JD&J for the cover work, to Abingdon Writers' Fiction Adult's Group for their honest critique and to my editor Emily Nemchick.

When I moved to Goa in the eighties it was a very different place to what it is today. Despite its westernisation, Goa still has a certain charm you won't find anywhere else. For me, it will always be home. The location of the Chupplejeep Mysteries is what makes the series so popular. I am forever indebted to the place and its inhabitants for inspiring me.

Thanks also to my readers. Without you there would be no *Kingfisher Blues*. Your support and kind reviews make this all worthwhile.

About the Author

Marissa de Luna is a passionate author who started writing in her late twenties. After spending her early years growing up in Goa, Marissa returned to England where she now lives with her husband and two children.

Other novels by Marissa de Luna

Goa Traffic

The Bittersweet Vine

Poison in the Water

Under the Coconut Tree – A Chupplejeep Mystery

The Body in the Bath – A Chupplejeep Mystery

Jackpot Jetty – A Chupplejeep Mystery

Miramar Monsoon – A Chupplejeep Mystery

A Slice of Murder – A Shilpa Solanki Mystery

Murder on the Menu – A Shilpa Solanki Mystery

Murder in the Mix – A Shilpa Solanki Mystery

Printed in Great Britain
by Amazon